CAUGHT UP BETWEEN SISTERS

BOOK THREE

The Queen

Printed in the United States of America
ISBN-13: 978-1-7336-442-4-2
ISBN-10: 1-7336-4424-2

For information regarding special ordering for bulk purchases, contact:
Queendom Dreams Publishing
Website: www.queendomdreamspublishing.com

Queendom Dreams Publishing

ACKNOWLEDGEMENTS

As always, I give all honor and thanks unto Jehovah God. For without His grace, no talent that I have been blessed with would come to fruition. I thank Him for the past, present, and the blessings to come.

Thank you to all along my path who have supported me in this journey. Anyone that's anyone knows who they are and don't need acknowledgment in a book to know how priceless they are in my life because I continually let you know personally.

My readers and fans of The Queen, words will never express the level of gratitude I have for you. Without you, I am just another person writing books. Prayerfully, you will stick with me along my journey and inspire me to want to give you more.

The Queen

CAUGHT UP BETWEEN SISTERS

BOOK THREE

The Queen

Queendom Dreams Publishing

www.QueendomDreamsPublishing.com

PROLOGUE

1

The Wiggins' families were all gathered for a Fourth of July celebration at Todd and Harmony's home. The weather was just perfect. While the kids were entertained by a moon bounce, a magician, and a clown, music was playing and card games were going. Almost everyone was happy.

Most of the Wiggins men were able to steal a moment away from their women to vent their frustrations to one another. One of the enclosed gazebos, large enough to accommodate four lounge chairs, seemed to be the safest location for venting, as it was far out of earshot of the women they loved. After slaving over smoking meats, manning the grill for hours, attending to guests, and juggling three teething babies, Todd made his escape to the gazebo with a few beers in tow to find Eric, Arnold, and Kevin deep in discussion.

"Arnold, why would you get married if you knew going in you wouldn't be getting any loving—ever?" Kevin asked.

Arnold's sunglasses were able to mask the hurt in his eyes, but they did nothing for the beat-down look of frustration on his face. "Hell, I thought she just needed a little time to heal from everything that happened to her. It's been almost a whole year since she was beaten and raped by the nut—" Just then, he realized Todd was entering into the gazebo. "No disrespect to you, Todd."

Todd nodded his head as he swallowed a swig of beer before spreading in his favorite lounge chair. "I understand."

Arnold continued. "The crazy thing is, her flapping-ass mouth is all healed, but not in the way that would make me happy. Every time I turn around she's bitching, nagging, or complaining about something. But don't let me try to bring up the subject of sex. Damn girl wants to get all emotional and starts accusing me of cheating and mess, or she'll say I want to cheat on her because she's not physically ready. I can't win."

"Damn, that's messed up," Todd said, and the others agreed.

"You think that's something?" Arnold stood up and became animated in a loud whisper. "I already spoke with her doctor, and Charise has green light. So, I ask, my brothas, what the hell is the problem? Why can't I get my dick sucked, a hand job, or something?"

The guys laughed.

"Not even a blow job?" Eric asked.

"Not even a hand job," Arnold answered. "And then to be accused of some shit I'm not doing on top of that? I don't know. I just don't know how much more I can take," he said, laughing through his frustration as he took his seat.

"Man, you think you've got troubles?" Eric laughed, his six-foot-eight frame shaking a little. "I have women trying to get with me every day, but my dumb ass is sitting around waiting for my daughter's mother to throw me what she feels like, when she feels like it. Sometimes I feel like Shawnee owns my life. She was cool about financing my restaurant and letting me live in her guest house so I could be near my daughter, but she doesn't throw me a bone unless her hormones are raging. Then she's quick to remind me that she if she finds out I'm messing with other women, she'll pull the plug on everything."

It was Eric's turn to be laughed at, and the men shared a laugh at his expense.

"Give me a guest house. I don't think I'd feel as bad if I had to stay in the guest house. It probably wouldn't hurt as bad, and I mean physically," Arnold replied, pointing to his genitals. The guys nodded. "Charise has this thing where she wants to walk around with nothing or next to nothing on, knowing it's arousing me. Then if I try to make my move, she shoots me down."

Todd interjected, "And they know what they are doing." Again, the guys acknowledged with nods and a collective "Uhm-hmm."

Arnold shook his head. "Man, I feel like a dude in jail that can only look and not touch. I mean, at least give me a conjugal visit or something. Hell, I think I'm a good looking guy. I know I'm in good shape—almost up there with Eric. What's the problem?"

After the guys laughed some more, Kevin asked, "Like I said before, why would you get married if you knew this was going to be a problem for you? I'm trying to find some sympathy for you, but . . . I don't know." He shook his head and chuckled.

"Who would have thought I'd still be waiting? I thought I was getting some on my wedding night. We checked with her doctor before we got married to make sure it would be all right," Arnold said.

Todd shifted his eyes to Kevin. "So, I take it your home life is all peaches and cream?"

"My problem is the complete opposite of theirs. Elaine has me cringing at the frequency. I go along with it because I'm half afraid to refuse her since I know a backup is only a phone call away. Other than that, we are perfectly paired. I wouldn't trade my wife in for all the money in the world," Kevin answered, smiling while the other guys had their mouths wide open from disbelief.

"Word! It's like that?" Eric asked, sitting up from his lounging position.

"Do you get the feeling he's trying to rub it in our faces?" Todd asked Eric and Arnold.

"What? What are you talking about? I thought you and Harmony were perfect?" Kevin asked Todd.

Todd put a finger in front of his lips. "Shhh! Harmony has bionic ears. She hears everything," Todd whispered as he peeped around to see if his wife was anywhere within earshot. "Hell no, we ain't perfect! Far from it. The babies will be a year in October. Harmony's still walking around looking eight months pregnant. You tell me what's perfect about that. If I gently suggest she try to get back in shape, all hell would break loose. That's like Pandora's box. So now I don't bother to bring that shit up—ever. Never ever. Hell, Arnold talks about his wife walking around with nothing on, mine does the same, but I wish she wouldn't for the opposite reason. I mean, I don't understand. Harmony was fine as hell—tall and sexy with everything in the right places. You remember, right?"

Eric and Arnold nodded since they remembered. Kevin didn't come along until she was already swollen from carrying triplets.

Todd continued. "She was intelligent and had it all together. Now, I don't know who the hell she is. Once upon a time she talked about keeping her career once we started our family. If I ask her about her plans to return to work in some capacity, she uses the babies as her crutch. Now all she does is play with the babies, sit on the sofa with her daily pint of Häagen-Dazs and Oreo cookies, while she psychoanalyzes the people on the Lifetime channel or *Dr. Phil*. She won't put on make-up or try to make herself slightly appealing." Todd cringed as if he had a disgusting thought.

"Don't you have a full-time nanny?" Eric asked.

"Yeah, we have a full-time nanny, and my mother spends more time here in Baldwin Hills than she does in Houston. My father has to fly out here when he wants to see my mom because she's always here, helping with the babies. My mom and our nanny use our gym, while Harmony won't as much as look in the room."

Todd peeped around outside of the gazebo again and whispered a little lower. "Now what I really don't understand is, Sandy had four children and looks damn good. Why can't Harmony at least try to get down to Sandy's size?"

Again, the guys nodded in agreement.

Todd shook his head. "And Eric, you think you've got it bad with women throwing themselves at you? I'm a damn doctor in Beverly Hills. Need I say more? I have twenty-five-year-old pussy thrown in my face every day. Sometimes they're younger than that. Half of my patients will find all kinds of reasons to have me examine their breast or genital areas."

Eric choked on his drink.

"Damn! That is hard," Arnold said with a chuckle.

"Yeah, I'm with you on that. I don't know if I could handle that one." Eric laughed, still trying to clear his airways.

"I love me some Elaine, but that would probably trip me up too," Kevin said, shaking his head.

"Man, I have mad respect for you," Eric added. "I never realized you had it so bad—or good." He laughed.

"Todd, are you in here talking about me?" Harmony asked, suddenly appearing in the gazebo. "I know I heard my name. What are you all in here talking about?"

The guys all looked at one another and tried to contain their laughter, as Todd was sure his heartbeat was audible outside of his body.

"No, dear. I was just telling the guys how much you dislike Kelly's husband. They were asking why he seems to be staying away from us, and I said that you don't like him because he wants to control your sister," Todd answered, as if Harmony would jump on him any moment. His eyes looked everywhere except at his wife's piercing eyes. She looked as if she wasn't buying it.

Arnold was impressed by Todd's quick comeback line to Harmony, so he tried to help cover. "Yeah, Harmony, I agree. I don't care much for him myself."

"Uhm-hmm, 'cause I'm pretty certain I heard something about women," Harmony responded, still suspicious. "Do I need to call my sisters over here?"

"No, honey. Kevin just asked why he keeps Kelly in his mess if he has all those women he works with," Todd timidly lied.

Kevin's eyes popped up at Todd from the surprise of being included in his deception.

Harmony rolled her eyes. "Don't get me started on his snake ass. I can't stand Kelly bringing his ass to our house, and then they hardly let his sons play with the other children. Those boys have been eyeing that moon bounce all afternoon. And do you see how her ass is over there looking like a damn Stepford Wife? She was in the kitchen with the rest of us and that bastard sent his sons in to get Kelly. I thought she might come back, but she never did. You're all some big, strong men. Can't you all get together and kick his ass so he'll get out of our family?"

The guys laughed, but Harmony was serious. She placed her hands on her large hips as she raised an eyebrow.

"Gee, I don't recall saying anything funny. I see I'm going to have to call my people in Detroit. They'd love an opportunity to kick someone's ass. They are serious gangsters, you know. All of you need to keep that in mind just in case you want to act a fool," Harmony said. She turned to walk away, but then looked back at her husband. "And Todd, I know you were out here talking about me, but we'll talk about that a little later."

The men remained silently still until they saw Harmony was back inside of the house more than fifty feet away. All but Todd broke out into a roaring laughter.

"Fuck . . . that . . . bitch! She ain't gonna say shit to me later," Todd whispered, still afraid for Harmony to hear him. "Then she thinks somebody is supposed to be afraid of her ghetto family in Detroit. A bunch of old hot air is all they are. I still want to smack her for inviting them to our wedding."

"You weren't lying about bionic ears," Eric said, still laughing. "How in the hell did she catch that shit? Man, I'd be scared to think around her."

Arnold said, "I think it's something in their family. If I didn't know any better, I'd swear Charise is a mind reader or something. I could be sitting there thinking some mean or crazy shit, and she'll just respond to it as if I said it out loud. That shit is creepy to me. I try to conceal my thoughts around her. Don't let some fine chick come on the television. She'll pick up on the ones that I find attractive."

Kevin shook his head. "Yeah, now that would scare me."

"What do you think would happen if we all got together and stood up to their asses once and for all?" Eric asked, sitting up in his lounge chair. "They can't keep treating us like this and thinking it's okay. We're all good looking men, doing well for ourselves. What can they do if we put our foot down?"

The men looked at each other before laughing at Eric.

"Oh, you are the foolish one, aren't you?" Todd asked. "If you talk shit, you'll have your jugular sliced by Shawnee. The whole damn family is rough around the edges. From what I've heard, their momma was rough. Always wanted to fight or cut somebody up. Shawnee is the mastermind of the family, and now she is a billionaire from that old guy she married. If I were you, I'd erase those thoughts. You can't win. Just face it— Shawnee owns you. She's the eldest. They all look up to her like she's the savior." Todd shook his head and reached over to pat Eric's shoulder. "Nah, my brother, let that one go."

Arnold and Kevin nodded in agreement.

"You don't want to bite the hand that feeds you—especially not Shawnee's hand. There's nothing more dangerous than a strong-minded woman who is intelligent, has power, money, and is rough around the edges. Oh no. Sorry, fam, but you're on your own with that one," Kevin said, shaking his head before chuckling. "Besides, my home is happy. I don't need anything shaking that up."

"I can't believe you all are going out like some punks. I am not Shawnee's bitch and she doesn't run me." Eric puffed up his chest, trying to look tough.

When no one else said anything, Arnold asked, "And just why are you sleeping in the guest house, waiting for her to summon you for sex?"

"Fuck you, man!" was all Eric could say as he sat back in his chair while the men broke into a roaring laughter once again. Even Eric had to laugh that time.

"Maybe we should get with Sean and find out how he does it," Arnold suggested. "He has her under total control. Look at them. Even the kids are in check. I kind of feel sorry for them, but at least his woman is in check."

"You better watch that thought before Charise picks up on it." Todd laughed.

"And then what? She's going to hold back on the sex?" He paused and answered before the others, "Uhps! Too late! She already held back. Bitch!"

"Hey! Hey! Hey! How are you gonna talk about your wife and mother of your son like that?" Kevin chuckled.

"You go damn near nine months with no action and see what you end up calling your wife," Arnold fired back. "Hell, you can have her."

"Nine months? Damn!" Eric asked in amazement. "I figured you were exaggerating with that nearly-a-year shit. You've only been married since April. How'd you get some nine months ago, but can't get any now?"

Arnold removed his sunglasses and shook his head. "Nobody said that it was Charise, did they?" Arnold answered with a "duh" expression before replacing his shades on his face.

Kevin shook his head. "That's the part I don't understand. You married the one who wouldn't give you any sex, but now you're pissed because you can't get any. Elaine and I chose to be celibate before marrying, but I knew there wasn't going to be any lacking once we were married. I don't think I could have married her if I knew there wasn't going to be some prize for my celibacy. I had been celibate a couple of years before marrying, but I wouldn't have married her if I knew I had to stay celibate."

Arnold answered, "That's just it. That's the part you seem to be missing: I didn't know I'd still be celibate. I thought I'd get some on my honeymoon. When I didn't get any, then I figured with a little time, Charise would be mentally, emotionally, and physically together where we could comfortably consummate our marriage. Charise is doing fine in every other area of her life, and you can't tell me she doesn't know what she's doing to me when she wants to cuddle naked or when she does all the other exhibitionist shit she does. I seriously think she gets off on fucking with my head. Hell, my dad told me I need to go find a piece on the side. I'm trying to be a man for my son, but she's breaking this man."

"Wow! That's not good. You can't let her break your manhood. Damn, I feel partly responsible. That was my son who caused Charise to be this way." Todd shook his head with distress.

"You can't blame yourself for what your son did. Hell, you remember how wild Charise was before that incident with your son. She didn't have a lick of respect for me or anyone else before then. If anything, it seems like she became a better woman as a result of that tragedy. Big thanks to Kevin also for helping her so much. It's just that I'm not receiving any physical benefits of that change. Nonetheless, my little man is happy having both his parents together. I do love seeing the way they both light up when they see each other now. You all know it wasn't like that not so long ago. Charise didn't have time or any desire to be a mother to our son. So, despite the blue balls, I am happy for that outcome."

"I know how you feel about trying to be a man for your son. That's how I feel about my daughter. I put up with Shawnee's shit because of my daughter. The thought of some other joker around my daughter makes me crazy. I would crush the motherfucker's skull if he got too close to her. So, to prevent all that, I have to jump through Shawnee's hoops. I mean, I'm grateful, because she could have not said anything about Shayla being mine. I would have just thought that old guy was her father."

Arnold raised his glasses up again to look at Eric as if he were crazy. "Eric, you can look right at Shayla and see she's your daughter. Shawnee couldn't have denied that if she wanted to."

Kevin and Todd nodded in agreement.

"Sure couldn't." Todd chuckled.

"Elaine and I never talked about having kids, but I'm kind of feeling jealous right now when I see how you guys light up when you talk about yours."

"I'll admit, I may talk a lot of mess, but I am so thankful to my wife for giving me three of the most gorgeous babies ever. I can't begin to explain how my babies make me feel inside. Sometimes I feel guilty, because when Harmony first got pregnant, I was secretly furious for her conveniently forgetting her birth control on our honeymoon and getting pregnant right away. I was even thinking of telling her to get an abortion, but I couldn't find the balls to say it to her. I really didn't want any more kids, since my boys were already grown.

Harmony was career oriented, and kids weren't on her list of priorities, even though her biological clock was ticking. I kind of felt like her ass tricked me. Now, I try to figure which of the three will be my favorite. Sometimes I hate leaving them to go to work. Maybe that's why Harmony hasn't gone back to work yet." Todd looked up into his thoughts.

"You know what I can't understand? How can a man pepper children all over the place and not feel any sense of attachment or obligation to them?" Arnold asked.

Eric reached over to Arnold for a fist-bump. "I have had many, many women in my life, but I wasn't about having children all over that I couldn't be there for. Shayla was created by super sperm, because both Shawnee and I were supposed to be protected. Shayla is my first and only. If I can't have more children with Shayla's mother, then I don't want any. Too many mommas are too much drama."

"Yes indeed!" Todd chimed in. "I couldn't see having kids and the woman was not my wife. To keep it real, sometimes I'm glad Harmony is there for the babies. It's good for their development."

Eric nodded. "Same here. I'm glad Shawnee's not trying to pawn our daughter off so she can travel around the world for her job. If Shayla's not with her, she's only allowed to be with me. I told her my mom is willing to come in town to babysit whenever we have a need. Shawnee's still trying to process the thought."

"I thought Shawnee gets along with your mother?" Arnold asked.

"Please! She's more worried about us appearing as a real family. They get along very well, and Shawnee trusts my mom, but it's just her trying to keep me at arm's length with her personally."

"We need to get together more often. This is like therapy for me," Todd said, finishing off his beer, and the other guys laughed when they realized he was serious.

"Therapy? Grown-ass men don't do therapy. That shit sounds gay. Get a grip." Eric laughed.

"Why do you need therapy? You're married to a psychologist," Arnold joked.

Todd shot Arnold a dirty look. "That's why I need therapy."

The guys all laughed.

"I don't know what you're talking about. I'd go to therapy," Kevin replied. "Heck, I've gone to talk to someone a time or two when things were getting rough."

"For the shit I put up with in my house, maybe I could use someone to talk to, to help figure out my damn wife. My moms is like my therapist, but she won't ever let me get a word in once she's on her anti-Charise roll." Arnold chuckled, but he was serious.

"Uh-oh, Harmony and Charise just came out of the house. You better be quiet and clear your thoughts," Kevin joked.

"Fuck them!" Todd whispered. The men laughed again.

"Uhps! There's my baby girl," Eric said, getting up from his chair when he spotted Shawnee coming out of the house with his daughter. "Check you all later."

The other men followed, joining the other women and enjoying their July Fourth celebration.

PROLOGUE

2

Kevin gave Sean a man-hug when he approached the table in the sports bar.

"Hey Sean, glad you were able to free up some time to join us."

"Yo, that was cool for you to include me. I thought I was supposed to be the outcast." He chuckled. "Are the other guys coming?"

"Yeah, they're running a bit late. We were just saying last month at the cookout how we need a monthly night for just the boys. Since it's NFL preseason time, there's no better time than the present. Also, with everyone's busy schedules, this was the earliest we were all able to coordinate."

Sean nodded. "I'm a NBA man myself, but this is cool. It's a nice distraction from home and office. All my boys work with me in the office, so when we do go out, we still talk shop."

"Yeah, I know what you mean. I stay involved in so many projects, and moments to just kick back and relax are a rare treat," Kevin said, trying to find a way to make conversation despite the awkwardness. "I'm a Clippers fan myself. What about you?"

"Oh no! Not the Clippers! Lakers all the way!" Sean laughed.

"Don't sleep on the Clippers. They're ranking better than the Lakers right now," Kevin argued.

"Yeah, yeah, yeah," Sean joked. But then he got serious. "Kevin, let me ask you a question before the others get here."

"Sure, man. What's on your mind?"

"So, what's up with this meeting? It's no secret there ain't no love. Or is that my imagination or what?"

"No hidden agenda. I just realized that we all have something in common: The Wiggins Sisters. None of us are in a position to judge anyone."

"Yeah, that's cool."

"Here come Arnold and Todd now," Kevin said pointing toward the door.

The guys exchanged a friendly greeting, but Arnold was seething inside at the idea of Sean being a part of their male bonding night out.

"Where's Eric? He couldn't sneak out?" Todd asked no one in particular as he situated his seat before sitting.

"He called and said he'd be here as soon as he could get away from the restaurant," Kevin answered, as the waitress was placing plates on the table. "I took the liberty of ordering some beers and wings just before you arrived."

Todd and Arnold looked at him strangely.

"You don't drink. What you doing ordering beer?" Arnold laughed. "Besides, I gave up alcohol after I learned I had a little one that came from having too many drinks."

"Yeah, right. That was your ass drinking up all the beers on the Fourth. Drunk so many, we didn't have enough for the other guests," Todd joked.

"I only had two, three, maybe four beers that day, but that was it," Arnold joked back. Then Arnold had a thought. "Damn man, you were sitting there counting what we ate and drank?" He tried to say it with a straight face but ended up laughing.

"You damn right!" Todd answered, also trying not to laugh.

"Now I did eat a whole slab of ribs. Those damn things were good as hell. I meant to ask you what you did to those things."

Todd acted shocked. "Man! Damn, Arnold, I didn't even get a rib. Ain't that about a bitch? You know how long I slaved over those things. All that and your ass ate a whole slab by yourself?"

The guys all laughed while Todd pretended to look sad. "Those were Texas-style. My great-granddaddy's recipe."

"Well you might want to take the matter up with Eric. That's a big one there. He looks like he could eat the whole pig by himself," Kevin added. "He'd scare a whole herd of pigs on sight alone."

"Hell, what are you, about six-four yourself? Eric my ass!" Todd said to Kevin. "You ate those ribs too."

Kevin laughed robustly as he held up his hands to indicate he was guilty as charged, and then he saw Eric entering the sports bar. "Look at him. He's coming in now."

"Damn, those girls are jocking him hard. They won't let him make it to the table," Arnold said.

"Maybe he'll bring some of that candy to the table with him. You know, something good to look at, maybe hold onto while we're watching the game," Sean chimed in, suddenly reminding the others of his unwanted presence.

The laughter faded and eyebrows rose. Sean could feel the instant chill.

When Eric approached and greeted everyone, he said, "Hey Sean, I didn't know you were joining us." His facial expression had difficulty hiding his disappointment. "I just hope we don't have to be sitting here biting our tongues."

"Hey, what's up? Yeah, I was surprised when Kevin called. But nah, you don't have to bite your tongue with me. It's all good wit' me. Hell, you might end up with an earful here," Sean answered and the guys just nodded.

Arnold tapped Eric's arm with the back of his hand. "E, Kev said you ate up all the ribs at the cookout."

Eric looked at a laughing Arnold, surprised. "Black man, please! Now you know damn well you ate those ribs up. Every time I turned around, you, Charise, and your shorty had a rib in your mouths." Eric made a comical reenactment of them shoving ribs in their mouths.

The guys all laughed and Arnold almost fell off of his stool from laughing so hard. "Todd knows it wasn't me 'cause I don't eat pork." He paused before saying, "Now, I *did* eat up that beef brisket." They all laughed again. "Hey, I'm a big man. I ain't got no shame," he said, hunching his shoulders and patting his tight belly.

"Damn, isn't it a liberating feeling to sit here and be so grammatically incorrect and not have to worry about someone correcting your ass?" Todd asked, beating his chest, pretending to be Tarzan.

"But then you come out with the 'isn't' instead of 'ain't.' We could use 'ain't' tonight and all the double negatives we want," Arnold scoffed. "That damn Charise. Every time I turn around, she's trying to correct me, but she can talk like a gangster, 'round-the-way girl whenever she wants." Arnold turned his focus to Kevin. "Kevin, I don't know whether to be grateful to you or kick your ass sometimes. When I see how much my girl has grown up and got her act together since you helped her start her magazine, I'm grateful to you. But when she starts with that whole trying-to-correct-my-grammar shit, I want to kick your ass for helping her."

The guys laughed.

Kevin put his hands up in defense. "She would have started that magazine eventually without my help. She has a way of going after what she wants and taking it. But really, that was a good investment for me I wasn't expecting a return on. She's doing a great job with her magazine."

"Yeah, I have to admit, I didn't think she had it in her. That's my baby," Arnold said, beaming with pride.

Taking note of the joyful smile on Arnold's face, Todd asked, "Oh, I take it you're getting some now."

Kevin and Eric erupted into laughter. Sean looked confused.

"Fuck you! Why you gotta go there?" Arnold shot back, instantly losing his smile. "Hell no I still haven't gotten any. Fuck her! See, you done gone and made me mad at her ass again."

The guys continued laughing as Arnold pouted and tried to maintain his serious face while shaking his head.

Sean wrinkled his brows. "I know y'all not talking about loving, are you?"

"Sure is," Eric answered, still laughing extra hard.

"Well when was your last crumb, Eric?" Arnold asked, trying to not look like the only fool at the table.

"Last night, this morning, and just before I came here. Now! What you got to say about that?!" Eric slammed his hand on the table, laughing even harder.

"Damn! For real, Eric? Don't play like that," Todd asked.

"Serious! I don't know what the hell happened, but I won't look a gift horse in the mouth. A brotha been feeling on top of his game lately. The Mandingo is back!" Eric responded.

Kevin raised his eyebrows. "So what you'd have us to believe is, Shawnee finally let you out of the guesthouse to live in the main house now? Is that what you are telling us here?"

"Hell no! There you go with that apples and oranges shit again. That's not what I said," Eric answered, while Todd and Arnold laughed and Sean was still trying to follow.

"Let me see if I got this right: So what you are saying is that you can't even live in the house with your woman?" Sean asked in disbelief, before propping his hand on his thigh and turning to Arnold. "And you can't get any loving at all from your own wife?" He blew out a deep breath and shook his head, chuckling. "That's some shit there."

"I take it your home life is all roses, huh, Sean?" Todd asked, feeling the need to defend his friends from the family enemy.

"I can't even imagine Kelly refusing me or disrespecting me. Trust when I tell you, my ship is tight," Sean answered, full of himself.

Todd, disgusted with Sean's smug attitude asked, already knowing the answer, "So what's up with that baby you mentioned back last Christmas?

You've been trying to get pregnant for some time now, huh?" He chuckled deviously.

Todd already knew through Harmony that Kelly had been secretly taking birth control pills to prevent getting pregnant, only Sean had no clue.

"We'll have our little one soon enough. My other two sons have been keeping her busy. She's getting her practice now at motherhood, and we're getting plenty of practice at making a baby," Sean defended, "if you know what I mean." He wiggled his hips in the seat.

"Damn, we're missing the game, and all we have is this bullshit tap beer to drink," Arnold said, not wanting to hear Sean's arrogance.

Eric examined and smelled one of the pitchers of beer. "Who ordered this shit?"

All fingers pointed to Kevin. He looked flushed with embarrassment as he looked at all dagger-like eyes on him.

"What? How was I supposed to know? I don't drink. I don't know one beer from another. I figured they all taste the same," Kevin said with a laugh.

"Ahhgg!! Next time leave the drink orders to us." Sean chuckled. Arnold gave him dap, momentarily forgetting his dislike.

Eric summoned a waitress. "Can we get some real beer over here? We're going to need some more wings also."

The waitress put her hand on Eric's large chest. "Oh I have to get you a large supply of wings. You're a big guy with big needs I bet," she said, cheesing closer to him than what should be appropriate with customers.

"Yeah, that big guy is married to a big woman who would make you wish you were never born," Todd shot at the waitress, startling her.

"You're blocking the man's action," Sean said when the waitress hurried away after taking the guys' drink orders.

"I'm not blocking anything," Todd answered. "Hell, you all know not to be doing shit I have to go home and lie about. You know Harmony's going to grill me when I get home, and I'll be the first to admit, I'm not a good liar."

"It's like that in your house?" Sean arrogantly asked, surprised.

"All of our houses," Arnold answered. "So that means you can do all kinds of shit in your house and your wife doesn't question you?" Arnold asked like a statement.

Sean puffed. "Hell no, my wife doesn't question me. There've been nights I haven't made it home and Kelly didn't question me."

The guys frowned up their faces, annoyed.

Intrigued by Sean's arrogance, Kevin asked, "So you stay out with other women and your wife doesn't say anything?"

"Most of the times I'm in the studio with clients all night. Every now and again, I like a little variety. Ain't nothing wrong with that. Every man needs some variety."

"I hate to disappoint you, but I am content being with just my wife," Kevin responded. He didn't care too much for Sean before, but this underscored his dislike for the man.

"Man, why you gotta go there? Now I have to hope Harmony doesn't ask me any questions when I get home. I don't want to tell her you're messing around on her sister."

"It's not that heavy, man. I'm not worried about Kelly going anywhere. We're solid. You don't have to lie to your wife on my account. I'd prefer no one doing or saying things to upset my wife, but if someone feels they must try to upset her then I'll be there for her," Sean answered with a matter-of-fact tone.

"Wow! That's some deep shit there," Eric said, shaking his head. "Who makes your wife feel better when it's you that's upsetting or hurting her? You really think you're not hurting her when you indulge in your 'variety?' What if she wanted some variety too?"

"OH! That shit would never happen!" Sean spat back. He was obviously rattled by the interrogation. "Kelly's not all petty and getting upset over some small shit like other women. She knows she's my wife and my number-one. That's all that matters. I go to work and take care of my wife. I give my wife plenty of good lovin'. She doesn't need anyone else, and she's not even thinking about going anywhere."

Arnold laughed at his own thoughts. "Yeah, you keep believing that shit if you want to. You'll be one of those niggas laid up in the hospital fighting for your life when she throws that pot of hot grits on your ass. It's always the ones who don't complain," Arnold told Sean. "But that's your business and your household, so you be the man of your house."

The others chimed in his background like an Amen choir. "No doubt," Sean answered, trying to contain his anger as his jaw tightened. "I'm going to be the man for sure.

The guys spent the rest of the time together mostly in silence, other than small talk about the game plays. They departed ways before the end of the fourth quarter.

PART ONE

Running Amuck

1

Todd

I'm going to have to get in Kevin's ass for inviting Sean to our first guys' night out. I needed to get some stuff out about what happened in the office earlier, but I wasn't going to talk in front of that fool. The other guys could help me sort out my mess, but if I would have talked in front of Sean, it would be back to Harmony before I could make it home from the sports bar. There's also no doubt he would have had word back to Shawnee if Eric had played around with that waitress. Any other night, I wouldn't give a damn who Eric's kickin' it with. But not in front of Sean. Hell, I wouldn't have minded some sexy girl on my lap while we watched the game, myself. But not with Sean around.

Miss Foster came in the office this afternoon for her quarterly-annual, meaning she comes in for her annual exams every three months rather than once a year like normal people. I don't know what it is about this woman that makes the blood rush to my lower head. She's one of the many who need me to check their breasts or vaginal areas rather than just going to their gynecologist as I would recommend. Probably ten percent of my patients are legitimately sick. The others just find any excuse for me to see them and behave like I've never seen tits and pussy before, and theirs is supposed to be like gold to me.

However, Miss Foster is different from the others. I have found myself making love to my wife (what few times I do), while pretending she was the gorgeous twenty-six-year-old. I've gotten to the point where I'm grateful for Miss Foster's excessive, unnecessary appointments. She'll also come if she had a runny nose that morning, saying she thinks she's coming down with the flu. If she gets a little pimple, she'll say she must be having an allergic reaction to something. She's nothing like my mother, who is a straight up hypochondriac. Oh no, Miss Foster just wants to get a visit with me.

Every time I see her tits, my mouth waters to lick them. When I see her ass, I just want to bend her over and fuck her senseless. Her advances have graduated way beyond what is appropriate for a doctor/patient relationship, but the thought of turning her away to another doctor hardly seems like an option. That would be the right thing to do, but my loins won't let me refuse the opportunity to see and touch her.

During one of her visits, she put her foot in my crotch. She picked up on my hesitation to push her away as I had previously. She took my hand in her hands to fondle her all natural, perky breasts during the so-called breast exam.

During her next visit she said, "It's okay if you enjoy touching my body. My body enjoys your touch." During both of her previous vaginal exams, she'd gyrate her genitals, but on the last of the two, she asked, "Do my pussy smell okay to you? I need to make sure my pussy is always fresh." She was sure to put extra emphasis on the word "pussy." Stupid me, I inhaled its scent, and it smelled so good. I wanted to lick it.

However, today a line was crossed that can't be repaired.

My dick was already looking forward to her quarterly- annual appointment this afternoon. When I came into her exam room, she still hadn't undressed and put on the gown as instructed by the nurse. I was about to step back out to allow her to change, but she insisted there was no need since I had already seen everything. Sounded like a convincing argument to me. Foolishly, I stayed while she seductively peeled off every item of clothing, including her thong.

My dick was ready to blow the zipper out of my pants. The stupid lab coat I put on to intentionally conceal the erection I get around Miss Foster didn't help one damn bit. Miss Foster saw the bulge as my eyes were hypnotized by her perfect naked body. She walked up to me and grabbed hold of my erection with one hand while taking my hand and placing it on her breast with her other hand. Mind you, she's not on the exam table yet.

I got caught up for a moment until I realized where I was at. I had both of my hands on her breasts. When I stopped myself, I had her get on the table and forgot to ask her any questions. I sat down between her legs and pulled the stirrups out and let her open up that fresh scent to my face. I also forgot to give her something to cover her naked body as she lay on the table. Had someone walked in the room, I would have been dead.

Additionally, I forgot to use the forceps waiting on the tray. Instead, I used my fingers. I then stood up on the other side of her for better positioning while my fingers were searching her pussy for some 'abnormality' and my other hand was checking her breast for an imaginary lump.

Miss Foster managed to get my trapped erection out of my zipper, and she fondled it as I had longed for. Her pussy juiced up all over my hand as my fingers went in deeper to examine her cervix. Her body was gyrating so seductively. Her eyes rolled up in her head, letting me know she found a place of ecstasy. I wanted my dick inside of her pussy like I never had with any other patient. When her tongue touched the tip of my shaft, I finally snapped back to reality.

"Oh my God! Oh my—I am so sorry," I said, hurrying to the sink to wash her cum from my hands.

"Don't be."

She came to the sink near me and pressed her breasts against my arm as she reached past me for some tissues.

I quickly moved away, saying, "I swear, I have never done anything like this before. I don't know what came over me."

"Doctor Palmer, trust me, everything is all good. I mean really good." She smiled while seductively wiping between her legs.

I tried not to look, but I was hypnotized until she covered her nudity.

She was cleaned up and redressed without ever getting a legitimate examination. She grabbed her pocketbook on the chair and pulled it open. She pulled something out and placed it in my shirt pocket.

"What's this?" I asked, trying to clear the frog from my throat while avoiding her seductive eyes.

"I figured I'd leave you with something to think about on a cold and lonely night, or maybe when you're having a rough day."

I began pulling the item from my pocket, seeing her phone number already written on the back of a wallet sized photo. She stopped my hand before I was able to get the picture fully out of my pocket. I didn't put up one ounce of resistance when she placed the photo back in my pocket and reached up to peck my lips.

"Later. There's no need to look now."

"Miss Foster, I am a ha-ha-happily married man. I'm flattered that you are interested, but—"

"That's not what my tingling pussy says." She smirked.

I couldn't think of anything to rebut. I mean, after all, I just finished fucking her with my hand, while her lips were on my meat. Who the hell was I trying to kid?

I wanted to apologize for crossing the line, but truthfully, I was not sorry. Instead, I opened the exam room door and tried to sound official. "We'll be in touch with your results in a few days."

She played along as she walked out of the room. "I'm definitely anxious to hear back." Then she was gone and I've been a mess since.

I ran to my office to examine the photo. I closed my door, unsure of what the photo may have revealed, yet hoping it was what I thought it might be. I pulled the photo from my pocket to find a nude Miss Foster with her legs opened wide enough for me to see the pink between her legs.

Since I couldn't bring myself to throw the photo away, now I have to find a place to hide it. I've looked at the picture about ten times since she gave it to me. The picture combined with the memory of my hand all up in her tight cavity is incredible. Damn, I wanted to lick her tits so bad. I don't know what stopped me. Hell, I already crossed the line. I should have let her suck my dick. No, instead, I'm trying to be the good husband. And who was I trying to fool with that "happily married" bullshit? My marriage is anything but. Even Miss Foster wasn't buying that line.

So after three beers at the sports bar with the guys, I'll take my horny ass in this house and hope Harmony will give me some pussy, so I can pretend that she's Miss Foster. Harmony has about 115—make that about 125—pounds more on her body than Miss Foster. That's going to require a lot of imagination. Then again, I could just call the number on the back of the photo and stop pretending. But what if she turns out to be some nutcase and starts making noise to mess up my marriage?

Funny, as I was driving home from the sports bar, they were playing that old song, "She's Got Papers on Me," by Richard "Dimples" Fields. I don't know if that's some kind of omen or what.

I swore after my last affair in Houston, while Harmony was in Los Angeles waiting for me to relocate, I would never cross the line again. That was Roxana Hampton, one of my former patients. When she heard I was leaving Houston she found me and reminded me of the times I rejected her advances because I was her doctor. I couldn't bring myself to leave Houston with always wondering what she would have felt like. So I tracked her down. Roxana was a bona fide freak. I was half tempted to stay in Houston and turn my back on Harmony and the babies. My mind tried to conjure all kinds of excuses so I didn't have to give up fucking Roxana at will. I certainly wasn't in a rush to get back to an oversized pregnant wife, who could no longer have sex. I needed to feel pussy on my dick. I couldn't be satisfied with just a blow job.

After Roxana, I vowed to myself I would forever be faithful to my wife, but, damn, it's almost a year later and Harmony weighs only five pounds less than she did right before she delivered the three babies. That's insane. Not only that, a C-section scar is not cute on a big woman, looking like she has yet to deliver, ten months later. Thankfully she's always too tired for sex. The sex she does give me is purely mercy sex, and in between that, she's always accusing me of wanting to fuck some skinny bitch.

Hello!! Newsflash!! You're damn right I want to fuck some skinny bitch. Try losing some fucking weight and maybe I'll want to fuck you beyond obligation or pretending you're someone else.

Then there is one of my nurses, Valerie, who, like Miss Foster, is also young enough to be my daughter. She lets it be known that she wants me. She doesn't have the prettiest face, but I'm sure her own mother loves it. Her hair weave looks like she practices on her own head to be a hair stylist in her spare time, and her teeth aren't in the greatest condition. She's no Miss Foster, but that day I saw her bending over and was able to see her boobs protruding from her bra, behind her scrubs, she made me want to see more. I know her bending was intentional, but I ain't mad at her. She bends her ass in my view all the time. It didn't affect me until that day I caught that glimpse of her nipples. Now when she bends that ass, I get turned on.

I can't fuck with Valerie, though. That would be a sexual harassment suit in the making. Not to mention I don't really find her attractive, but I could fantasize. She's always squeezing by me, making sure to rub her breast against my back. Now if I rubbed my dick against her ass, she'd be screaming "lawsuit." Valerie also tries to hang around until everyone else is gone and ask personal questions about my favorite foods, drinks, and music. The situation makes me uncomfortable, so I typically send her home or leave. It makes me uncomfortable because sometimes I want to fuck her but can't.

The one woman I have fantasized about more than anything or anyone would be my wife's sister, Elaine. I remember the first day I laid eyes on her in D.C. when I went to help Harmony with her move to Houston. I can't tell you how bad I wanted to leave Harmony's ass in D.C. and take Elaine instead.

I can't explain the power she has over me. So many times I've wondered if she fantasizes about me as well. Hell, I understood Shawnee's first husband, Robert, when he went through all he went through just to have a chance to fuck Elaine. Sometimes I want to ask Eric what was it like to fuck Elaine, but then I start wondering if Shawnee is the better fuck since she's the one he's hung up on. Hell, I wouldn't mind doing Shawnee just once either. I already know she's a big freak, just from Harmony telling me some of the antics she's used to climb the corporate ladder, and ultimately own the whole damn company—the company that should have been left to my sister.

But still, if I had to choose, I would pick Elaine out of all the sisters. My heart sank when Kevin talked about his oversexed marriage. That's the woman I need: A sexy-ass woman who is totally concerned about keeping fit, and is a sexaholic. I love everything about Elaine, down to her sexy footwear and her always pedicured feet. Unlike Harmony's daily ponytail, Elaine generally keeps her hair styled, but still long. When she does have a ponytail, she's still looking damn good enough to eat. Her ass sits out, screaming, "Todd, come fuck me," while her tits stand up saying, "Come lick me." Not an ounce of fat jiggling on her body.

Before Harmony got pregnant, I fucked her and imagined she was Elaine instead. I did it on our honeymoon. I was pissed off at my own wedding because I was marrying Elaine's sister instead of Elaine. I wanted her so bad when I saw her in her skimpy bathing suits in Cancun, especially the thong bikini. Even seeing her in her designer gown got a rise out of me. My brothers Kyle and Kenny also agreed she should have been my bride. Thankfully I have two brothers I can tell anything to and don't have to worry about hearing it again. You remember the singing group, Sister Sledge, and how they were all attractive, but each had a uniqueness about them? That's the Wiggins women, with Elaine being the most captivating.

I don't know what it is about those Wiggins sisters. Even my oldest son, Andre, was captivated by Charise. Now he'll die in prison as a result since he beat and raped her with objects because he thought she infected him with HIV. Turned out Charise wasn't positive. If he didn't try to kill her, at least I could still have him in my life.

Then again, we'd probably still be in Houston, and I wouldn't have ever had a chance to experience Roxana or to meet Miss Foster. Talk about a tradeoff.

When I really think about it, it may have been best that Sean came out tonight. I don't think it really would have been a good idea telling the guys about my encounter with Miss Foster. They would most certainly try to talk me out of bothering with her. They'd convince me to throw away the picture, and then I'd be kicking myself for the next three months (until her next quarterly appointment).

Damn, I don't want to go in this house. I want to sit in the car and just stare at this photo all night. Damn, I should have sucked those tits. I should have let her take my dick in her mouth and suck the testicle out. I should have licked that pussy. I forgot to do her rectal exam. I could call the number I have already memorized, or I could wait for her next appointment and get some cheap thrills.

2

Arnold

This is Arnold," I answered on my speaker phone sitting in my posh Downtown L.A. office with a view to kill for. I work as a Global Implementation Manager and my new office is one of the fruits of my labor.

"Hey, stranger. Did I catch you at a bad time?"

I snatched up the receiver and looked out of the glass walls, afraid someone may have heard my ex-girlfriend calling me. "Samantha? How are you?"

"I'm doing good. I'm sure I'd be much better if you were here with me in Houston."

I nervously chuckled. "Wow, it's really good to hear your voice." I had to double check my cell phone to make sure my line wasn't accidentally opened, somehow allowing my wife to overhear me talking to the woman she despises.

"How is Jarrod? I miss that little boy," she said to fill in after an awkward silence.

"He's doing good."

"I bet he had the most fabulous second birthday ever?"

"Yeah, that was a few months ago. He's getting big. He's talking up a storm. Now he's looking forward to seeing his family for Labor Day this weekend. I'm kind of psyched up myself. I love getting together with the guys."

"Is your family flying in, or are you referring to your in- laws?"

"Both. My brother, my sister Junie, and my parents are coming with the kids, and then there are my in-laws also."

Samantha caught me off guard when she asked, "So let's be honest. Was marrying your son's mother all that you thought it would be?"

I debated whether to answer honestly or not. The mere sound of Samantha's voice made me feel guilty. Almost a whole sexless year, what I would give just for one of those many nights we shared together. Samantha is a woman who knows how to treat her man. It killed me to let her go to pursue my foolish fantasy of being married and raising my children with both parents, as my parents had.

"Honestly, things are really good." I decided to lie. I didn't dare tell her I was in a sexless marriage.

"So I guess meeting me for lunch one day next month when I arrive in L.A. is out of the question? 'Cause you know I wouldn't want to intrude upon your happy life," she teased.

"You-you'll be in L.A. next month?" I stuttered. "Business?"

"To be quite honest, I miss you and want to see you. I was hoping by now you'd realize you were with the wrong woman and Charise would have left me an opening to come and reclaim the best man I have ever had."

Now how do I respond to that? The last pussy I had was hers. The last massage or bubble bath I had was with Samantha. The last dick sucking I had was from Samantha.

"Sam, I have to ask, are you coming to create drama? Because I really would like to see you, but I don't want to have any craziness."

"Crazy?" Samantha erupted in laughter. "Crazy is your son's mother, who I know you don't truly love, but married out of obligation. You know me, Arnold. I'm not about drama. Over the past year, I've had time to think about things. I realize that I'd be happier with a part of you than to have none of you. You could sit there all you want and tell me things are good for you, but I know better. I'm willing to accept whatever portion of you that you are willing to give me, but having no part of you is killing me. You do know you have lovemaking skills that should be bottled and sold, right?"

See, that's the shit I need. Samantha strokes my ego. With Charise, I can't do anything right. Why should I keep sexually depriving myself? It's not like I won't still be a good father for my son.

"Sam, I'm looking forward to seeing you next month," I confessed. "How long will you be in town?"

"It depends on you. I've been offered an opportunity in L.A., but will only consider it if I know that you will keep me in your life. Otherwise, I'll be in town for only two weeks. I finally took a vacation."

"Vacation? I didn't think they let you have such extravagances." I laughed.

"Well, if you remember correctly, I was returning from vacation in Cancun when we met on the flight to Houston on Valentine's Day."

"How could I forget that day? Talk about an emotional rollercoaster. Thankfully it ended on a high."

"Glad I could be a part of that high. Arnold, you don't know how much I missed you. Even Momma told me to go get my man."

"How is your mother? Tell her I said hello."

"She's doing great. I'll tell her I talked to you. That'll make her day. Well, I'm not going to hold you up. I'll give you a call when I get in town. Enjoy your holiday festivities."

"For sure. And Sam, thanks for reaching out to a brotha. You just made my day much brighter."

"No, thank you for not shooting me down. I can't wait to see you," she seductively whispered in the phone, enhancing my erection.

After I hung up from Sam, I called my mom, who is like my best, best friend. I told her about my conversation with Samantha.

My mother will never, under any circumstance, like Charise, and she was mad I listened to my dad and married her. My mother doesn't feel Charise has changed one bit from who she was before being hospitalized. She also thinks

Charise is sleeping with someone else and that's the reason she won't sleep with me. She says Charise is afraid of losing custody of our son once again. I don't know what I would do if I found out that was true. I have been sexually deprived for damn near a year. I wouldn't *try* to kill her; I *would* kill her.

Labor Day weekend is going to be kind of rough. My mom doesn't bite her tongue to Charise that she doesn't like her. Then Charise always wants me to try controlling my mother. My mother is probably the one person Charise is intimidated by. When Mom is around, Charise behaves like mother of the year.

My mother hasn't come face-to-face with Charise since our wedding back in April. Mom's more pissed off about my blue balls than I am. I'm hoping she doesn't confront Charise about it. She promised me she wouldn't, but Mom can be a firecracker at times. My pops said he'll help to keep the two apart.

My younger sister Jamika refuses to get anywhere near Charise. She wants to fight Charise since all the mess we went through in Houston. My oldest sister Joanie doesn't like family gatherings that include anyone outside of our immediate family. Junie gets along with everyone, even Charise.

Charise will talk mad shit about Junie and the rest of my family every time she gets mad at me for one thing or another.

"You know, I used to like and respect that girl, but what a damn fool she must be to give up her whole life to sit around being someone's mistress in hopes of one day being the missus."

"Mom, people do that when they find that love they think is worth holding on for."

"What, like the love you thought you had for that nasty-ass Charise? You were—as a matter of fact, still is—a real fool for chasing behind Charise not once, but twice. If Samantha has no qualms about being the chick on the side, then do what you must and go for self. Particularly because I think that whore you married is doing so already. There ain't no way that tramp is still traumatized."

"Mom, that's my wife and son's mother you're talking about. Stop it."

"Ok, deep breath. I'm taking a deep breath. Well, at least the tramp makes beautiful babies. I do love my grandbaby." She chuckled. "I can't wait to see my Snookums."

I just shook my head. There is no changing my mother's mind when it comes to Charise. She went on and on before I finally interrupted her. "Mom . . . Mom, I have to go. I'm at work. I'll call you later."

"Don't you be trying to rush me off just because you don't wanna hear what I have to say. You know I'm right. I always am, and I know your gut is telling you she's a tramp, stringing you along. If Sam is willing, go for yours. I won't respect her anymore, but do what you have to do."

"Okay, Mom. Thanks for the advice. Love you. Bye!" I said, quickly ending the call.

If I don't know anything else, I know one damn thing: Arnold Hamilton is about to get him some pussy. I just have to make it through this month. Woo-hoo! Hopefully my wife will give me some before then. But if she doesn't . . .

3

Kevin

How am I in this predicament, again? I thought I was done with all the secrets and skeletons and crap. If I wasn't so paranoid about Elaine reverting to prostitution, I wouldn't be having more sex than I could stand, and I would not have succumbed to the temptation.

It was hard as hell to resist. I don't know when my feelings developed, but when she stripped naked and placed my hands on her large breasts, I realized that she had to be sent from hell. The devil tends to play on our weaknesses. I was able to abstain for a few years before marrying Elaine. That's how I know my weakness wasn't the flesh; it was my feelings.

I believed Elaine was everything I could ever want or need. Yet I touched *her* forbidden body and had no one I could tell. She's like poison to her own family. I kissed her poisoned lips as my loins ached to be inside of her. Yet I didn't tell my wife and my friend of the deception they are living? What would be the price to be paid if they knew? What would happen if the one secret I've held back from my wife were to ever come to light? Where would that leave us all?

Several years ago, Yolanda Banks was the woman I loved and wanted to spend the rest of my life with, but Yolanda had a sister with her own agenda. No, sex wasn't her agenda. Getting high was. She enjoyed smoking pot. She'd spend a lot of time at the house even when Yolanda was away on business. There were never any trust issues.

One Friday when Yolanda was away, her sister came by to fix my dinner, as she had many times in the past. When I came home, I found her out back smoking marijuana. Somehow that one day I was getting turned on by her being there high. She was as sexy as Yolanda, but she had this more carefree spirit compared to Yolanda's strictly business side.

That night I offered her a drink to go with the marijuana. When she was good and toasted, I made my move and she cooperated. We were at it for hours. She stayed with me all night and into the morning, but then I got greedy and wanted more of the loving with her in her right mind. While I was mid-stroke, Yolanda walked in totally shocked by the scene. Yolanda ran out, and I tried to run after her, not sure what I would say if I caught up to her. Before I could make it to the door, she was already speeding off in her car.

It was two days later when I received the phone call that my Yolanda was dead. They found her car down off the coast. To make matters worse, her sister committed suicide when she found out about Yolanda. I couldn't bring myself to attend either funeral.

I was been celibate from that time until the day I married Elaine. Now my demons are visiting me once again.

The week after the Fourth of July cookout, Charise stopped by my home office to go over some numbers for her magazine. I wasn't quite sure why she felt the need to see me about her magazine financials when I hadn't asked her for anything. Then again, it was her quarter end, so I figured it must have been legit. Still, she always gave anything I needed to see to Elaine to give to me.

I was reviewing her financials and she excused herself to the restroom. Next thing I know, I looked up and she was standing directly in front of me wearing only a thong. She bent to kiss my speechless lips as she took my hands to her double-D's. They were beautiful and felt good in my hands. I was seeing the body I had longed to see many times before, and kissing the lips that caused me to lick my own lips.

When she saw no resistance from me, she straddled my lap and guided my hand on her breast to touch her alcove. My member rose to the occasion inside of my Sean John sweat pants. My mouth wouldn't let go of her mouth the whole time. My hands feverishly searched her body. I let go of her mouth in exchange for a breast. I lost all concept of reality or consequences, until she reached inside of my pants to pull out my trapped member, and the soreness brought me back to the realization of the hell I had just entered. The soreness was caused by my excessive sexual relations with my wife—the sister of the woman who I was touching and kissing. I snapped back to my senses and sent Charise out of my home. I have been imprisoned by the memory ever since.

Somehow I had developed a special bond with Charise over the past year. Although I had never thought of that bond as being romantic or anything like it, I would find my thoughts imagining her naked whenever Arnold would talk about how she'd walk around with nothing on. I've heard so many erotic stories involving Charise and would envision them as they were told to me. Still, I never had any desire to be with her sexually.

Seeing her nakedness in front of me caused me to become aroused. Suddenly I desired to have her. I then understood how Sandy's husband was also taken in by her sexuality. Once upon a time, I sat in judgment, thinking that was the sickest and most despicable thing ever, but now I find myself in this position. Not once, but twice now. I thought I'd learned from the whole Yolanda experience, but I'm not sure I've learned anything now.

The one secret I never told my wife was about Yolanda. I never wanted her to have to worry about what Sandy had to deal with. I didn't want Elaine to know I could be such a despicable person and risk that she may not want me in her life at all.

Now the woman I have somehow developed feelings for has placed me in an even more difficult position than before.

She came by my office yesterday saying, "We need to finish what we started."

"Huh?" I asked, surprised by her boldness.

"I could see how bad you wanted me at the Labor Day cookout."

She was right. I did.

"And I could see your mouth watering when I was seductively sucking on that rib bone." She inserted her finger deep into her mouth before drawing it out.

Again, she was right.

"Charise, you have to stop this. I have a wife and you have a husband," I tried to remind her as firmly as I could.

"Please! Don't nobody want Arnold's boring ass. The only reason I hang on is for my son. If he leaves, he'll leave with my son and that's the only child I'll ever have. Besides, your wife is a prostitute and always will be, and you should have what you want just like she's having what she wants."

It was as if Charise could read my vulnerability when it came to dealing with Elaine's past.

"Why are you making this so unnecessarily difficult, Kevin? You have already made it perfectly clear that you want me."

"Charise, please leave and do not return with this craziness. Otherwise I will have to tell Elaine what you're up to." I tried to sound serious.

She laughed. "Fine, I'll be sure to tell Elaine about our first time together and how you sucked these beauties," she said, cupping her breasts, "and how those big, thick fingers were deep inside of my hot, wet pussy. Oh, and how I held that great big meaty, cock in my hand."

"Charise . . ." I wasn't sure what I could say to get her to back off.

"I'd highly suggest you give us what we both want and need so no one gets hurt. You wouldn't want to be responsible for tearing the family apart, now would you?" She headed for the door and turned back. "I'll give you until tomorrow to make a decision, or else the can of worms will begin to open and it'll all be your fault."

When she left, I tried to act like I could actually get work done after that conversation. There was no use.

I didn't know what to do about her ultimatum. I wished I would have told Elaine when Charise first came to me. Better yet, I wish I hadn't gotten so carried away that time. I would have probably gone all the way, but the soreness saved me. It was also difficult looking at Arnold at our guys' night out and the Labor Day cookout, so innocent and unsuspecting and unable to get any sex from his own wife. At the very least, I should have told him what his wife was all about. Then again, I don't want any harm to come to Charise, nor do I want her to lose her son again.

Not knowing where else to turn, I called Todd. He was probably the best one to advise me on how to handle Charise, since he fights off temptation every day.

"Damn, it sounds like she has you in a pickle. I feel bad for Arnold," Todd said after I filled him in. "She duped him into a sexless marriage just to regain custody of her son. I hope you're not even thinking about giving her what she wants. You can't give her what she wants; otherwise she'd have you forever. That shouldn't even be an option—unless you really *are* trying to hit it."

I could only groan into the phone. I wasn't sure what I wanted. I didn't know what to say.

"How far did things get the first time she approached you? Why would she think she has something to blackmail you with? Why didn't you tell Arnold when we got together? You should have exposed her ass!"

"Too far to tell my wife or Arnold."

"What? Damn, Kevin! How'd you, of all people, let that happen?"

I put my face to my desk in frustration and then lifted it back up to answer, "I don't know, Todd. When she was standing in front of me naked, it was like I blacked out. You know Charise is large up top—well, big on the bottom also, but I couldn't help it. When she touched my sore dick, it brought everything to a halt, and I snapped back to reality."

Todd laughed. "So what you're telling me is, if your dick wasn't already pussy-burned, you would have been up inside of her?"

"Pussy-burned? Is that a real word?"

"Never mind all of that. I just made it a word. Just stick to the issues here. So am I hearing you would have tapped that ass, Kevin?"

"I don't know. I don't want to think about it. The crazy thing is, we hear so many 'Charise' tales. Sure, I would visualize her each time, but never in a million years did I think I'd be a part of her tales. When I actually saw the real thing, I just lost myself. Hell, Arnold would die if he knew I was imagining his wife in erotic positions."

Again, Todd chuckled. "Oh, trust me; I understand, but you're going to have to come clean with Elaine. That sounds like your only option. If you fuck Charise, you're going to have to get used to having both women on a regular, and Elaine already got you pussy burned. How do you think you can handle two highly-sexual Wiggins women? There is no way you're going to get with Charise once, and she won't bother you anymore. Then you also have to worry about what Arnold is going to do to you when he finds out you're the reason he's not getting any. He'll think you've been sticking her all along, and you know his momma stays in his ear about her screwing around on him."

"Okay. Say I tell Elaine and she gets mad enough to go back to prostituting. According to Charise, Elaine's already doing it."

"Charise told you that?" Todd laughed. "Yes. I don't know what to make of it."

"Do you think Charise heard something from one of the other sisters?"

I shook my head. "Your guess is as good as mine. If I find out for sure that my wife is back prostituting . . . Let's just say that better not be the case."

"I know damn well Charise would not have that kind of information before Harmony, and Harmony definitely would have told me if Elaine was doing something." Todd laughed at a thought. "I just remembered something I never did tell you."

"What's that?" I asked.

"According to Harmony, Elaine thinks you're a sex fiend and that you are wearing her out trying to keep you satisfied."

"*I'm* a sex fiend? Hell, I'm only trying to keep her from wanting to be with other men. I don't need sex as often as we do."

Todd paused for a beat. "Hmm, that might hurt you if she thinks you're a sex fiend and now you want her sister in addition."

"Oh, this is crazy. I remember as clear as yesterday, their brother Angelo warned me about trying to help Charise, because she'd only be interested in my penis."

"I could have told you that myself. I used to wonder why you would break your neck to help that girl. I felt partly responsible for what my son did to her, but you helped her more than I did."

"I liked Elaine and wanted to do whatever I could to help and support her. I mean, do you see Elaine? It's not like I was going to find another her anywhere, anytime soon. When everyone warned me about how difficult Charise was, I stepped it up because of my feelings for Elaine. I tried to be there however I could for her brother as well, but now I'm in this mess."

"Just tell your wife everything. Wasn't that your philosophy? 'Come clean and be set free?'" Todd reminded me.

At first I wondered if Todd had a motive for telling me to confess to my wife. I wondered if maybe he was hoping to snag Elaine for himself if we were to break up. I couldn't blame him for wanting her.

After some thought, I realized I was just being paranoid. "Okay, I guess that's what I'll have to do then."

"You better do it tonight, 'cause I sure plan on telling Harmony tonight. It's hard to discuss Charise because Harmony thinks I'm angry at her because my son went to prison behind her. I keep trying to telling her that I'm not angry with Charise, and I thought my talking my own son into pleading guilty was proof of that. Honestly, between you and I, now this pisses me off because she obviously hasn't changed one bit. Harmony is so blinded by Charise—she's completely duped by her, and I plan on exposing her. Now I don't know who's going to tell Arnold. I'm staying out of that one."

"That's a tough one. Let me just start with my own wife first."

"So I'm sure you and Elaine won't be attending the babies' first birthday party next month? I hate that Charise has to bring her son."

"No, I don't think that would be a good idea. I need to keep my wife away from Charise. I don't need any extra details coming out beyond what I tell."

"I do understand."

"Thanks, Todd."

"Anytime. I might need you one day. Sooner than you think."

"Sounds like a story there." I chuckled.

"Yes, indeed there is. Anyway, good luck with that, and I'll catch up with you tomorrow."

After hanging up, I spent the rest of the afternoon practicing what to say to Elaine. I pondered which parts to omit and which to reveal, and I can only hope that Charise won't reveal the omitted parts. If I'm lucky, Elaine won't believe a word out of Charise's mouth.

4

Eric

Eric, I have to ask you a question, and I need you to be honest. I just received a very disturbing call from Elaine."

Oh lord! Now what kind of shit am I caught up in?

I haven't touched Elaine since I found out she was Shawnee's sister. Shawnee didn't give a damn that I used to date Sandy, so I can't imagine what Elaine would be filling her head with now. When I'm at my new restaurant, which Shawnee financed, women throw themselves at me all day, every day. I keep my body very fit, which attracts women young and old. I am a big guy and was once an internationally known exotic dancer known as Mandingo. My decision to become an exotic dancer caused my break-up with Sandy, and it was during one of my Mandingo parties that I met both Elaine and Shawnee—separately.

I hate that Elaine and her people often come to my restaurant. I always feel like I'm under a microscope and like she's looking for some dirt to run back and tell Shawnee.

Shawnee is the one woman I have loved beyond my own comprehension. My family and friends call me a fool for being stuck on her, but they just don't understand that I have never had one woman make me feel as fulfilled as

Shawnee has. I have completely turned in my Playa Card. I even dropped the name 'Mandingo' because she didn't like it.

When we first met, Shawnee was married. She divorced him and later fucked me up by marrying some old white guy. Shawnee and I lost contact for a while, but when we hooked back up, she wasn't married to the old guy yet. I understood that he was hooking her up financially, and I didn't want to interfere with her getting hers, yet she'd always make waves if I tried to hook up with another chick. I couldn't top what he could do for her, but it hurt me that she didn't love me enough to walk away to be with me.

I probably wouldn't even be on Shawnee's radar right now had our daughter not been miraculously conceived despite a condom and birth control pills. The old guy she married passed away earlier this year from prostate cancer. Turned out he was an old freak doing Shawnee, some of his other employees, and one of Todd's sisters, who is fine as hell, if I must say so myself. She reminds me of that actress, Salli Richardson, but taller. Just fine for no reason. I never told Shawnee that she and I went to lunch one day when she was in New York. I would have hooked up with her, but she had her own agenda, which was getting me back with Shawnee so she could be with the old guy, who was their boss. Shawnee also doesn't know I saw a video of the old guy and Todd's sister doing the do. I even made a copy for my files. I jerked off on that shit a few times.

I believe fate is everything, though. Shayla was conceived right before Shawnee married the old guy. He left Shawnee his entire estate and even set my daughter up for life before he died shortly before Shayla was born. The timing of it all gave me the opportunity to be in Shayla's life from day one, and ever since. If Shawnee was still married, I probably would have been deprived of my daughter. When the old guy died, I understood that Shawnee was grieving, so I didn't press her about us being together. In my heart, though, I was rejoicing at the chance for us to be a real family.

Having to live in the damn guest house doesn't sit well with me. It's not quite my idea of being a real family. What's worse is now Shawnee's suggesting

I find someone special to date, but then asks that I don't bring them on her property or around our daughter. The big slap in the face was when she had me babysit while she went on a date with some other dude.

Sometimes I want to say, "Fuck this bitch," but she did finance my top-tier restaurant, which has been a lifelong dream of mine, and then there's my daughter. For those two reasons, I can handle humility. I still hold out hope for us to marry someday.

Somehow our sexual relationship has increased tremendously. Not too long ago, it was almost non-existent. I don't know what brought the change about, but I'm happy. I'm not too happy when she kicks me back out of her bed when she's sexually satisfied.

I just want to be able to hold her sometimes, but she ain't having that. I held her more while we were sneaking to be together when she was with old dude. I hate these mixed signals. She's giving me more sex, but telling me to go find someone else while she's dating other guys. She plays too many games if you ask me.

So now she wants to ask me about some shit that she talked to Elaine about. I can't imagine what Elaine would be trying to dime me out on. She's been pretty cool with me despite our brief history. So why would she be trying to say something about me now?

"I can't imagine what Elaine could be trying to tell you about me. You already know where my heart is," I defend.

Shawnee looks at me as if I were stupid. "Huh? What the fuck are you talking about? No one said anything about what *you* did. I said I wanted to ask you a question based on something Elaine just told me. That's a big difference from Elaine told me something disturbing about YOU." She shakes her head and gives a disgusted laugh. "Stay focused here. Everything is not about Eric, you know?"

Damn, I want to knock the shit out of her sometimes—particularly in her damn mouth. But I still love her.

"Okay, it's not about me. So what's up?" I ask, trying to keep my attitude in check. I'm still waiting for my ration of pussy for the night.

"Apparently Charise has made a move on Kevin. He just came clean to Elaine about it because Charise is now trying to blackmail him into fucking her, or else she'll tell the family that he's been putting the moves on her. Something about his ass has the ring of sneaky. I wouldn't be surprised if his overly righteous ass already fucked her. Now, of course you know I don't put a damn thing past Charise and I'm not quite buying into that whole *rehabilitated* act like the others are. My question that I need you to answer honestly is, has Charise tried to make a move on you, and would you tell me?"

"Huh? Damn, that's fucked up," I say, blown away. Not Kevin. "Damn, wasn't Kevin the one who helped Charise with her whole recovery process and her magazine? And that's how she did him. That's some foul shit. But to answer your questions, no, she's never been around me alone. She's come to the restaurant on the occasions I've told you about, but she was never alone. Would I tell you if she came at me incorrectly? Hell yeah! That's some sheisty shit there. I'm glad Kevin had sense enough to tell Elaine what was up."

"Well it seems he wasn't going to say anything had Charise not blackmailed him. The bitch also told Kevin that Elaine is currently hooking and he is the only one who doesn't know it," Shawnee adds.

I can't even speak. My mouth is opened, but no words will come out. That damn Charise is no joke. I see I need to stay far away from her ass. I did want to ask Shawnee why she would think Kevin messed with Charise, if Charise had to blackmail him to sleep with her. I can't stand Shawnee always having her jacked up opinions and comments about every- damn-body, but she's perfect. I wasn't saying shit that would keep me from getting some ass tonight, and asking that question would be the makings of a fight. An unnecessary fight, no less.

"How often does she come by the restaurant?" Shawnee probes.

"Hell, I don't know. To my knowledge, she's only been there on the occasions I mentioned to you. Now you're going to have me paranoid about her coming through there trying to rope me in to some of her stupid shit," I say, trying to control my anger about Shawnee now questioning me about that little tramp-ass sister of hers.

"Yeah, that was my concern also. Well, I'm sure I don't have to remind you what's at stake if you cross that line. You know she better not bring her silly ass to the birthday party next month, 'cause I will expose the bitch."

I can't stand her constant reminders of stripping me of everything if I'm not obedient.

She stands up in front of me like she's going to kick my ass. "This brings me to my next subject. I have to fly to Europe next week, so we need to make some arrangements for Shayla. You know I don't want any of your bitches around my daughter. I'm okay if your mom wants to watch her. If not, we'll have to figure something out. I know you're not too keen on the idea of my taking her with me for this trip. Actually, I'm not feeling that either. So what do you think?"

I hate when Shawnee stands in front of me in a tee-shirt with no bra. It looks like her big nipples just hardened, and now I can't concentrate. My dick is getting hard. If I don't focus and answer her, she's going to get pissed off and I won't be sucking on those nipples tonight.

So I give the safe answer. "Whatever you feel is best, I'll support you."

"Okay, then we'll just call your mom tomorrow. Tonight, you have something I want," she says as she comes and sits on my lap.

YES!

My mouth doesn't waste any time going for those nipples. Her shorts allow my fingers easy access to the pussy. Damn! I don't have a condom nearby. I have to finesse her to her bedroom, where I know she keeps her condom supply big enough for me. If I let Shawnee get hers first and she realizes we have to stop to go get a condom, she will end the session. Shawnee is totally into my fingers in her pussy, so I pick her up and carry her to her bedroom before she can climax. I receive no objections.

Yes! Again!

5

Sean

I can't believe I gave up time in the studio to hang with those lame-ass niggas who can't run their households. The first lesson they need to learn is how to control their bitches. I don't know why I went with them again after that first time. First off, I don't even like football, and then they're all uptight and act like they're scared of those bitches. There isn't a damn thing that Kelly wouldn't do for me. I make sure to consume her time with my sons to keep her from getting into any trouble. Early in our marriage, she tried to get all jiggy like those bitch-sisters of hers, but when I pulled my piece out, she immediately knew her place. When my sons first came and I let her know she'd be watching them and taking care of them, she tried to put up some resistance. I lifted that bitch off her feet by her throat, and she's been mommy of the year ever since. I'm still not understanding why she hasn't gotten pregnant yet. All of her sisters have kids except her. Oh, and that hooker, Elaine. I hope I didn't catch a barren bitch.

Kelly's family got long dollars, which I can have them putting in my company in no time. That's why I bother going to the sports bar and cookouts with their asses. Kelly don't have shit anymore. We put everything she had into my company.

She asked about working her event planning business so she could earn some dough, but I am not going to have a bunch of niggas trying to get at my wife. Then she'll let people in her ear and try to give me grief. No, she can stay her ass right at home with my sons. I got plenty of money. If she wants to work on getting me some more money, then she better hit up those highfalutin, bitch-ass sisters. Hell, even their husbands got big dollars. Todd is a doctor that owns his spot. Kevin is some millionaire investment broker, banker, or something. Arnold has some big position with that international company, and Eric has that preppy-ass restaurant. They got it going on, which is why I don't understand why they put up with shit from those bitches.

On the real tip, I would love to smack that ass on Kelly's sister Charise. Her ass just says, "Pow! Here I am." I heard she's hot in the ass and does all kind of freaky shit. I see the bitch all the time 'cause somehow her magazine office is in the next building from my office.

I can tell she wants to get with me. She's always flirting with me and my homies. My boys said she's probably trying to trap me so she could run and tell Kelly. Shit! Let me slide my dick up it in that ass one time, and she'll be hooked like Kelly was.

Kelly started off as a tough nut to crack with that three- month rule bullshit. That was an easy fix once I put something in her drink. I fucked her so good she's been hooked ever since then. Bitch had me spending all kinds of loot to get at her, but now I got her dollars.

Let me get Charise alone one time and she'll be begging for it to be her turn from then on. I can tell she ain't even into her so-called husband. He's too stupid to figure that out. How you gonna have a wife you never fucked since you've been married? If that nigga could see how she's out flirting, he'd smash her face in. I saw the way she was sucking on a rib bone at the cookout the other week when Arnold wasn't looking. I was trying to figure out who she was performing for. I know Kevin saw that freak, 'cause he looked right at me when she did it. I wish Kelly would try some stupid shit like that. I should have told

Arnold about his wife when he was talking shit at the bar, like she is so perfect. But not before I get that ass and maybe some dollars out of her.

One day I was coming out of my office building with one of my honeys. Charise looked the girl up and down like she was fucking me herself. Now, when she sees me, she's cheesing with that "come tap this ass" look. It's also strange how often I see her. If I didn't know any better, I'd say her ass is scoping me out. I saw this fine honey only twice in a year, who works in the same building as Charise. Coincidence? You tell me. All of the buildings on Avenue of the Stars, and she's in the next building from me? I know she must have wanted me when she picked that spot for her office. I'm sure Kelly told her where my studio was at.

Some call me the man they love to hate. I was raised by a single struggling mother in Oakland. Then when she was tired of struggling, she had all kinds of niggas up in there fucking her, but she was getting paid.

She gave me my first lesson in manhood when I was like nine years old. She had me watching her when niggas were banging her. She said there ain't nothing worse than a man with a big dick who doesn't know how to use it. It was weird at first, but then I wanted to watch all the time. She also taught me how to know when a bitch is faking. She'd let me know which niggas fucked her right and which ones she had to fake it with. She didn't want me to ever have to worry about some bitch faking on me and then trash talking her baby when they got around their friends.

By the time I was thirteen, she got this grown woman to give me my first piece of real pussy. I say real, because those knucklehead little girls I was fucking before then, acted all scary and didn't want to try shit. After that first woman, I didn't want to fuck with any more little girls. Yeah, I knew they were faking at first like they were enjoying it, with the "Ooh-Ahh" shit.

By the time I was fifteen, I had all these women screaming and scratching up walls. At first my moms was paying these hoes to give me my practice, but after a while, I had hoes paying me.

Now I make my sons watch me when I fuck Kelly, so they can learn just the same. Kelly tried to make noise at first, talking about that's not healthy behavior for children, and it makes her feel uncomfortable. Slap a bitch in her mouth and see how quick she shuts the fuck up. Hell, I turned out just fine. Her talking that shit is like her trying to say something's wrong with me or something's wrong with my momma. Don't nobody talk shit about my momma. That's an ass beating due a motherfucker. All niggas need to learn to take a page out of my book. Teach the kids right.

I always had a thing with music. I had my own DJ equipment since I was sixteen. Being a DJ gets you a whole lot of pussy.

Then I stepped up my game and started my own record company, Top-Load Records. I started in my mom's crib, but that day when I left home to move to the L.A. area and was able to go pay for my own office on Avenue of the Stars, I knew I had arrived. Something about having your own office in L.A. makes you feel all important.

My sons' mother helped a lot. She's fourteen years older than me. She had big dollars and I had big dreams. The problem was that I didn't have any love for her, only my dreams. Now she did have a younger cousin who I loved fucking, but then the bitch went and caught feelings, and wanted to throw salt in my game. My kids' mother went and got the house out in Salt Lake City like she was punishing me or something. The problem with knocking a bitch out too much is they eventually become immune and some get balls even bigger than yours. Even though the bitch left to Salt Lake, she wouldn't stop trying to get me back.

The rock I put on Kelly's finger, my kid's momma bought. She bought it for us to get married. Like I said, I didn't have any love for the bitch. Come to think of it, half of the shit I gave Kelly came from her. Her silly ass filed for child support just to piss me off. I'm not sure why, because she always gave me the money whenever I came and fucked her. She was originally from East Oakland and had a violent side to her, which helped me get custody of my boys. She wasn't stupid enough to get violent with me, but she'd usually go after women she knew I was fucking with.

When I filed for custody, my lawyer said I didn't have much of a chance of getting custody because all of my assets were tied up in my business, I wasn't married, and I didn't have anything stable to offer. That was an easy fix. Her name was Kelly.

I met Kelly at some industry party she coordinated. Something about her screamed "class." She wasn't one of those fake bitches trying to ride my jock. After a brief conversation, I found out she had her own successful event planning company, she had a successful family with dollars, she had no children, and she was looking to be in a committed relationship. Sounded like the perfect target to me.

I won't lie. I did end up catching feelings for her before I was able to get the goodies. It was something about her strength and resistance that had me. I also loved her reaction whenever I gave her something nice or did something for her. She wasn't like some of those other bitches always waiting with her hand out, and she wasn't looking to buy a man out of some desperation.

Nonetheless, I had to speed up the process since I was trying to get custody of my boys. That's when I spiked her drink that night. She was already drinking, but with Kelly, that didn't mean shit. That girl could drink a sailor up under the table and still be in her right mind. When I put that roofie in her drink, that was all she wrote. The freak sure came out that night. The freak's been out ever since then.

Still, I'm a man who likes variety. I like having two women fucking me and working each other. Kelly's not with that program. I thought about forcing the issue, but then it would be my luck, the bitch would turn my wife out and try to take her away from me.

I tried forcing the kids' momma and she ended up biting the other girl's nipple off. She beat the shit out of the girl and told her she'd kill her if she ever fucked with me again. Although that was funny as hell, I never tried the shit again with that crazy bitch.

Being in the music industry gives me access to all kinds of variety. We could be in the studio laying a track, and I'll have some bitch giving me head in front of everyone. On occasion, we get the hoes who want me and my boys to run a train on them. I also have a few bitches giving me their hard-earned cash just to fuck them. Sean Greene doesn't discriminate when it comes to the dollars.

Thankfully I have one of those dicks that takes a lickin' and keeps on tickin'. I have plenty to go around. Now if I could just tap that ass on Charise, I'd be A-OK. I know it's just a matter of time. Every time Kelly would tell me crazy stories about Charise's sexcapades, my dick would get hard. I'd fuck Kelly, thinking about the shit she told me about her sister. Now with that no boundaries-having bitch always flirting with me, I can almost feel that pussy on this big black dick.

6

Todd

Dr. Palmer, we received the results from Miss Foster's pelvic exam, and the lab said there was not enough specimen to do the tests. Should I call Miss Foster and let her know we have to repeat the exam, or would you prefer to call?" Valerie asked me with a look of suspicion on her face and in her body language.

Damn, I just noticed Valerie isn't wearing a bra. I can see her nipples protruding through her yellow scrubs when she just folded her arms across her chest. Surely she had a bra on earlier. Did she remove it after everyone else left? And why is she just mentioning those results when all reports are delivered first thing in the morning? Come to think of it, that was a whole month ago.

"I could call her since I'm sure you need to get going for the evening." I hoped I didn't show any anticipation about calling the lovely Miss Foster.

"I'm in no rush. It wouldn't be a bother for me to call her myself. I know you don't need to be bothered with such tedious items such as this," she suggested.

I gave in. "Fine, you can call her then."

I figured it was best I didn't call, being I could end up in a heap of trouble. I had been able to resist the temptation for one month now. I was thankful she hadn't been back with a pimple or the sniffles.

"Okay, I'm going to change out of these scrubs and then I'll make the call," Valerie told me.

I wasn't sure why she felt the need to tell me she was going to change, since she had never announced such in the past.

"Valerie, just give me the chart. I'll make the call myself. She'll probably ask to speak with me anyhow."

Valerie handed the chart to me, clearly annoyed. When she left my office, she didn't bother to close my door. I figured she left it open so she could eavesdrop.

I took a deep breath before picking up the phone to make that call. I felt like I was walking down to the gas chamber. I wasn't sure what would come as a result of talking to her. I ended up letting Kevin talk me down when I told him about the photo she gave me last month. I think a big part of me was afraid of the consequences. That's what stopped me from calling her. Now I have to call her about this shit.

"Hi, this is Dr. Palmer. I'm trying to reach Cynnyyah Foster," I said.

"Dr. Palmer, glad you finally called. I was almost ready to give up on you," she responded.

"Well actually, I'm calling regarding your test results. There seems to be a problem with the sample, and we are going to have to repeat your exam," I said, trying to sound as official as I could, since I knew Valerie was somewhere in hearing distance.

She laughed. "Oh, okay, the sample you never got around to taking? That's okay. You tell me when you want to see me to complete my exam and I'm there. Well unless you'd prefer to come to my place."

Now I understood why Valerie left my office door open. She went into one of the offices on the other side of the nurse's station and decided to change from her scrubs. She kept the light off in the office, but she left the door fully open for me to catch a glimpse.

Damn! My dick was ready to bust out of my pants. Just as I thought, she didn't have on a bra. She slowly stripped down to her thong before taking her sweet time to redress in street clothes. I don't know what the hell Miss Foster was on the phone talking about, because I couldn't take my focus off of Valerie. I know she knew I was completely engrossed.

Damn, Valerie is sexier than I thought. Well at least her body is.

I found myself standing for a better, unobstructed view of her ass and all. I'm not sure at what point Miss Foster hung up, because I was holding a phone to my ear with a dial tone.

Once Valerie was dressed, I quickly took my seat before she looked at me looking at her. Valerie gathered her things and returned to my office.

"How did she take the news when you told her she had to be rescheduled?" Valerie asked as if nothing happened. "I can tell she has a thing for you, so I'm sure she's glad to have an opportunity to see you again."

"She said she'd have to check her schedule and call me right back," I lied.

"She won't be calling you tonight. The phones are on answering service already. She'll probably have to get scheduled tomorrow morning," she answered, sounding almost pleased that Miss Foster wasn't going to reach me.

I knew I should've said something to Valerie about her inappropriate actions, but my dick wouldn't let me say a word. It didn't want to close the door on another opportunity to see Valerie in the flesh. She was standing in my doorway with a tight, pink, deep v-cut, cropped tee-shirt, revealing her perky cleavage, still with nipples poking through. The shirt exposed her navel ring, and her thong rose above her low-rise Guess jeans. *Oh man, this girl is sexy and she knows it.*

Valerie went on and on about something, but my brain was still stuck on her body. I couldn't even be discreet and act like I wasn't looking. I did manage to hear her say, "Do you need anything else from me tonight before I leave?"

I wanted to say, "Hell yeah I want something else from you!" but I didn't. Instead, after looking down at my kids' pictures, I said, "No, that'll be all. Have a good night, Valerie."

Then she was gone. *What am I gonna do?* I could never look at Valerie the same again.

I remembered I still needed to call Miss Foster back. She probably tried calling me back but couldn't get through.

"Hi Miss Foster. This is Dr. Palmer calling you back," I said when she answered again.

"I was wondering what happened, but then I figured my cell phone must have entered a dead-zone or something. Dr. Palmer, if it's possible, I'd like to stop by the office this evening for my exam."

The dick rose back up. "Oh, Miss Foster, the office is already closed for the day. Everyone is already gone."

"Well, all I need is for you to do my exam. Who else do we need?"

"I need to get home myself. It's getting kind of late. How about you call the office in the morning to get on my schedule?" I answered.

"I'd prefer to come this evening. After all, I need my results as soon as possible, and it's already been a whole month. Someone could have called me earlier today or before today, but didn't. Therefore, I want my exam completed this evening," she demanded.

"You're absolutely correct. Someone should have called you earlier. Fine then," I conceded. "How soon could you be here? I really do have to get home."

"Ten minutes. I'm not too far away right now. I'll see you in ten minutes, Doctor."

Before I could say another word, the call was ended. My dick wouldn't go down. Miss Foster was not going to simply let me do her exam and then leave.

This might be it: the day my fantasy becomes real. Damn, why did Valerie have to leave? At least she could have saved me from the clutches of Miss Foster. Then again, who would save me from Valerie? Maybe I should call Kevin.

Ten minutes seemed almost like ten seconds. Before I knew it, there was a knock at the door. I didn't have time to call Kevin. I put my lab coat on to attempt to mask my erection that wouldn't leave me. I opened the door to find Miss Cynnyyah Foster wearing a plaid mini skirt with no stockings. Her five-foot, four-inch frame was held up on a pair of red five-inch stilettos, which matched her candy apple red halter top.

"Good evening," I said as she entered. "I didn't have a chance to get the exam room ready. If you could just have a seat, I'll be with you in a minute."

"No problem. I have time." She took a seat, instantly providing a glimpse of her upper thigh and ass when she crossed her legs.

I went into my office and pulled a photo of my wife out to help me stay in check. Instead, I saw an overweight, undesirable woman who made me want to fuck someone else. Then I pulled out some photos of my babies. That did the trick. My erection went away. I went and prepped an exam room then went to let her know the room was ready. When she entered the room, I held a gown in my hand for her to change into. She had her own plans.

She looked me in my eyes as she unfastened her halter top, letting it fall and expose those nipples I desired to lick. She kept her eyes on my eyes as she unfastened her skirt, causing it to fall to the floor. This time, there were no panties or anything else. My poor babies lost this battle. My erection was back and harder than before.

Miss Foster climbed onto the exam table with her knees up, showing me her beautiful pussy. She didn't bother to put her feet in the stirrups, nor had she removed her shoes.

"M-miss F-foster, I'm going to need you to remove your shoes so we could get your feet properly in the stirrups," I stuttered.

She silently obliged. Her silence scared me. I was able to get her test swabs without any interruptions, but I knew it was too easy. After I collected the specimens, she took my hand and massaged her pussy with it. When she realized my hand no longer needed her assistance, she took my other hand and placed it on her tits. She didn't have to help me massage her tits.

My brain was screaming, "Suck them! Suck them!" I tried to fight the voice in my head, but knew I was fighting a losing battle once she started gyrating her hips. My mouth went for it. There was no turning back. I sucked, licked, and teased those nipples like I had dreamed of so many times.

My fingers crept deeper and deeper in the depths of her vagina. Miss Foster's body was going crazy, and she freely let out the moans she sequestered on the last visit. I felt her hot juices squirting on my fingers. Her pussy called out to me, and my mouth found its way to answer the call. I ate the hell out of that pussy. That pussy juice was in my nose. Her body tried to run, but I kept pulling it back to me.

My dick was dying as it was still trapped in my closed trousers. I repositioned myself to allow Miss Foster's hand to do me the favor of freeing him. She graciously did and went the extra step of taking him into her mouth. She sucked my dick skillfully, her mouth just the right amount of wet. She managed to turn her body across the exam table, allowing her to suck my dick, while giving me access to keep eating her pussy. Although her upper torso was hanging off the table, she held on and did the damn thing.

When I came close to erupting, I stopped her. I couldn't bear the thought of letting Miss Foster go without getting into her pussy. The part that was driving me crazy was, I knew only a few feet away there was a drawer full of condoms that we give our patients, but my dick wanted to feel the hot wetness of Miss Foster.

I turned her pussy to face me. I touched it one more time as if anticipating how I was going to fuck it. Her titties called for me to suck them some more. As I was sucking them, my hand helped my dick find its entrance into her tight pussy. Hell, I was ready to explode on contact, but I managed to hold onto my soldiers. Her pussy sucked my dick just as good as her mouth did. The pussy was marvelous! I wanted to stop right there to smoke a cigarette. (I don't smoke.) I wouldn't be satisfied if I didn't get to bend her over and fuck her from the back, so I repositioned her body on the table and fucked the shit out of her. When I knew I was ready to let go, I had her come back and suck every drop of cum out of my dick. She swallowed without losing any. I don't know why her swallowing made me want to kiss her, but I did.

After we cleaned ourselves up in silence, I saw Miss Foster to the door and told her we'd call her with her results. I guess I should have been checking her results before fucking her. Without words, she gently grabbed my crotch, pulled my neck down to kiss me, and was out the door.

When she left, I loudly chanted, "Yeah, you the man!" as I was cleaning up the exam room. I returned to my office feeling like the man—

"What the hell?" I said when I saw Valerie sitting in my chair behind my desk wearing makeup.

"Now I don't understand, what does that bitch have to offer you that I don't?" she asked. "Obviously you are not worried about your wife or lawsuits from sleeping with your patients. So why won't you touch me, Todd?"

I was speechless. I didn't know what to say. How long was she here? She did leave, didn't she? She must have been in the bathroom putting on makeup when I thought she had left. All I could manage to say is, "Valerie."

"I kind of had a feeling you had something going on with her. Particularly when her test swabs from her pelvic exam showed no signs of specimen, and you certainly examined her last month when she was here, because the paper on the exam table was wet. Probably from her cum." She stood from my chair and came to stand close enough in front of me, with her breast touching my chest. "Do you not find me attractive? I see how you look at me. I saw you watching me earlier while I changed clothes. I know you want me, Dr. Palmer, so what's stopping you? I obviously want you too. I want you to examine my body too."

I found my voice and moved past her to the other side of my desk, where I figured it was safe, as I sat down. "Valerie, yes you are very attractive," I kind of lied, "but I can't afford to get caught up in some sexual harassment situation, nor do I want to make our working together awkward."

Valerie peeled off her tight pink tee-shirt and stepped back in front of me, with her beautiful tits exposed before my eyes. She took my hands, which were folded in front of me, and placed them on her twenty-five-year-old breasts. "Tell me you didn't want to touch them when you saw them earlier. Tell me you didn't want to suck them as I see in your eyes right now."

She was right, because I grabbed her arms and pulled one of those tits into my mouth. I couldn't stop squeezing the other. While I was squeezing and sucking, she was coming out of those jeans and moving her thong to the side. There was no more "guessing." When the way was clear, my hand found her clit.

I couldn't believe myself. Not only did I cheat on my wife once that evening—not only did I fuck the woman unprotected—not only did I fuck a patient, but there I was about to fuck one of my nurses that I have to work with day in and day out.

Valerie wasn't going to allow me to give her any less than what she knew I gave Miss Foster. Once again I was eating pussy, finger and dick fucking, as well as getting my dick sucked. Valerie wanted to give me one up on Miss Foster: Her booty. Yep! Valerie let me into her booty hole. The last piece of booty I got was Roxana. I'd been craving Roxana so many times just because of that. Well that and the sex was great overall.

Valerie probably got more fucking from me than Miss Foster, because I wasn't able to ejaculate as quickly as with the first round. There wasn't going to be any quickies this go-round. Nope! I fucked Valerie in two different exam rooms, in my office, on top of the nurse's station, on the floor in the carpeted waiting area, and in one of the bathrooms. I sucked her tits until her nipples were chafed. When my dick wasn't up in that asshole, you can bet my fingers were. Valerie was like an acrobat. I was able to do her in all kinds of positions. That makeup she carefully put on was sweated off.

Sex with Valerie had me wanting to get with Miss Foster again just to see what tricks she could do beyond that exam table. Judging by her loose rectum, I already knew she was also into the anal sex. I just didn't think to go there with her. Maybe there would be another opportunity with her.

The crazy thing was, as much as I was enjoying fucking Valerie, it was my thoughts of fucking Miss Foster in the ass that made me finally cum inside of Valerie's pussy. At least this time I had sense enough to find a condom—well not right away. I didn't use the condom until after I went into her ass. I wanted to feel her pussy on my dick. I don't like condoms, and she didn't seem to have any objections until after I went into her ass and was going back into her pussy. Okay, maybe it wasn't me coming to my senses, but her.

Working together from now on is going to be a beast. Now each time I look at Valerie's ass, I'm going to have a flashback.

I did break down and call Cynnyyah Foster that very next evening. I had to see what all she was about. Just as I thought, Cynnyyah could dance circles around Valerie. Maybe it was because I find Cynnyyah more attractive than Valerie.

The more I fuck Cynnyyah Foster, the more I despise my wife. At this point, I don't think there is a damn thing Harmony could do to make me want her like when I first met her. Even if she lost a hundred pounds, I'm already turned off from her sexually. I still love her, but I just don't want to fuck her anymore. Both Cynnyyah and Valerie have no problem sharing me and filling my void from home.

7

Sean

I'm starting to think you wait out here for me intentionally," I said to Charise when I saw her outside my building for the second time that week.

She had on this sexy, apple-green mini-skirt suit, showing off her bronze-colored, muscular legs in some four-inch sandals that made her calves appear bowed. She had a cell phone to her ear, giving orders to the person on the other end. Sounded like business. When she turned around to face me as I approached her, I saw her ample bosom bulging from her suit jacket. She obviously wasn't wearing more than a low-cut bra, if anything. The sight was okay in my book, along with every other dude walking by, and some women as well.

She ended her phone call and said to me, "Why exactly would I be waiting out here for you?" she said all snobby. "I work in this building right here in case you haven't noticed." She pointed to the adjoining building.

"If you say so," I replied, letting her know I was onto the bullshit. "Have you had dinner yet? I'm heading over to Roscoe's to get some grub. You want to join me?"

"Why would I want to join you for dinner?" she asked with attitude. "Where's your entourage? Where's your bunch of bitches I always see you with?"

She asked about 'my bitches' and not my wife. *Good sign. I got her ass.*

"Stop trying to play all hard. Just join me for dinner. What harm can come from dinner in a public place? I need to eat, you need to eat; it's dinnertime and maybe a good time for you and I to finally sit and chat. You've never taken the time to get to know me for yourself. You only know the gossip and the rumors."

I could see her pondering the thought. "So you're saying all the things I've heard about you aren't true?" she asked, raising an eyebrow and still trying to maintain her tough front.

"I don't know what things they are. I'm a keep-it-real nigga. I'm not one of those fake niggas," I said, stepping into her space.

She stepped back. "So what about all those bitches I always see you flaunting?"

"Charise, I'm alone right now. Either you want to have dinner with me or you don't. I'm not asking to take you out on a date. I simply asked if you want to join me for dinner. If it's going to be this much of a problem, then never mind."

She took the bait. "Fine! Just dinner. I guess this would be a good time to get to know more about you for myself," she said, looking at my body like a pork chop sandwich.

We arrived at the restaurant and I led her to my usual table in the corner, close to the door. She asked all kinds of questions about me and never one time mentioned her sister, Kelly. She didn't have any alcohol, but certainly was getting more and more comfortable with me as if she were drinking.

She was getting more flirtatious when she'd put her fork to her mouth. I knew she was going to be mine that night when she asked, "So what I really want to know, is it true that most guys who work in the music business have big dicks? Is that like some criteria or a fallacy?"

I was kind of shocked by her out of the blue question. I answered, "I don't know about theirs, but I know mine is big."

"What do you call big? Most guys claim to have big dicks, but then they turn out to have some knockwurst, or worse than that, a wiener."

"Hey, I don't have a problem if you need to see for yourself. Hell, you can reach underneath the table and feel it. I can tell you it's ten inches, but you don't seem like the type who will just take my word for it."

"Ten inches, huh?" she asked, looking intrigued while biting down on her bottom lip. "I guess that is pretty decent."

I was hoping she'd want to touch it. I could see she wanted to play games, so I said, "I can see you work out. It looks good on you."

She was just a cheesing. "You think so?"

"Hell yeah! Your legs look great in that skirt. Sexy as hell, and that skirt does your ass serious justice, not that you need it. When I first saw you from the back, I was hoping you were someone else."

"Why did you hope I was someone else?" she asked.

"'Cause I would have loved to feel those legs. They are so perfectly sculpted," I said, dragging the words like a melody.

Again I could see the wheels turning in that pretty head. "Well, I guess there wouldn't be any harm in letting you touch my legs. Just don't be trying to get all carried away."

My dick was hard. *I am so in there.*

She moved her seat close to me. I noticed her mini skirt was up kind of high; at the threshold. I reached under the table and let my hand glide down her leg. Then as my hand was gliding back up her leg, I noticed the slight parting of her upper thighs. When the base of my hand made contact with her pelvic bone, I moved my hand from her leg and placed it back on the table. Then I said, "Nice. Real nice."

She in turn decided to take me up on my earlier offer and let her hand size up my Johnson through my pants. Thankfully it was hardened. She said, "Very impressive." When she put her hand back on the table, she said, "The sad thing with some men having big dicks, is they are scared to use it."

My dick hardened another ten degrees. She just don't know. That's just what my momma taught me.

Then Charise really fucked me up when she took a piece of ice from her cup and dropped it in her cleavage. The look on her face made me think of her having an orgasm. She took it a step further by asking me to reach in and get the ice out before it melted.

I looked around to see if there were any spectators. When I saw there were none, I went in for the gold. Now my dick was ready to break out. It took me a minute to get hold of that ice, but I did get a hold of a healthy portion of tits. Charise has some big tits and they are real. A lot of bitches pay to have what she has naturally.

Maybe because of the height difference, Charise has a more compact frame that gives her five foot, three-inch body more voluptuous curves. Kelly, on the other hand, is not as voluptuous at five feet, seven inches. Kelly has a nice body, but Charise's is more of a turn-on. Charise definitely got more tits and a fatter ass.

When I replaced my hand on the table, she took it and put back on her thigh. She massaged my Johnson through my pants. I responded by rubbing her thighs and ultimately between her thighs. I managed to let a finger get inside her thong. Then I had this thought about how this trick teases her own husband and won't give him any pussy. I figured I better get out before she got me.

"Well, we better get going. I have to get back to the office. I also don't want to get in any trouble," I said, hoping she'd fall for the game again.

"Back to the office? I thought you were done for the evening. And why would you get in any trouble? We're adults."

"I still have work waiting for me in the office, plus I don't want to get in any trouble with your husband. It's one thing to have dinner, but it's another to be touchy-feely," I insincerely responded.

"Husband? Pulease!! That motherfucker is a joke. I wish everybody would get off that 'my husband' bullshit. He's a fucking joke, okay? What about you? Are you a joke?" she challenged me.

Damn! She didn't bite her tongue about that lame-ass nigga of hers. I defended myself. "Far from it. I can show you my office if you have time."

"I would love to see your *office,* Sean," she said.

It was on then. We barely made it in my office good before Charise was undressing. I could only watch. I sat at my desk watching her strip.

When she was down to just her bra and thong, she walked over and stood between my desk and my chair. Then she unfastened her bra, exposing a lovely set of tits. Then she turned her back to me and bent over, laying her upper body on my desk, still with the thong on. That ass was staring me in my face. She spread her ass cheeks and showed me her pussy before sitting on my lap and giving me a lap dance.

I reached around her fondled her tits with one hand, while the other hand massaged her pelvic area. This girl gave a lap dance like a fucking professional. She had her pussy aligned with the head of my dick, which was still in my pants, and worked that ass in my lap. That shit felt almost as good as if my dick were up in the pussy already. I knew this bitch was going to have skills just from looking at her.

I had to push her off of me because I was ready to cum. I laid her back on my desk. I stood up to suck those voluptuous melons and then licked my way down to the pussy. I slid her thong over to lick, but she moved my face away. Instead, she masturbated herself like you see in some porno flick.

She picked up this glass paperweight and rubbed her pussy with it. She turned from her back to her front on her knees, on my desk, and she worked it. She had pussy juice coming out on my desk. She eventually let me join in with masturbating her and let me taste that pussy. I buried my face in her ass.

Then it was my turn to show her what I could do. I flipped her on her back and she was going crazy. I kept a tight grip on her thighs to keep her in place. Those strong-ass thighs were powerful, and at times were locking my head in between her legs. Oh but when she climaxed, my head felt like a helpless nut between a nutcracker. This bitch shook something loose inside my head with her grip.

At least she wasn't a selfish bitch. After she got hers, she got up and opened my shirt and pants, releasing my manhood. She licked and teased my nipples while she gently massaged my dick. She then worked her way down, as I rested my head back on my chair. She took her time. She licked the shaft, up and down, front and back, licked my balls, and teased my head with her tongue before swallowing all ten inches of my dick in her throat. *This bitch needs to be getting paid for her service. Hell, I'd pay for this shit.* She would not let up. She sucked my dick until I came. I was worried about cumming and not being able to slide my dick up in that ass, but like I said, I was dealing with a fucking professional.

Charise took my dick in between her two melons and sensuously massaged it as she licked the head. When my dick was beginning to get hard, she sat her fat ass back on my lap, taking my dick sideways as she rubbed her pussy juices back and forth. Every now and again, the tip of the head would meet up with the mouth of her pussy. I would be ready to slide it on up in there, but she wouldn't let it go in. That shit was driving me crazy.

Then she stood and faced me. She straddled me in my chair again, grinding on my dick still without letting it go in. Her ass felt so good against the palms of my hands. I got a finger in her asshole. As my middle finger went in, my dick reached its maximum erection.

Charise lifted herself just so my dick was able to make its full entrance into that pussy. Oh, it felt so damn good, and she certainly knew how to move her body. When she tried to wrap her legs around my neck, I stood up for better positioning to fuck her. Instead, I turned her around and laid her facedown on my desk. She wrapped her legs around my waist while I pounded that pussy. I was spanking the hell out of that ass.

I never locked the door when we came back to my office. My boy Deondre came walking in while I was fucking Charise. Charise looked at him and didn't miss a beat. When it became apparent to Deondre that Charise wasn't bothered by his presence, he stood and kept watching. Charise seemed to become more turned on and acted like she was fucking for a camera. She pissed me off when she summoned Deondre to come join in. I wanted her all to myself. He happily obliged her summons. When he was near, she stopped me, sat me back in my chair, and then placed her ass back on my lap.

She took Dre's face and guided it to her tits as she directed him to suck on them. She then took one of his hands to massage her clit. Now I was really getting pissed. I share bitches with Dre all the time, but this was one pussy I didn't want to have to share.

Dre was thoroughly enjoying himself. When Charise had him fully into the groove, she again rubbed her pussy along the side of my dick until she had my erection back, which had started to go down. When my dick was stiff, she lifted herself and guided my dick into her asshole. I wasn't pissed anymore. She had Dre's fingers all the way in her pussy while he sucked on one tit, and I fondled the other. Her ass took my dick in as easy as her pussy did.

Now this is the shit I wish my sons could watch me fuck. This girl is spectacular.

She had Dre stand up and sucked his dick while she was sitting on my dick. She raised up off my dick, like mid-stroke. I was wondering what she was about to do next.

She laid Deondre down on the floor, straddled him, put his dick in her pussy, and then summoned me to get back in her asshole. We had this bitch in a sandwich. We were amazed how this girl just ran the whole show. I think we all came within just a matter of minutes.

Hell, I wish I could have her and Kelly fuck me at the same time. At least I wouldn't have to worry about Charise taking Kelly away. I've had sisters in a threesome before. They fucked each other like they weren't even sisters. That shit turned me the hell on, but I had to get rid of those hoes 'cause they always had their hands out. Somehow, I don't think Charise or Kelly would get with that kind of threesome.

When me and my boy finished fucking her, Charise went on her merry way, back to her husband, perpetrating as though she ain't fucking. She's a real ho! Too bad Arnold can't handle his bitch.

8

Arnold

Oh baby, you don't know how much I missed this body up against mine." On the real tip, I was just happy to finally have some pussy. Any would have done.

Another month had gone by and now I was three weeks shy of a year.

I met Samantha at the Circa 55 inside the Beverly-Hilton, for lunch. We never got around to ordering. As quick as I laid eyes on her, I wanted to take her. Thankfully she didn't put up an ounce of resistance. She showed me to her suite and I spent the next two hours making up for the whole year of sexual deprivation.

For whatever reason or another, I didn't feel any guilt. This was Charise's fault. I tried to be a hundred percent devoted and committed to her and our marriage. All she had to do is suck a dick or something. Throw me some type of bone other than having to look at her naked body without being able to touch. If it weren't for her, I certainly wouldn't have been lying there with Samantha.

"I wish there was a way you could spend the night with me tonight," Samantha said.

"Unfortunately, with the baby's mother I have, I wasn't able to get any cooperation for arrangements for my son. My sister-in-law is going to keep him tomorrow night for me. That'll give us tomorrow night to spend together," I answered.

"I guess that means your wife is still living up to her 'Mother of the Year' award?" Samantha laughed. "Your wife won't watch her own child overnight even if you tell her you're going out of town on business?"

"She doesn't want me to go out of town. She's home every night with our son, but she just feels he needs us both in his life. When I told her I had to go, she told me I need to find a babysitter because she wasn't going to be at home while I'm out cheating on her."

"She thinks you're cheating on her? Why?"

I sat up on the side of the bed, facing the window instead of Samantha. The conversation was disturbing and I didn't want her to see just how bad I was feeling about my living situation. "She accuses me all the time, and I don't know why. Every time she sees women looking at me, she accuses me of trying to be slick and hook up with them."

"So she's okay with your sister-in-law babysitting while you supposedly cheat on her?" she asked, also sitting up in the center of the bed.

"Well . . . actually, she doesn't know her sister is watching the baby for me. She doesn't know that Sandy and I have become really tight over the past year. This is the sister whose husband she was sleeping with. We both think if Charise knew we so much as communicate, she'd think I'm hooking up with her sister just to pay her back."

Samantha wasn't having me continually looking away from her while we spoke. She stood on her knees behind me and gently cupped my chin to turn in her direction, and then she laid back down. "So where did you tell her sister you were going tomorrow?"

"Believe it or not, I told her the truth. I told her you were coming to town and I wanted to spend some time with you."

She sat up and scoffed with disbelief. "You have got to be kidding! And she's okay with it?"

"Sandy is really, really cool. She knows Charise is her sister and that's where her loyalty is supposed to lie, but she feels I should have never left you to be with Charise and feels I at least owe it to myself to see if there was something left between us . . . or not."

Reality: my dick was so happy being up in some pussy, but I didn't know about all those other feelings, though. I tend to lose respect for a woman who is willing to share a man. Now I was kind of hoping Charise is cheating on me. It would help me feel less guilt about cheating on her.

"Wow! I like her. Is that the same one who called asking to help get Charise's attacker prosecuted last year? There are so many of them that it's hard to keep track."

"Yeah, that's Sandy."

"Oh, ok. Yeah, she was kind of cool. I didn't know if she was just acting like that because she needed my help for her sister or was she genuinely a nice person."

"She's definitely good people." I laughed at a thought. "What's so funny?"

"I just thought how she might even grill me for details of you and me. That's how she is."

Samantha looked surprised. "That would be awkward, wouldn't it?"

"You'd be surprised. I wish you could just hang out with us sometime. She is so raw and down to earth. Like I said, she's definitely good people."

Samantha pulled me backwards, rolled on top of me, and began kissing my neck. "Well, I want to make sure you have plenty to talk about. You wouldn't want to disappoint your friend, now would you?" she asked, kissing my lips before I could answer.

𝓂

"So how was your date?" Sandy asked when we met for what has become our weekly lunch. I hadn't sat down good yet.

Sandy, next to my own mother, is like a best friend. She's easy to talk to and real down to earth. I don't feel so bad about sneaking to hang out with Sandy, because Eric also sneaks to hang out with her. Sometimes the three of us would get together to hang. The difference is, I never slept with Sandy.

Eric and Sandy's relationship was long ago, but because Eric is now with Shawnee, Eric and Sandy have to sneak around as though they are messing around. Shawnee would die if she knew they were anywhere together alone. I can't say I'd blame her, because if I didn't really know what time it was with Eric and Sandy, I'd be beside myself just the same.

Charise also would lose her ever-loving mind if she knew I was sneaking around with the sister *she* betrayed to no end. Our relationship is like a brother-sister relationship, but I don't think neither Shawnee nor Charise would appreciate or understand it. That's because neither of them have any respect for boundaries. Sandy and Kelly are probably the only ones who have any sense of boundaries, and that's why I respect them both.

I just feel bad for Kelly's entanglement with Sean. That nigga is a loser for sure. I don't know how she got caught up with that one. I often find myself thinking of ways to get his ass out of her life. She deserves so much better. I was hoping he didn't show up for our Guy's Night out a few weeks ago. He makes me not want to go anymore.

"It was okay," I answered Sandy.

"Okay? That doesn't sound too good. Hell, at least I hope your loins are happy." She laughed before cramming a forkful of her chicken, prosciutto, arugula, and asiago salad into her mouth.

"Oh yeah, the loins are happy," I laughed back, "but to be honest, that feeling I used to have is not the same anymore. I had such great respect for Sam, but now . . . I don't know what I feel."

We got quiet when the waiter came and took my usual order of chicken salad on wheat sandwich with an unsweetened iced tea.

"I know men often mistake a woman trying to stay in her man's corner and let him know that she'll always have his back as a sign of weakness on the woman's part," Sandy continued as soon as the coast was clear. "Actually, it takes a stronger woman to stand behind that man. The problem is, most men don't deserve or appreciate that type of woman. Also, most men don't realize what they had in that woman until they can no longer have her."

"That goes the other way for women too. Hell, it took me to be gone for Charise to realize she had a good man, and even with me back, she doesn't seem to appreciate me," I rebutted.

"Uh, look who we're talking about. You said a mouthful when you said 'Charise.' You can't put *Charise* and a *woman* in the same sentence," Sandy sarcastically stated, then laughed. "Charise is a breed all of her own. I know that's my sister and I love her, but she doesn't count when talking about a 'real woman.' Samantha, she's a real woman. She might even be a fool for love woman, but a real woman no less. If not her, that's the type of woman you should be with. You need someone who's going to be woman enough to be a mother to your son, like Sam was before you foolishly left her to pursue the biological mother who shows you time and time again that she will never be that woman."

"You must have been talking to my moms. The two of you say the same things. She thinks Charise only got back with me because she can't have kids anymore and I had custody, but that doesn't make too much sense, because Charise won't seem to be bothered with Jarrod unless I am around. She won't keep him alone. If she was trying to get our son from me, I would think she'd always want to keep him and try to get me out of the picture."

Sandy shook her head and laughed. "Again, we're talking about Charise. There is no rhyme or reason to her logic. Maybe she keeps you on a short leash because she's afraid someone will do to her what she's done to others. It could also be that she's worried that if you leave her for another woman, you'll take her only child from her again."

"Not if she ain't giving me any!" I shot back. "What marriage have you ever heard of where the man ain't getting any cookies? I could get my marriage annulled right now because it has never been consummated. We've been married six damn months."

"You already know how I feel on that subject. You're a damn fool. That's all there is to it. That girl is playing you like a fiddle. Ain't no telling how many guys she's screwing around with. That's why I try to encourage you to get yours.

I think of my two boys when I hear about this mess you're living in with my sister, and I have to tell you, I'd not only kick their asses for being so dumb, but I'd be just like your mother, always looking for the first opportunity to kick that girl's ass.

"Every time you and I talk, I run home and try to school my boys on what not to tolerate from a woman. Don't worry, I don't mention your name." She laughed. "But for real, whether you want a chick on the side or you need to kick Charise to the curb, you need to look out for you and your son. I don't particularly condone the whole adultery thing, but you need to stand up and be the man when it comes to Charise. Even if that means leaving," Sandy strongly advised me again.

The waiter brought my order and we got quiet again. I could tell he was a nosey, gossiping one who was on the prowl for dirt to talk about.

As soon as he was out of earshot, I asked, "Do you really think she's messing with other dudes? My mom says the exact same thing"

Sandy looked down and away. "I don't know. It wouldn't surprise me. I'm just saying. You need to listen to your mother."

I was about to take a bite out of my sandwich when I noticed her demeanor change and her shifting in her seat. "Okay, you just pulled an 'I'm lying' move. What the hell?"

"Huh?"

"Your eyes. They went every which way, and you are not a good liar. I know you too well. What have you heard or know?"

"I don't know what you're talking about," she said in a higher pitched tone that confirmed her lying, while she tried to look me in my eyes, but still couldn't.

"Come on, Sandy. I thought we were better than that. She's fucking someone and you know all about it, right?" I asked, getting angry.

Sandy closed her eyes and took a deep breath. "Please Arnold, don't put me in an impossible situation. Right now, I really can't say, but I just don't want you to be any fool. You don't deserve what Charise offers. That's why I just wish you'd leave her dumb ass."

"Damn, the conversation must be intense here. I could feel the tension," Eric said, pulling up a chair to the table laughing, with the waiter following behind him. "What did I miss?"

"Sandy was about to tell me that my wife is cheating on me," I responded, looking directly at Sandy. At that moment, I didn't even care about the waiter's presence. He hurried off, but I knew he was still trying to stay within earshot.

Eric choked and looked away as though he also knew something. He looked like he was about to run from that chair he was about to take a seat in. I watched them both for a reaction as their eyes played with one another.

"Well maybe I better leave you two to finish your conversation then," Eric responded, standing back up ready to run.

"Oh no! No, no, no, no! You are going to sit your ass right back here with Sandy and tell me what you know. Both of you obviously know something," I demanded.

Eric sat back down. The waiter was heading back to the table to get Eric's order, but he just held his hand up and shook his head letting the waiter know he wouldn't be ordering.

"Arnold, just let it go. As long as you are doing your thing, to hell with what my sister is doing," Sandy answered.

"Do both of you understand how difficult it has been for me to be celibate with a fucking wife lying butt naked near me and won't let me touch her for a whole fucking year?"

I saw the waiter's eyebrows raise up even though he was a couple of tables away. His radar was definitely tuned in to our conversation.

I continued. "All along I'm thinking she's just a little messed up still about being raped and beaten by Todd's son. I'm sitting here trying to be the loving and supportive husband and father. I want the truth and I want it now."

"That nosey waiter is over there listening, you know?" Sandy asked.

"Fuck him! Let him get an earful then!" I yelled, and then watched the waiter take off when he saw us all looking at him.

Eric put his hands up in defense. "Man, I didn't know. I just heard. And yeah, you have every reason to be pissed, but I'm with Sandy on this. You need to let it go since you've already made up your mind to cross the line with Sam. What can you say at this point? Not much. You didn't cheat on your wife because you thought she was cheating on you. You cheated on your wife—period. Now just let it go."

I looked at Eric as if I could actually kick his ass. "Let it go?!" I asked disgusted. "How would you feel if it were Shawnee? You wouldn't just let it go."

"Oh? How the hell do you think I felt the other night when she had me babysitting because she had the nerve to go out on a date with some other nigga? And that wasn't the first time she did that shit."

Sandy scrunched her face as though she ate something sour. "Now that's messed up, Eric. I can't believe Shawnee would do that to you. I thought the two of you were doing well."

"You thought like I thought. She plays too many games for me. She told me I was free to date but I couldn't bring anyone to the house or the restaurant she paid for. She really got me feeling like some bitch. Who stands for that kind of shit? Your woman telling you she's dating other men, and then she wants to tell me I can't have women in the restaurant because she bought it for me. I wish I could just give her back her dough that she put up for the restaurant, and then she couldn't talk shit to me. Then to top it off, she won't let me just go get my own crib because she said she's not going to have 'her daughter' in some nasty bachelor pad where I'd supposedly be screwing all of my women."

"Yo man, I'm sorry," I told Eric, who looked on the verge of tears. "I didn't realize things were so bad for you. I guess the big difference here is I *do* have the power to walk away at any time, and no one has any holds or power over me." I paused as I thought on my own words. "That's just it! I need to get my confirmation and walk away from Charise once and for all. If I have to cheat, then I probably don't need to be in that relationship."

Sandy clapped her hands. "He finally gets it," she said to no one in particular.

"Now one of you can tell me how to get the confirmation I need that my wife is cheating on me and not just trying to play me to regain custody of my son."

Sandy and Eric looked at each other. Their eyes debated whether to tell me what they obviously knew or not.

"Okay, I will tell you this much, but I won't tell you all or how I came upon the info," Sandy offered.

I kept quiet, waiting to hear whatever piece of information she was willing to share. I could feel my insides turning. I felt the air diminishing as I waited to hear my worst fear.

Sandy continued. "Your wife absolutely does not have any problems having sexual relations. She does not have any psychological hang ups, and to top matters off, the bitch is still as wicked as the day before she was beaten and raped. She has fooled us all. Maybe initially she was sincere, but somewhere along the way, she shifted back into her manipulative and deceptive ways."

I sat stunned by Sandy's harsh words regarding her sister. I didn't want to accept or hear them, but I knew she would not blatantly lie to me.

I also was able to read the hurt in Eric's face as Sandy spoke the words that he obviously already knew. I wanted more details. I needed to know how and where their information came from, but it was already stipulated that she would not say.

As my mind raced, I tried to use deductive reasoning. *How would both Sandy and Eric know? Had Sandy had a previous conversation with Eric? Was Shawnee the source of Sandy and Eric's information? But how would Shawnee know what Charise does? They barely speak.*

I had to ask, "I need to know how you know. How are you so certain? How do I know you are telling me the truth and not just trying to get back at my wife for what she did to your marriage?" I said, almost irritated toward Sandy.

Sandy looked shocked by my words, but didn't speak. She looked offended, like she'd kick my ass for accusing her of lying.

"Trust me," Eric spoke up, "Sandy is not lying to you. Sandy and I have never had a single conversation on the subject, but I also know this to be a fact. The whole situation is all fucked up and puts everyone in a very difficult position. Even I felt like a weasel every time I'd speak to you and then had to keep silent."

"Oh no he didn't call me a liar," Sandy interjected to no one with her arms folded across her chest.

"So I take it Shawnee would have been the one to tell both you and Sandy, but how would Shawnee know anything about Charise's life? They barely speak to one another."

"Arnold! I am begging you, just let this go! No good will come of your pursuing this. You just need to use your energies on moving on with your life and your son."

The waiter was at the next table nodding in agreement and no longer concealing the fact that he had been listening to our conversation.

I shook my head and laughed. "No, I don't think so. I gave up my life, and sex for a whole fucking year. I left a good relationship with a good woman and brought confusion into my son's life. Letting it go is probably the last thing I'm going to do."

"Man, I know how you are feeling, but you have to walk away. You're going to do something stupid and end up locked up behind some ho," the waiter came and boldly stated.

We all looked at him as if he was stupid, and he took his cue and hurried off again.

"Well, one thing he got right, she is a ho." Eric laughed and then turned to Sandy as he caught himself. "Oops! No disrespect to you, Sandy, but you know what I mean."

"Don't worry. I agree with you," she answered.

"If the two of you won't tell me, then I'll get a private investigator to get my answers," I said.

Sandy looked at Eric, and then to me. "I guess that might be good. If you need closure to help you move on, then a private investigator might be a good thing. In the meantime, you really need to make plans for you and your son. You need to walk away from that girl."

"Well it would be easier if the two of you would just tell me what you know."

"I don't think so. You need to get concrete information for yourself, and I don't think you'll have too much of a hard time getting it," Eric said.

Sandy rose up from her seat to reach over to hug me. "I'm sorry, Arnold, that I can't say any more than I've already said. I'm sorry that you are going through this shit. Eric and I will be here to help you get through this. I've been through this and it can be done. Yours is not the first marriage to fail, but just know that life will go on beyond this turmoil."

"Yeah, and I gotta figure how to work through my own turmoil." Eric painfully laughed.

"Awww!!" Sandy said reaching to then hug Eric. "Don't worry, both of you will be all right. Eric, you just have to show less interest in Shawnee, and she'll turn around. She'll want you more if you are less available. Right now, she thinks she has you wrapped around her finger. Stop being so readily available and she might stop taking you for granted."

"Isn't this something?" Eric laughed. "My ex-girlfriend, who is now my best friend, is giving me advice on how to keep my current girlfriend, who is her sister. Who would have guessed it?"

"Seems like you chose the wrong sister. Hell, seems like I chose the wrong sister." I laughed despite my circumstances.

"Well I'm glad to see both of you smiling again. I was starting to get embarrassed by you guys," she said.

"Embarrassed? By us?" Eric asked.

"Yeah, embarrassed. I'm sitting here with two of the finest guys in town, and every chick walking by is watching. They're probably thinking I was just busted in a love triangle because of the intensity and emotions of the conversation."

"There she goes stroking our egos again, Eric."

"Well at least the nosey-ass waiter will set the record straight and let them know the two guys are knuckleheads who don't know how to handle their women," he responded.

We all laughed and agreed to change the subject. Eric summoned the waiter back to the table to get his food order and we finally got to eat our lunch.

In the back of my mind, I still contemplated what I was going to do to Charise when I got proof of her affair.

9

Kevin

Y ou've got problems brewing," Eric said when he arrived to my office shortly after leaving his lunch with Arnold.

I automatically knew my trouble had Charise's name on it. "I'm almost afraid to ask. It has to be Charise related, huh?"

"In a nutshell: yes. Arnold is now on her trail, and I'm trying to keep you in the clear. I don't want our bond destroyed behind her."

"Maybe I need to just speak with him myself. I didn't want to be the one to tell him his wife has been deceiving him for a whole year," I said to Eric.

"I'd want you to tell me if it were Shawnee. Arnold's going to mainly be mad that you didn't say anything to him before."

"I feel horrible about the entire situation. I wasn't going to say anything to anyone had Charise not blackmailed me." I took a long pause and deep breath. "Between you and I, the worst part is that I can't get the whole scenario out of my mind. I keep praying about it, but the thoughts won't go away."

"Like lustful thoughts?"

"Yes, lustful thoughts. Part of the story told got chopped away, such as how Charise was able to blackmail me," I confessed.

"Damn! I just heard she tried to come on to you and came at you naked. I didn't know there was more, Kev," he said, shaking his head.

"Unfortunately, there was much more. I try not to think about it."

"Did you get with her or is it that you want to get with her?"

"No. I didn't sleep with her, and I don't want to sleep with her, but I constantly find myself wondering what it would have been like."

"I don't understand. You say you didn't sleep with her, but there was more to the story. What are you not telling me then?"

"Things went a lot further than Charise simply stripping and telling me to have sex with her. I kissed her. I touched her."

Eric took a long pause as he looked around in thought. "Now when you say you kissed her, was that like a peck-kiss or a slob-kiss? And when you say you touched her . . ."

I looked down in shame. "It was a kiss-kiss and an uninhibited touch."

"Aw! No! No, dawg! Oh no, man, she didn't get you like that, did she? Please tell me she didn't get you like that, Kev."

"She got me. She got me good. I almost lost my head completely, and now I keep replaying it over and over in my mind. It was one thing to imagine her doing all of those things I've heard about, but when you have real, live flesh to go with that imagination, it's an entirely different story. Now I feel like it's hard to face Arnold just because of my lustful thoughts. It was hard hanging out at the sports bar together knowing what I knew about his wife. It's hard looking into Elaine's eyes because she trusts me implicitly, and I feel deceptive."

"So this happened before we went to the sports bar? The first time or the second time?"

"It happened the week after our July Fourth gathering. The blackmail didn't come until after the first sports bar gathering, shortly after Labor Day. By the time we went to the sports bar the first time, I began to dismiss the whole thing, but I still felt guilty hanging around Arnold. It was really, really difficult for me when we got together the last time. I started to cancel, but I didn't want to let you guys down." I paused. "Another confession—I invited Sean along because I wanted to keep the focus off of me. Truth be known, I don't like the character, but I figured there wouldn't have been any intimate conversations to make things more difficult for myself."

"Oh man, this is not good. It sounds like you do want to sleep with Charise, otherwise you wouldn't be having such guilt. I guess you already know not to cross that line any further than you have already done, and I think maybe it's best you don't have that conversation with Arnold after all. Maybe because I'm a man, I can see that look in your eyes, but it looks like you really want to hit it. It's like you've been kicking yourself ever since for not hitting that ass already."

Damn! He could see all of that?

"I don't know what I think or feel anymore, Eric. I think I may have developed feelings for her somewhere during my time of helping her. Otherwise I would have been able to resist her. She's not the first person to try hitting on me, but I could always resist."

"I think you may be right. Do you know how many beautiful women here in L.A. alone, that have come on to me, exposed themselves to me, or something? I haven't touched one of them. I should have based on how Shawnee treats me, but I have not. If you weren't feeling some kind of lust or whatever before, she wouldn't have had any effect on you."

"So what do I do? How do I deal with this situation? I invested in her magazine. It's not like we won't ever come into contact again. I mean I told Elaine because that seemed like the right thing to do. I have never felt this weak or vulnerable when it comes to a woman."

"I don't know what to tell you. When you have to see her for business, just be sure to have someone else around. Have Elaine there when you meet her."

"That would be a disaster waiting to happen. Charise would fill in the blanks that I didn't tell Elaine. And just like you said, my eyes can't hide the lust, Elaine would pick up on it immediately. Furthermore, Elaine wants nothing more to do with Charise."

"Sounds like you've got a problem. Just so you know, Arnold is getting a private eye to tail Charise. Just make sure you are not part of any findings. That wouldn't be good."

"Thanks for the heads up. I don't see myself being a part of those findings, but I'm sure some unsuspecting creature will be." I nervously chuckled.

"That's for sure. Anyway, I better get going. I have 'Shawnee's' restaurant to run," Eric said sarcastically.

"I'd buy her out for you and rescue you from your misery, but she'd have my head on a platter. Then my wife would be getting on my case for getting involved, but I do sympathize if that helps. I feel your pain." I chuckled again.

Eric laughed. "Yeah, and painful it is. You're right. Shawnee would slay you or anyone else trying to help me get an upper hand on her."

We laughed as I walked Eric out to the elevators.

I don't know why I couldn't bring myself to confess to Eric about Charise's phone call to me just that morning. It may have been the reason my eyes were presently filled with lust.

She called and said, "I don't know why you wasted your time telling my sister I tried to come on to you. You're only going to make it harder on yourself to get this pussy that I know you haven't stopped thinking about since you touched it. I bet you still smell your fingers, hoping to catch a whiff of my scent again. And let's not forget how your mouth watered on these tits. I bet you didn't tell Elaine that part or how your tongue was down my throat. But that's okay. I kept your secret for you when she confronted me—for now at least. I didn't want to make your life miserable. Actually, I'm trying to make your life more pleasant. The same way I made Sean's life a bit happier."

"What did you just say?" I finally interrupted, most annoyed by her last comment.

"You heard correctly. Sean wanted this pussy also, and I granted him his wish. You dragged your feet. He let me see how he has a big dick that matches his big feet. He didn't drag those big feet of his at all."

I wasn't sure why I was fuming. I was beyond angry. I was jealous.

"Why would you sleep with Sean, Charise? What would make you let that character touch your body?" I asked.

Charise laughed. "I would have preferred if it were you, and it still could be. Sean's just a rebound. It's up to you. Trust me, I would love to feel your fingers inside of me again. I haven't forgotten how good they made me feel. I would love to kiss those succulent lips again. I would also love the opportunity to kiss that big dick I felt inside of your pants. I know your dick is bigger than Sean's."

I was at a loss for words. My dick hardened immediately. My dick wanted her lips to kiss it. I put my fingers to my nose as she spoke and tried to recollect the scent of her wet pussy juices on them almost three months ago. I wanted her at that moment.

She continued. "So if you would prefer to have my pussy instead of Sean having it, then I suggest you get with the program real soon. This pussy could be yours whenever you want it. Your choice. Talk to you later," she said before she abruptly hung up.

My mind was like a pendulum. I was angry about her being with Sean in one thought, but then I wanted to be with her in the other thought.

Why is she doing this? Why must she target all of her sisters' husbands? She won't even sleep with her own husband. Why won't she sleep with her own husband? How much longer will she target me for sex? Do I tell anyone about her and Sean without them seeing my anger? My jealousy?

With much thought, I called Sean after Eric left my office. I needed to get to the bottom of this.

"Hey Sean, I'm sorry to bother you, but I just received a disturbing phone call that I was hoping was false," I said when he answered.

"Sure, what's up?" he asked. "I'm always the subject of rumors anyway." He chuckled.

"I was told that you are sleeping with Charise. That isn't true, is it?"

"Who told you that? Why do anyone give a damn what I do?" He now sounded agitated. "That's a bitch-move, Kev."

"To be quite honest, it was Charise who called and told me. I wasn't sure what the purpose was of her telling me that or why. I was just hoping there was no truth to her statement."

He laughed. "Oh, she told you that? That girl is crazy. Why would she tell you that other than to try making you jealous? Let me ask you, are *you* sleeping with her?"

I wasn't expecting his question. "Of course not!" I probably said louder than needed.

"Well I'll just say this much—if that's what she's telling you for whatever reason she's telling you, then we'll just go with that then. I'm a busy man, and I have to go now." Then he hung up.

I wasn't sure what to take from his response. He didn't exactly deny sleeping with her, but neither did he confirm.

What did I really expect him to say? "Yeah, I slept with her." I know he better never put his grimy hands on her again.

10

Todd

Momma, I don't know what else to say or do to get my wife to lose the weight. She's not making any effort at all. The kids just had their first birthday, and Harmony looks like she's about to give birth all over again. Do you know how embarrassing it was when we were out together and someone asked how far along she is and if she's having multiples again? Then every conversation we have is either about the babies or her family drama, and you know how I feel about her nutty family."

"Cheating on your wife is not the answer, Toddy. I can't imagine she hasn't figured it out yet."

"Well how did *you* figure it out?" I asked my mother, who stays with us more than she stays in Houston.

"Your schedule changed for one. You never used to come home this late. More so, because you almost seem happy or satisfied in some way, and since I haven't noticed any improvements in your home life, the only logical explanation is another woman."

I rubbed my brows. I got up from the kitchen stool and walked around the island, trying to process my thoughts. I was frustrated as hell by having to live my secret life. I felt like I was going to explode from keeping it to myself.

Here was a good time to let out my true feelings. "Momma, I can't make love to my own wife. Not that I really have much desire to touch her because of how she let herself go physically, but then if I try, she's always shooting me down for one reason or another. I do have needs, Ma."

"I understand, son, but I'd just hate for you to lose your family over this. Perhaps she already knows you're cheating on her and that's why she doesn't want you to touch her. She might be silent only because she knows it will destroy her family."

"You think?"

She didn't respond but raised a brow and pursed her lips with an obvious unspoken "Yes." It looked as if she were speaking of her own experiences.

I sat back down next to her. "What am I supposed to do then?" I asked when she said nothing.

"Why don't you try dating your wife again? That might help the sparks."

"You forget that we tried that. You've offered to keep the kids while we went out on the town. We were home within forty-five minutes because she didn't feel right being out socially, while leaving the babies. I couldn't take it anymore, so now I'm doing what makes me happy."

"Well, just be careful, son. I want my children to be happy, and if she's not trying to make her husband happy, then that's on her."

I leaned over to kiss my mom on her weary forehead. "Thanks, Mom. I knew you'd understand."

"That's what moms are for." She smiled nervously as she got up and left the kitchen where we have the majority of our powwows after Harmony is asleep.

I quickly became bored with both Cynnyyah and Valerie. The sex was great, but then I realized there were many more Cynnyyah's coming into my office for more than medical reasons.

Maria Littleton didn't beat around the bush like Miss Foster did initially. It was only her second time coming to see me as her doctor and she told me that she wanted to feel all of me inside of her. She said she had fantasized about me every day since the first time she saw me six months prior. When she came this time, she was there for her full annual checkup. She said she typically goes to her GYN for her pelvic and breast exam.

I think Valerie zones in on the women she thinks may be interested in me romantically, because she always tries to cock block by trying to be in the room for the exam, especially the younger women. But she failed to pick up on Maria's interest in me. Maria had beautiful, full breasts with large nipples. Since Valerie wasn't in the room, I was able to take my time on the breast exam. One of her breasts fit in my two hands, but they didn't sag one bit. When it came to her pelvic exam, I was able to inhale the smell of her pussy, and it smelled good enough to eat.

The difference this time was I didn't hook up with Miss Littleton until all of her test results came back clean. Then I went by her small apartment and tore that pussy up across every square inch of the place. When I finished with her, she had to put an ice pack down there and take some Motrin to make the swelling go down. Maria Littleton was a one-shot deal. I don't like a woman without creativity. I also don't like one who wants to initiate some shit she can't finish.

Added to the list were Tonia Walker, Muriel Webster, and Erica Jones. I had so much pussy that I didn't know what to do with it all, and not a one of them were over the age of thirty. The beauty of it was that it was all "no-strings attached" pussy.

The crazy thing was, Valerie would be in the office spending her days trying to do things to keep me turned on, but somehow it just turned me on for all the other women who came through the door. Well, at least the young, sexy ones. I would try to pick up on the slightest hint of the woman being interested in me, and it was on from there. However, damn near every day before I'd leave the office, I'd have Valerie's tits in my mouth. That was her big thing. She wanted me to suck on her tits and finger-fuck her. That would be the foreplay, which would hold me over until I made it to one of the other women's house.

In six weeks, I only fucked my wife one time. If it were left up to me, I wouldn't have touched her then, but since she wanted to have sex, I had to perform my husband duties.

The irony is she made me wear a damn condom. The only pleasure I had out of that episode was pretending she was Tonia.

Tonia was five-foot, ten-inches like Harmony, but the big difference was about 130 pounds. Tonia was a model— gorgeous to look at and sexy to fuck. Hell, I was thinking about Tonia when Valerie was sucking my dick. There was something about Tonia's lips that turned me on when she spoke. Her lips were like Naomi Campbell's—another I'd like on my "to do" list.

Muriel had a nice fat ass sitting on her five-foot, five-inch frame. She wasn't fat at all, but her ass just protruded out. She was an exotic dancer who made a good chunk of change making that booty clap. At first I didn't find her attractive, but when she demonstrated to me, during her exam, how she wraps her legs behind her neck to make the guys at the club go crazy, I suddenly found myself wanting her. She reminded me a lot of Charise. Not that I'd want to fuck Charise, but she has an ass to make any man cry, and she's a freak.

Then there's Erica. She was one of those sneaky-freaks—totally on the conservative side. I was surprised when she came on to me. She also just put it out there that she wanted to spend time with me. There wasn't anything particular about her that would immediately grab my attention and cause me to look twice. I decided to fuck her for the hell of it. That girl had so much bottled up energy, I thought she was going to kill me. She still wouldn't be my first choice to call if I had to choose. That would probably be between Tonia and Cynnyyah. Those two turn me on the most even when they're nowhere around. I'm now looking forward to going to see Roxana. I have to fly to Houston next week to see my other sons. When I would go in the past, I wouldn't contact Roxana, trying to be a good husband. This time I let her know I'd be in town, and she was excited.

Valerie came to my office to announce the surprise of my life.

"There's a Mrs. Dobbs here to see you."

I tried to place the name. I could tell the woman must be attractive in a threatening way by Valerie's attitude. The only Dobbs I knew was Kevin. Mrs. Dobbs would be Elaine. I didn't think she ever used her married name.

Still skeptical, I instructed Valerie to send her in.

Valerie stared at me long and hard before rolling her eyes. "Uhm, if you say so."

See, this was the shit I knew would make working with and fucking Valerie complicated.

Sure enough, it was Elaine walking into my office. I was stunned. I stood to greet her. I think my dick stood as well, happy for this pleasant surprise.

"Elaine! What a surprise," I said, barely able to contain my excitement. I offered her a seat, while taking my own.

She was absolutely stunning. Looking at her made me despise being burdened with Harmony.

"I'll just get right to the point, Todd," she said abrasively. "Are you cheating on my sister, and why?"

I choked at her directness. I quickly ran to close the door that I mistakenly left open. Where was this coming from?

Obviously Harmony must be saying something to her sisters. *Bitch!*

"No! Why would you ask me that?" I lied in a whisper.

She looked as if studying my body language, then answered, "I was becoming concerned by my sister's mood change. She mentioned that you're barely home anymore and feels you don't love her anymore."

"But why wouldn't Harmony say something to me if she had concerns? I don't understand how you became involved," I said. I was half annoyed but didn't want to rattle Elaine.

"I'm not quite sure why Harmony won't just speak up for herself. She's an expert on speaking for everyone else. I really didn't want to cross the line into someone else's marriage when I have my own marriage being targeted by my fool-ass younger sister. You know I love my family and I don't want to see them hurting. If there is anything I could do to help, I'm going to try.

"I will be the first to admit, my sister has let her physical appearance go to hell in a hand basket since she's had the children. I try talking to her about trying to make herself more appealing for her husband, but she seems almost depressed. I don't know why she seems like she doesn't care anymore. The only thing I could come up with is that you must be cheating on her. You know she's the psychologist, and she's typically the one who keeps everything together, but now that she's letting her own self go, I feel like it's my place to step up to help my family. I mean you come from a large family, so surely you could understand trying to be there for your family members in crisis."

I'm not sure what all Elaine was talking about. I know I heard her mention the word "ass," and my brain locked up right there.

"I'm not sure what to say, Elaine." Her long pause made it obvious that it was my turn to say something. "I talk to Harmony all the time, but she's never mentioned any problems or concerns. I have tried many things to get our marriage on track—"

"Ah-ha! So you would admit the marriage is off track?" Elaine asked as if she caught me in a lie.

"Uh, well, yeah. I guess I would venture to say that. I don't think it's so off that it can't be fixed. I'm still just surprised by your visit. Harmony typically is very assertive and speaks her mind in our relationship. I figured that was a Wiggins characteristic," I chuckled.

"So am I—surprised, that is. I usually tend to avoid the family drama. I did suggest to Harmony that she goes with you to Houston next week. I know you want to go visit your sons, but I thought it was a good opportunity for the two of you to get away together. Kevin and I could probably help your mom and nanny with the babies," she suggested.

IS SHE CRAZY?! Did she just suggest I take Harmony to Houston with me and give up 'Roxana sex'?

"That would have been all right, but you know there's bad blood between Harmony and my sisters. I also don't think she'd be okay with visiting my son

Andre in prison as a romantic getaway. A vacation would be nice, but I already know Harmony is not interested in going anywhere unless the children go."

"Please tell me my sister didn't say that. This is bad. We have to figure something out because I would hate for your marriage to fall apart or you to start cheating on her," she said, raising an eyebrow.

Too late! The kids are the only thing holding my marriage together.

"Speaking of cheating," she continued. "How much do you know about Charise coming on to my husband? Has Kevin told you more than he's admitted to me because he's worried about my reaction? It doesn't take a rocket scientist to know Charise must have something on him to be able to blackmail him. He did something with her, didn't he?"

"No. I don't think so," I lied again.

Valerie rudely knocked on the door, walked in before I could answer, looked Elaine up and down, and then said in her most ghetto fashion, "Your two o'clock is waiting for you. She's been waiting for some time now and she wants to know what's taking so long."

"Valerie, I'll be there shortly. I'm meeting with my sister- in-law," I tried to hint to Valerie.

She picked up on my signal and changed her whole attitude. "Oh, I'm sorry. I'll let the patient know you'll be with her shortly," Valerie said with a smile before walking out and closing the door.

Elaine's demeanor as she watched Valerie even after the door was closed said that Valerie was setting herself up for a good old-fashion beat down.

Elaine stood to leave. "Well, I'm not going to hold you up. I just want you to let me know how I can help in any way." She reached over and gave me a hug when I stood to get the door for her.

OH!! OH!!! The feel of her body next to mine has my dick throbbing. Not just hard, but throbbing. Why can't Elaine be like Charise, and have no problems fucking her sisters' husbands? Damn, she feels good and smells good.

"And tell that skank ho she better find her own man," Elaine stopped and said as she was going out of my office.

"Who? What?" I asked, confused.

"The help—that ghetto-ass Valerie. I can see the bitch wants you. Tell her it ain't about to happen."

Just then Valerie was approaching. I was thinking, *Oh Lord, please don't let Valerie say shit about us being together.* Instead, she said, "Excuse me? Did I hear my name?"

"Perhaps," Elaine said deliberately as she walked past Valerie in a confrontational manner. She paused and looked at Valerie as if she would kick Valerie's ass if she breathed improperly.

Girl Fight! Or so I was hoping. Damn, I would love to see that shit: Two women fighting and ripping each other's shirts off, and their titties popping out while they're fighting. Damn, the thought was making me hard.

Somehow, as refined as her front was, Elaine seemed like she could get real hood and smack the taste out of Valerie's mouth. That would be a short fight and I wouldn't get to see any tits flying out. Valerie has a little hood in her, but definitely not the same hood as Elaine. Elaine's body, although sexy as I don't know what, is a lot more solid than Valerie's. Like I said, she'd hurt Valerie's ass. Come to think of it, Shawnee, Harmony, and Sandy look like they would put a hurting on the poor fool who crossed their paths incorrectly, but all of them are fine as hell. Sexy. Well, now with the exception of Harmony.

With Elaine now gone, it was Valerie wanting to know about Elaine. I reminded her that Elaine was my sister-in-law and was acting that way because I'm married to her sister. I went on to warn her not to get into any types of confrontations with any of them, because things would be very ugly for her. That made her back off from her probing.

I could still smell Elaine's perfume lingering in my office and on my jacket. Elaine is like a cross of Halle Berry and Lisa Raye. There is just no sense in how one woman could be so fine. It took every bit of my energy not to cup her ass and let her feel my throbbing meat when I hugged her.

Whew! Elaine, Elaine, Elaine. She just doesn't know! I want her in the worst way.

11

Sean

I think your sister is fucking your brother-in-law." "Which sister and which brother-in-law?" Kelly asked. "Kevin and Charise."

Kelly laughed. "I don't think that would ever happen. Kevin would never let that happen.

"What makes you so certain?" I asked.

"I heard Charise tried to come on to him, but he told Elaine. I guess he's too smart to get caught out there by Charise."

"I think he fucked her," I rebutted, annoyed by her praise of Kevin.

"Why do you say that?" she asked. "You must have heard something,"

"Kevin called me twice now all rattled because he said Charise told him I was sleeping with her."

Kelly's face showed instant disturbance. She damn sure wasn't going to fix her mouth to ask if there was any truth to the statement.

"Why would she tell him something so absurd?" she safely asked.

"I figured she was trying to make him jealous. I believe there's more to that story about her coming on to him and him rejecting her. I bet you he waxed that ass."

Kelly folded her arms across her chest. She was pissed but wasn't going to say anything.

"What you all pissed about? What, you don't want to hear me tell you how he waxed that fat ass?" I laughed.

Damn, the thought of that ass made my dick hard, so I fondled myself.

"All that talk got my dick hard. Come here and suck my dick," I told Kelly.

"Do you think you could make it sound a bit more appealing? Could we go to the bedroom?" Her expression made it obvious that she didn't want to, but like I said before, my bitch is well trained not to refuse.

"I'm sitting here on the sofa. What the fuck we gotta go to the bedroom for? My dick is hard here. It might not be hard when we get to the bedroom. Why all the conversation when I tell you to come suck my dick?"

Kelly gave up her protest. I know she was worried the boys would walk in at any moment. Kelly was doing a half-ass job sucking my dick, so I stopped her.

"Fuck it! You want to act like you don't know how to suck a dick all of a sudden? I'm going back to the studio. Surely I could find me a good dick sucking there."

I could see the mixture of emotions flooding Kelly's eyes, but her lips remained silent.

"And don't be getting on the phone with your nosey-ass sisters telling them what I said about Mr. Goodie-Two-Shoes. We're gonna hit that money-bag up for some cash one day, so I don't need him getting all pissed off at us. If he wants to wax that ass, then that's his business. He just don't need to be calling and questioning me."

I got down to the studio looking for someone I wanted my dick sucked by. Dick sucking is like an art. Not everyone can do it, so I have to be selective with the one I pick.

I found this groupie bitch named Lillian. She was like eighteen or nineteen years old at the most and one of those chicks down for whatever. I had her in my office on her knees sucking when Deondre came walking in my office unannounced as always.

"Yo, you got a visitor."

"I'm busy," I said, pointing down to Lillian.

"Charise," he responded.

I pushed Lillian off my dick. "For real? She's here now?" I said, getting happy.

Deondre waved Charise in my office while I was still packing my Johnson back into my pants.

"Anything she could do, I could do better," Charise sang, walking toward my desk and looking Lillian in the eyes.

"I'm sure you can, shorty," I answered.

"I say make it a party," Deondre suggested. "I already know Lillian got skills, what about you?

"Skills? What kind of skills are you talking about?" Charise asked with annoyance in her voice.

"My man likes his threesomes. Can you hang?" he asked Charise.

"I thought you already got that answer," she responded, full of herself.

"Wrong answer! He likes two women at a time," Deondre educated Charise about my preferences.

Charise got quiet and her confidence went out my twenty-third-story window. She obviously didn't possess those skills. Lillian laughed.

"Well since you're here, now's a good time to learn some new skills," I encouraged.

"She obviously doesn't have what it takes, Sean," Lillian taunted Charise.

"I'm strictly dick, so no, I don't need to learn anything new," Charise tried to bark back.

"Then I hate to do this, but I'm going to have to ask you to leave. I have Lillian to do what you could do." I challenged Charise.

Lillian was beaming with pride and flashing all thirty-two of her teeth. She waved Charise off. "Bye-bye. Come back when you grow up."

"Grow up?! Oh trust me, I am grown up!" Charise said. "What are you, about fifteen?"

Lillian just laughed and shrugged her shoulders. Deondre left my office. Ignoring Charise, I went and pulled my fold-out bed out. "Come on, Lillian. Just ignore her."

Lillian happily obliged. She stripped down to her g-string and sprawled out on the bed. Charise was frozen in her tracks. She stood watching helplessly as I licked Lillian's breasts and rubbed between her thighs. Lillian pulled my Johnson from my pants and started sucking. I was so caught up in the rapture, I didn't notice Charise stripping down to just her thong. She walked up to kiss me in the mouth.

I pulled Lillian up and had her kiss Charise in the mouth. At first Charise resisted, but she got with it when she saw I wasn't going to back off. Lillian fondled Charise's breasts before bending to feast on them. Charise was clearly uncomfortable.

I had the two of them lay on the bed as Lillian continued on Charise's breasts. I think Lillian was enjoying the hell out of Charise's tits. I rubbed between Charise's legs until Lillian's hand took over massaging Charise's clit. Slowly but surely, Charise was loosening up.

Lillian was bent over Charise from the side. I inserted my fingers into Lillian's pussy, and she buried her face between Charise's legs. Charise tried to resist at first, but eventually began fondling Lillian's pussy and tits. Lillian straddled Charise's face and the two were in a 69 position. Since Charise was a beginner and Lillian was an expert, Lillian controlled the pace until they were both exploding.

I couldn't make up my mind which one I wanted to fuck first. I settled on Lillian, since she had the skills to keep working on Charise. I raised Lillian's pussy from Charise's clutches and got up over Charise and was able to put my dick into Lillian's pussy from the back. Lillian had Charise going crazy. Charise had one hand massaging Lillian's clit as I was fucking her, while her other hand rubbed my balls.

We changed up positions with me lying on my back, Lillian's pussy in my mouth and Charise riding my dick. Charise and Lillian were kissing one another and enjoying each other's tits. We changed positions a few more times and without fail, my boy Dre had to come join in on the action. He fucked Lillian while I finished up Charise, and Charise and Lillian were still working each other.

I guess Charise got what she came for because she left without ever saying why she came.

When I got home later that night, I could tell Kelly had been crying. I rubbed her shoulders and asked, "What have you been crying about?"

"Nothing," she answered.

I stopped rubbing her shoulders. "What have I told you about lying to me? Now what were you crying about?"

She hesitated for a beat. "I don't understand how you feel it's okay for you to be with other women and it's not supposed to upset me. Why can't I have the husband I loved and fell in love with? He would never disrespect me the way you have been treating me lately."

"Tell me how do I disrespect you, Kelly? Wasn't I going to make love to you earlier, but you wanted to act all brand new with my dick?"

"Sean, your sons were going to be home any minute. They came in ten minutes after you left. I don't feel comfortable being with you in front of them."

"I don't know why you insist on going down this road again. Kelly, they have seen every inch of your body already. What's the big deal if they would have walked in? Would you prefer my sons watching me fuck another woman? You tell me, 'cause one way or another, my sons are going to learn just like my moms taught me. Trust me, there's always a bitch lined up trying to take your place as my wife, and they don't have all those silly hang-ups like you do. I'm trying to be with you and only you, but you don't make it easy. I bet your sister wouldn't have all those hang-ups. She would fuck me anytime, anywhere and not give a damn who was around. Maybe she should have been my wife."

"My sister?" Kelly asked boldly. "You're fucking my sister?"

"Did I say all that? I said she wouldn't have your silly hang-ups. Now if you want me to give you another chance, you can come suck my dick properly. I'll take care of you after. If not, then shut the fuck up with that noise."

"That's okay. I can do without tonight." She went to walk away.

I snatched her by her hair, turning her back to me. She squealed out, but certain not to be loud and draw anyone's attention.

"Why, you had some nigga up in here fucking you? You had some other nigga up in MY pussy?" I said, raising my voice as I put my hand on my piece.

I will kill this bitch up in here tonight!

I saw my sons peeping out from their room. They looked scared, but they needed to learn how to treat a bitch when she starts acting stupid.

Her eyes filled with terror as she watched my hand wrap around my gun. "No, I wasn't with anyone. I swear. I-I just didn't want any more problems tonight."

"Well then I suggest you get to sucking—and you better suck it right this time, Kelly. And take all that shit off." I motioned with my gun to her clothes.

"Y'all can come and watch if you want," I called out to my boys. I had them take a seat right there in the living room with us so they could get a close up of all the details.

Kelly did as she was instructed and was rewarded for doing a good job. I fucked her good. Hopefully we'll get that baby soon.

12

Eric

It's been over a month since Shawnee has given me any ass. Sometimes I feel like killing her. Last night was definitely one of those times. I kept Shayla while her mother was out on her date. It was like three in the morning when Shayla woke me up. After I got her back to sleep, I noticed a dim light coming from Shawnee's bedroom window. It was enough light to cast a shadow of two people together. I came and stood outside, not sure why. I heard the screams of my woman being fucked by some other man.

I didn't know what to do. I paced back and forth. I wanted to do a Rambo on that bitch. If I confronted her, then there would've been problems. If I said nothing, then I'm like her little bitch.

I was trying to stay focused for my little girl. I had to think of some way to escape Shawnee's hold on me. I didn't think I could love her after this shit. I have always held onto hope for us to one day be married and be a happy family. Maybe have more children—a son. Now, I just wanted my daughter, my restaurant, and my freedom. Shawnee could be with whoever the fuck she wanted to be with. She was acting like a stank ho like her sister Charise.

My loins were hungry. It'd been so long since I'd had relief. I was half tempted to try and get some from Sandy for old time's sake, but I didn't want to mess up the friendship she and I built over the past several months. I don't know why I didn't stick with Sandy in the first place. Oh yeah. I didn't want to raise her kids and she didn't want to deal with my stripping. Hell, if Elaine wasn't married, I could have hit her up again.

Damn! I'm getting desperate.

But none of that was necessary, because Michelle was standing in front of me begging to make it all right. Michelle had been trying to be with me since she first came to work for me.

Michelle was my Pastry Chef and fine as hell, but I had been blowing her off because I felt I had to be faithful to Shawnee. I was also always paranoid that Shawnee had the restaurant bugged with wires and videos I didn't know about. There were many women trying to get at me, but I'd think that Shawnee was setting me up with her secret spies. I refused to take the bait.

Now that Shawnee cut off my sex supply and brought some man into her home to fuck her, everything was fair game. At least she wasn't doing me like Charise was doing Arnold. Shawnee straight up told me her intentions and suggested I do the same, but I didn't think she would bring 'em to the crib, though.

"Eric, why are you playing so hard to get? I know you find me attractive. You know I'm not trying to make any waves or any bullshit, and I wouldn't try to interfere with your home life. Would you at least touch them?" Michelle said, standing in my office with her shirt unbuttoned and two lovely grapefruits staring me in the face. "Please, Eric. If you can touch them and not feel anything, then I'll back off. I'll know that you are not into me like I think you are. Since your eyes haven't moved from them, I know you want to touch them."

She just didn't know how right she was. I was so paranoid. I was trying to push away my fears of Shawnee and just go for the gusto.

Michelle pushed the fear for me. She stepped close enough to where her breasts were touching my face. She cradled my head in her bosom. I gave up my fight and opened my mouth to receive her hardened nipple. I savagely sucked both breasts. She moaned lightly. I groped her ass, which was barely covered by her short-shorts. It wasn't exactly short-shorts weather outside. It's November for crying out loud, but I was appreciative of them.

My hands made their way into her shorts and found a wet pussy. I dug in for gold as I slid the shorts off to the floor. The deeper I dug, the more her legs buckled from beneath her.

She managed to get her hands in my pants and freed Big Willie. Willie is 14 inches long, and many women can't handle him. I sat Michelle on my lap facing me. I didn't put my dick in her. I just let her hot pussy glide up and down the trunk. She grinded her clit and was having an orgasm. My dick wanted to get up inside of her. I tried to maneuver to search for a condom, while keeping her in position. I checked my desk drawers, my pockets, and my wallet.

NONE! Oh hell! I'm not putting my dick in no one unwrapped.

"Michelle . . . Michelle, we're going to have to stop. I don't have a condom."

"Don't need one," she answered.

Michelle positioned her pussy against the base of my dick and testicles. She pressed her body closer to mine to enclose Willie in between our bodies. She moved her body so perfectly until my volcano was ready to erupt.

"You like that?" she sensually asked. It was obvious that she was feeling good.

"Uhm-hmm." She was working magic on Big Willie. I felt really good.

She kept working her clit up against my shaft until my eruption was emptied. That was almost as good as the real thing. *Not!* But she helped me get my nut out. I still wanted to get inside that pussy. I couldn't stop kissing her. I was so happy.

That moment made me decide I wasn't going to be Shawnee's bitch any longer. Suddenly I wasn't afraid. I found my balls, and Michelle would be the first of many to come. I was on a mission. I had to conquer all pussy. I was the man. Thanksgiving was getting near and I was going to give myself something to be thankful for.

The next morning, I went out to find my own place away from Shawnee. I found this efficiency not too far from the restaurant. It was certainly overpriced for the size, but for the sake of Big Willie's happiness, no price would be too high. After all, I am a man.

By that following night, my Willie was in search of his Cinderella (not everyone can fit this dick in them). Michelle would be my first tryout. Michelle was not a fit, but that's okay because my hostess, Karen, was willing to give it a shot. Karen was a better fit.

Me and Willie had a lot of time to make up for, so I found the numbers to thirty different women who passed me their numbers at some time or another. If I kept the number, that's because I held on to them as a possibility just in case Shawnee and I didn't work out.

Thankfully, some women are dumb like that, where you can just call them months later, out of the blue. So in week one alone, I got to try my "shoe" on in thirty-three women. Oh, I forgot to mention one of my waitresses, Ariana. Willie liked Ariana. She was only one of seven that'd get a call back for the next week.

Yep! I am the man, and there is no stopping me now.

This was how Shawnee wanted things. Well now she had it. Mandingo was back in action.

13

Arnold

It's been six weeks since I had the private investigator start following Charise. She only went to work, to get something to eat, and home. She had her one quarterly meeting with Kevin, but nothing else. I think Sandy was wrong about Charise cheating on me. If Charise was having sex, she wouldn't have been able to make it six weeks without, and she obviously hadn't been anywhere to have sex. That or someone had to tip her off to my investigation. Nah! I knew Sandy wouldn't say shit, and I knew Eric was far from fond of her. Maybe my wife was on the up and up.

I was so thankful yesterday, when Charise let me touch her. Words can't express how good it felt. I still didn't get to penetrate because she was still a little afraid. Hopefully soon I could have my wife completely. I was more than thankful for the blow job she gave me, and for her letting me grind on that booty and suck those tits.

My moms was not happy about the report from the private investigator. She said I need to get my money back. She refuses to trust Charise. I let Eric know about the results and he seemed disappointed. I thought for sure he'd be happy for me.

Our guys' night out fell by the wayside. Everyone was always too busy. I was half tempted to call Sean to see what was up with him these days, but then I couldn't stand to listen to him talk about all the women he is fucking while he leaves his poor wife at home with his sons.

Kevin's involved with so many business ventures and projects; he barely has time to talk on the phone. When I talk to Todd, he doesn't mention his wife one time. He definitely sounds happier these days. Hopefully that's a good thing.

After last night, I've been beating myself up about cheating on Charise. I let Samantha know I couldn't see her again because I would be working on my marriage. Life had been a battleground at home. Both of us have been keeping heavy schedules. I think I've been burying myself in work because I didn't want to deal with the possibility of my wife cheating on me. Now that I know she's not and we're finally getting to a point of intimacy, I could cut my workload down. I could work on my marriage and loving my wife. Samantha can finally stay in the past where she belongs.

14

Kevin

I swore I'd be able to resist. I took all these precautions and at the last minute, shot that precaution to hell. I never thought the day would come: I cheated on my wife. I'm glad there are no plans for a Thanksgiving family dinner. That would have been a rough one.

Last month Charise had to come see me with her quarterly statements for the magazine. I set the meeting up for four other people to attend, who also had to present financials for companies I am vested in. Generally, I deal with them individually, but this was my way of safeguarding myself from Charise.

My contradictory thoughts that something would happen, had me foolishly schedule the meeting at my home office. The meeting was scheduled for 10:30 that morning. At 9:30, I called and rescheduled the other four. My nerves started getting the better of me, so I called Charise at 10:00 to cancel also. She didn't answer her phone. I repeatedly called, but she wouldn't answer the phone. I began praying and reading scriptures to keep me from doing any wrong, because I could have just left the house, but didn't.

She arrived at 10:23am.

"Where is everyone? I thought the other companies were supposed to be here?"

"Lauren? What are you doing here? I left a message to reschedule almost an hour ago. The meeting has been cancelled. Your secretary put you on the calendar for next Tuesday, and said she'd let you know the meeting was being rescheduled."

Lauren laughed. "Now Kevin, if you wanted to see me alone, you didn't have to try tricking me. You know I have always been attracted to you. I was disappointed when you went and married that shoe saleslady, but however you want to do this is fine with me."

I suddenly noticed the sexy red wrap dress Lauren was wearing. She looked professional, but her exposed cleavage was anything but professional. My eyes locked onto her cleavage and wouldn't budge.

I met Lauren about four years ago through a mutual friend who wanted me to see if I could help take Lauren's catering company to the next level. Lauren is a very attractive woman, with piercing hazel eyes. Typically when we'd meet, she'd wear business suits that didn't do her half the justice that the red dress she was wearing for the meeting was doing her. She just never had any sex appeal. But this day, she looked like she'd been on someone's makeover television show. Her make-up was beautiful. Her dress accentuated her hourglass figure. Her bangs were cut perfectly right above her eyebrows, while the rest of her hair rested just on her shoulders. I even noticed the red nail polish on her pedicured toes. She was beautiful.

Damn! She'd give Elaine a run for her money with this look.

"Kevin, I understand that you didn't want anyone else here with us." She laughed.

"No, really, call your secretary. She'll tell you. I called an hour ago. I tried to cancel," I said with a choked whisper as I watched that wrap dress come unwrapped, exposing her beautiful breasts in a half cupped lace bra, and a matching laced thong.

The dress dropped to the floor. She stepped directly in front of me, where I was sitting on the corner of my desk. She took my arms and wrapped them around her waist and pressed her body against my erection. She wrapped her arms around my neck and reached up to take my hungry mouth into hers. My hands caressed her body.

I knew I was in trouble when I unsnapped her bra from the back. She let the bra straps fall from her shoulders, and I helped it to fall from her breasts. I bent down to remove her thong. I kissed her thighs and ass as I made my way back up. I stepped away from her so my eyes could fully absorb Lauren's beauty. And to think, I was worried about sleeping with Charise.

I picked her up and carried her to my office sofa. I laid her back and let my mouth explore her body. My tongue left her mouth to tease each nipple and her navel before it went in search of her cave. I inhaled its scent before I allowed my tongue to search for treasures. I had her legs up in the air as I took her to a seventh heaven.

Her loud screams made me a bit nervous that someone might call the police or come knock on my door to see what was happening, not that my neighbors are close enough to hear. What was weird is I somehow had Charise on the brain as my tongue was so deep inside Lauren.

"You do know this bitch has to go?!"

I jumped up with Lauren's juices still on my mouth. Lauren tried to find cover.

"Charise? How did you get in? The meeting was cancelled."

"Oh? Is this why you wanted to cancel the meeting? Lauren, correct?" she asked, redirecting her attention to Lauren.

"How long have you been trying to fuck my sister's husband?" Charise stepped up on Lauren as if she was going to jump on her. Lauren was trying to quickly gather her things and ran out of my office with just her dress wrapped around her, but not on her. One of my office doors opens to the foyer within my house, while the other leads directly outside. Lauren was lucky to make it through the door leading to my foyer. I held Charise from going after her so she could get the chance to at least put her dress back on before going out of my house.

"Stop this!" I demanded. "What are you doing here? How did you get in my house, Charise?"

"How about your dumb ass didn't lock the door? I thought we had a meeting scheduled at 10:30. I didn't think I had to ring any bells. Is this bitch the reason you won't fuck me, Kevin? Oh, you know what time it is now. You know I will not only let Elaine know, but Lauren's husband as well. I think you better go wash that bitch's pussy from your face and get to fucking, motherfucker. You're going to fuck *this* pussy, not that pussy. How dare you fuck that bitch, Kevin? How long has that shit been happening? That's what I want to know."

Damn, Charise sounded worse than what I think it would have been like getting caught by my own wife.

"Go wash that bitch's pussy off your fucking mouth! I can't believe you," she demanded, and I did as I was told.

I didn't know what to say or think. I wanted to go see about Lauren, but I knew Charise wasn't going to let that happen. I didn't want to go too far away from Charise, because I didn't want her to try going after Lauren. I know Charise wasn't going to let me off from fucking her now. There was no way to get out of it. She had me good. There was no way I'd be able to explain my way out of this to Elaine. Elaine would be especially pissed because she likes Lauren. She gives Lauren discounts on her shoes all the time, and she doesn't do that for almost anyone. Damn, I wonder if Elaine was the one who got the makeover for Lauren. That's the type of thing Elaine would do when she saw people looking tacky (in her opinion).

What am I going to do about Charise? If I fuck her this once, she'll never back off.

As I was washing my face in the bathroom, I heard Charise going into the main house from my office door. I didn't know what she was up to, but I had to find out quickly. I was hoping Lauren was good and gone, otherwise there would be real hell to pay.

I came out the bathroom to search for Charise. I saw her heading up the steps. I went up after her. Upstairs is certainly off limits in my house. Charise went into what was obviously my master bedroom. She climbed onto mine and Elaine's bed.

"This is where you are going to fuck me—right here and right now."

"Charise, would you please come out of here? Elaine certainly wouldn't appreciate you in our bed. Please go back downstairs. This can't happen. You need to leave," I tried to reason.

Charise just ignored me as she stripped off her jean suit that looked painted on her ass. She kicked her shoes in two different directions.

I didn't know what to do. I didn't know how to get this girl out of my bed. However, when Charise was laying in the middle of my extra large king size bed butt naked, my fight started bailing on me. I tried to look away, but when she laid back and started fingering her own pussy, I couldn't stop looking. Her mouth reached her own breast to suck. She "oohed and ahhed" as if she were having an orgasm. I was hypnotized. She had me in a trance.

I peeled my own clothes off and climbed in between Charise's legs and put my train up in her tunnel. No foreplay or anything. Just straight up in the pussy. I let my dick go in and out and watched her cum increase on my dick with each stroke.

"Ooh baby! I knew that big dick was going to fit perfectly in this pussy. Sssss… Fuck this pussy good! Sssss… Ooh damn baby! Fuck me!" She moved her body with each of my strokes that began slowly and gradually increased.

"Stir it up!"

I was stroking her as if I had all the time in the world. Then she turned her big ass around to me in a doggy-style position.

I had to just look at her ass and palm those big cheeks before I went back up in that pussy. After my dick was repositioned, I reached around and grabbed her healthy breasts. I slapped that ass a few times. I had to palm her ass some more just to compare her ass size to my hand size. I loved it. I brought her to the edge of the bed and held her in a wheelbarrow position. The pussy was to die for. I heard about all the freaky things Charise did, but I didn't want any of that. I just wanted to fuck her pussy. I had imagined fucking this sensational pussy a million times.

For the next 45 minutes or so, I enjoyed my sister-in-law in my wife's bed. I kept trying to stop, but then couldn't get enough of feeling her pussy on my dick. Every time she'd try to step away from me, I just had to kiss those breasts one more time. I didn't want her to go. Ever.

"Don't worry, Kevin, we'll have time together again. This doesn't have to be the end if you don't want it to be," she said, as if reading my thoughts.

"This has to be the last time. We can't chance being found out," I reasoned. "You are absolutely wonderful. You're sexy and gorgeous. I can't get enough of you," I said, taking her nipple back in my mouth.

Charise pulled away. "Well I guess you better plan on seeing me again. I want you to have this as often as you'd like. I like how good you make my body feel, Kevin. I want to feel it again and again just the same. And I want you to think of me every time you lay in this bed, while you are fucking my sister. I want you to be thinking of all the things you and I have yet to do."

My dick was hard. I picked her up, carrying her back to my bed and entered her once again. I was hooked on her loving. I wanted it all the time. Every day.

I knew then I'd be Charise's love slave—waiting to steal a moment together. I also knew then, that I was in love with Charise, and Lauren would be a distant memory. Before making love to Charise, I had every intention to finish with Lauren, but I no longer had any desire to finish what I started with her.

After I was able to finally let her go that day, I beat myself up big time. I don't think my marriage has been the same since then. I want so desperately to have sex with Elaine as often as we were just the month before, but now it's hard without always seeing Charise. In our bed, no less.

To make myself feel better about the betrayal, I went out and bought a collection of diamonds for my wife. She seemed a bit suspicious, but I assured her it was just a token of my love for her. The first time I betrayed Elaine, I gifted her with an income property I owned in Arizona. Since the betrayal was greater this time, my gift had to be greater to help alleviate my guilt.

The guilt has been overwhelming, but not so overwhelming that I didn't indulge with Charise once more yesterday. It was only the second time I had been with her. I did let her know to be careful because Arnold was having her followed. I had her meet me at a back service entrance of the building where she works. I took her to a nearby hotel and returned her to her office two hours later.

I promised myself that would be the very last time. I love my wife and I don't want to lose Elaine. I have to find a way to fix things at home and I have to shed my guilt so I could face my wife like I'm supposed to.

Since she likes investments, I think I'll buy her another property or something that will provide her with long term income. That should level the field back out. It's Thanksgiving, and I'm thankful for my wife. I have to fight for this marriage, even though she has no idea our marriage is under serious attack—by my actions.

Elaine has been whipping out all kinds of sexy lingerie. I know she's trying to keep my attention, but lately, I have been spending most of my time downstairs in my home office while she's in the house doing whatever.

I only recently became obsessed with being in my office when Charise began emailing me photos of her, either wearing some sexy lingerie or nothing at all. She sent me pics of her legs wide open showing me the pink inside of her brown pussy. She also sent a photo of a dildo inside of her. She'd send me various images of her playing with herself, using different sex toys or just her fingers.

Mine and Elaine's sex sessions would last hours in the past. Now when I looked at the emails from Charise and tried to make love to my wife, I exploded pretty much as quickly as I entered her. I sometimes wonder if Elaine suspects my infidelity, but then I doubt it because I know she would never understand or forgive me if she knew.

During the days while Elaine was gone, I'd pull those photos up and jerk off. Each time Charise sent me a new photo, she'd write the words, "Think about 'this' while you are fucking her tonight," and I'd do just that. I'd try to play it off as though Elaine's new lingerie had me so excited, I could barely contain myself.

When I couldn't take the torture anymore, I just decided to throw all caution to the wind and go meet up with Charise. That time I took some of my own photos. I took photos with my dick in her mouth, my dick in her pussy, and my dick in her asshole. She took photos of me sucking her tits and pussy. I loaded the photos on my password protected computers in both of my offices and they were available for my viewing any time of any day.

My guilt has been fading away each day. If anything, I started feeling if Elaine wasn't so busy with everything she has going on, I wouldn't have fallen into this trap. In essence, this is her fault.

15

Todd

This girl has to know she's making me crazy. I've been trying to figure out what she's up to. Since that one visit to my office to find out if I was cheating on my wife, Elaine and I have been out to lunch four times and to dinner three times. She really fucked me up when she had me going bathing suit and Victoria Secret shopping with her. She tried on some skimpy shit and wanted to model it for me, and then asked if I thought Kevin would like them. I also noticed her hugs seemed to be a little longer each time we'd meet. A lot more intimate. It's clear she wants me as bad as I want to fuck the shit out of her. Either that or she's laying a trap for me so she could tell my wife, which is why I just follow her lead.

"I think Kevin and I are drifting apart from each other," she casually said while we were having lunch in the food court of the mall where she modeled for me.

"Huh? Really?" I asked, trying not to sound too excited. I'm not sure what good I thought would come of it, but somehow it made me feel better to think Kevin wasn't touching her body.

"Yeah. Things seem so different with him and he's always preoccupied with his work even when he's at home. I mean, we still get along well, but just a lot more distant. I'm not really sure if I should read much into it. Every time I turn around he's buying me gifts. Expensive things. I don't know if that's just how he is or if he's trying to compensate for some wrong."

"Elaine, you are his wife, he has great wealth and an empire to run. He should be buying you gifts. You deserve them."

"Do you buy your wife gifts?" she asked, ruining my appetite for both my food and the conversation with her.

"I try to when I can. I can't afford all the things that Kevin can afford since I am running a medical practice and have three babies, but I do what I can to provide well."

"You should buy her something now, while we're here at the mall," she suggested with a smile.

I looked at my watch, tapped it, and said, "Oh, would you look at the time? I have to get back to the office. Maybe next time. I guess you better get back to your boutique before your brother chews you out again."

She laughed and put her hand over mine. "You're right. You would think he's my boss the way he acts. However, next time, I'm going to help you pick out something nice for my sister. I know you're just trying to get away from the conversation right now."

"No, really, I have to get back. You know I always enjoy hanging out with my dearest sister-in-law."

"Aww, how sweet. Okay, I'll let you off this time. I'm going to call you in a couple of weeks so we can go shopping—"

"Oh, I don't know. This is a really busy time of the year for me. Most of my patients are getting set to travel for the holidays and like to get checked out or their flu shots and stuff," I half lied. Actually, that was true, but I wasn't trying to go shopping for my wife with the sister-in-law that I wanted to fuck.

Elaine made a sad, pouty face. "Ohhh, I was hoping you could help me find a nice gown for the holiday parties I need to attend next month."

Well since she put it like that. "Just call me and I'll see what my schedule is like then. I can't make any promises, though."

"I understand, Doctor." She seductively smiled.

She stood and I followed her lead as we left back to our own lives.

She had me sneaking out on that shopping adventure to search for some gowns. Since she didn't mention anything about shopping for Harmony, I went on and cleared my schedule for a few hours. Honestly, I thought this shopping trip was a ploy, because Elaine had access to the most famous international designers, and she had no need to shop in any boutique or mall for any dress. She dragged me to some swanky, overpriced store that specialized in formal wear. Thankfully there was no more mention of what to buy for my wife. Thankfully there was nothing in the store that would have fit my wife even if she was mentioned.

She collected a few gowns and had me sitting in the back so she could model each one for me. I was already having a hard time, but when she left the door partially open, and I could see her nude body, I thought I would burst out of my damn pants.

There was something more intriguing about the idea of her totally nude. The lingerie and swimsuits I saw her model were quite revealing, but now she's totally naked. I couldn't stop staring at her body. I didn't pay any attention to her watching me stare at her. Hell, at that point, I didn't give a damn if she knew I was staring.

My dick first became hard when she modeled the previous neutral-colored dress that fit her body like a pair of opaque pantyhose. I could see every blood vessel in her elliptical areolae. Her nipples sat up in the dress, begging to be sucked. She's not my wife, but I would be mad at her for wearing the dress beyond the bedroom. But then she removes that dress and leaves the door open?

She covered her nakedness with one of the gowns. "Todd, could you come and help me with this fastener?"

I didn't want to have to get up. I had an erection to hide.

"Sure," I answered, but I felt like I was headed to my hanging.

The dress had a back out that dipped to her ass. The clasps were around the neck. Those were the hardest clasps I had ever fastened in my life. The beaded dress was stunning on Elaine. We stepped out of the dressing room so she could model it for me. I liked the dress, but it still didn't seem like Elaine. Somehow a rack dress didn't seem to be her style.

When she was done modeling that one, she had me follow her back to her dressing room to help her unfasten the clasps. When she had me fasten the clasps, she held the front of the dress securely to her chest. However, when she had me unfasten them, she "forgot" to hold the front of the dress. The dress fell, exposing her breasts and then her entire body. She was literally inches away from me. Naked!

She decided to hold a superficial conversation as though she didn't know how she was affecting me. I was mesmerized. I can't tell you what she was talking about at that point. She no longer made me wait on the other side of the door as she changed into another gown that was held up on her body by her own curves. She remained inside of the dressing quarters to model that one in front of the multiple mirrors. She didn't bother asking my opinion of it. She just removed it.

The coup de grâce was after she removed the dress, she stood in front of me naked once again and asked, "Todd, you're a doctor, and you do breast exams right?"

I snapped back to reality from my fantasy place within my mind and hesitantly said, "Yeah." I was waiting to find out where her question was going to take me. She knew damn well I was a doctor and performed breast exams.

"What is the proper technique for a breast exam? My gynecologist says one thing, but then my primary says another."

I held up my arm and tried to demonstrate on myself in the large dressing room.

"Well, you're a doctor. I think I could trust you to demonstrate on me. It's not like you really have any boobs to demonstrate the proper techniques." She laughed. She was sounding like one of my patients finding a bogus reason for me to touch them.

My dick was so hard. I didn't want to have to touch Elaine's breast. My dick was already pressing on my zipper screaming to get out. I tried to find a good position to stand to give this demonstration.

"You could stand behind me if that would make it less awkward. That way we could see the full mirror as you demonstrate. I'm not making you uncomfortable, am I?"

"Uh… No-No. I'm okay," I said probably an octave too high.

I was afraid to stand behind her because she might feel my erection up against her bare ass. It was killing me to view her beautiful waxed pubic area through the mirror. I wanted to grope it. She held both of her arms up behind her head, although I would generally only suggest one arm up at a time. I stood behind her. I hesitantly put my hand on one of her breast for the demonstration. I barely got to touch it. She jumped as her nipple immediately hardened more than it was already. Her jumping pressed her ass against my erection.

She laughed. "Oh my! I wasn't expecting cold hands. I'm sorry. You could try it again."

I attempted the demonstration once again. *Oh My Lord! Beautiful! They're so soft and full. Oh Elaine!* As I continued with the demonstration she subtly continued to rub her ass against my hard dick. Eventually she stopped being subtle and just let her body rest up against mine as she rubbed. I stopped the bullshit breast exam and just cupped both of her breasts, and squeezed. I closed my eyes and got lost in the moment. I couldn't believe this was real. I didn't want to open my eyes and find out it wasn't real. Worse, I didn't want to open my eyes and find Harmony's breasts in my hands.

One hand held her breast for dear life while the other hand inched its way down to her trembling clit. I pressed myself harder against her ass as I panted. Her legs slightly parted, allowing one finger access to her pussy. As the one finger inched in, her legs allowed another finger to pass into her pussy. She turned her head so I was able to get my lips onto her lips, and she gave me her tongue.

I opened my pants and pulled my dick out to fuck her in that dressing room on that eighth day of December. My hard dick rubbed her bare ass while my fingers were in her pussy. She was totally into it. Her thighs were apart enough for me to get three fingers inside of her. I reached again for those titties. As she bent over, the head of my dick found the wetness from between her legs that was now pouring out.

I pulled my fingers out to help guide my dick into her opening. Her pussy juices were all on my dick. I was trying to line my dick's head to push it in her pussy opening. Her moans were getting louder as I tried to muffle it with my mouth. I hadn't got in it yet, and I was ready to blow.

Before I could get it in, some bitch disturbed us by opening the door. She quickly closed the door when she realized what was up. I was going to keep on, but that was enough to bring Elaine to her senses of what we were doing.

"Oh my God! What are we doing?"

I begged Elaine, "Just let me get my dick in there. I need to feel your vaginal walls contract on my dick. Please!"

She wasn't going for it.

"I'm so sorry. I'm sorry," she repeatedly apologized with tears in her eyes. "Please don't let this get back to my sister. I don't know what came over me. Please, Todd, forgive me," she said as she tried to quickly dress.

I don't know what part she was sorry about. She didn't have to worry about me saying a word. She didn't purchase anything and ended up skipping our lunch.

Damn! Damn! Damn!

Two weeks later, Elaine called.

"Todd, I need for you to meet me in Long Beach. I just want to talk."

Talking isn't exactly what I wanted to hear from Elaine. A few days after our last meeting, I went back to the store and purchased the glove-like, opaque dress for her, for *only* $1,259. I didn't know when the opportunity would present itself for her to wear it just for me, but I definitely wanted her to have it, with the hopes that the day would come.

However, her voice sounded flat and I could tell she was troubled. I wasn't sure if that would be the best time to give her the gift, with the demand that she never wears it for Kevin, but continuing to hide the dress in my office was making me very nervous.

"Sure. Where and what time?" I agreed.

"You can meet me at the Maya, and I promise I will not take advantage of you as I did in the dressing room."

"The hotel, Maya, near the Queen Mary?"

"Yes, Todd. The Maya-Double Tree."

Well damn! I might not be the brightest star in the sky, but a hotel room doesn't seem like a good place to "just talk." No restaurant, no mall, just the hotel room.

I bet she hasn't stopped thinking about how this dick would have felt inside of her since we parted ways.

I hesitantly answered, "Okay, I can be there after my last patient. Say maybe around four-thirty?"

"That'll be fine. I'll text you the room number and will see you then." She quickly hung up.

I actually had more patients that would have had me working until after six, but I'll be damned if I was going to pass up this opportunity.

Talk, my ass. She can talk right into this microphone I got down here for her. Not after what she started, and she can start by modeling the dress I bought for her.

As soon as she opened the room door, I took her. She actually tried to put up some resistance with that exaggerated, "Stop, Todd! We can't do this," shit. I ignored her and kept kissing her neck while unbuttoning her blouse.

"We can't cross the line. The dressing room was a big mistake," she said, acting like she was trying to pull away. "We really need to talk."

Yeah right. A mistake my ass. *That's why you wanted to meet in a fucking hotel. And speaking of fucking, that's just what I came to do: fuck!*

Hell, the head of my dick was already less than an inch away from her pussy in that dressing room. It was so close, I felt the heat. My dick felt that wetness. It was going all the way in on this day. *Talk, my ass. I came to suck up those titties she made me feel on for some bogus breast exam.*

Elaine was delicious. I could eat her pussy for breakfast, lunch, and dinner. I was even happier she didn't make me wear a condom. I would have hated to been so close in her pussy the other week, and not be able to feel her completely now. I most enjoyed her straddled facing away from me, riding my dick while I looked up in her pussy. She definitely had skills in those hips. I enjoyed watching my dick go in and out of it and seeing her cum covering my dick.

I enjoyed Elaine from head to toe, literally, 'cause I sucked her pretty-ass toes as well. I had her from the front, from the back, lying down, standing up, sitting down, and upside down. My mouth examined her breasts to make sure they were as perfect as they looked. I licked her pussy from the clit to her asshole. I refused to leave anything undone that I would regret not having done at a later time. I even loved burying my face in her sweet smelling ass, while letting my nose tickle her erogenous zones. Even better, she didn't make me pull out of that good pussy each time I was ready to cum. My shit was strong enough to blow the cervix off of her uterus. Now if she were to come up pregnant, I don't know what I'd do, but for the moment, I didn't care. She was so perfect for me. It was the best Christmas present ever. I couldn't ask for better.

When we parted ways, we did so in silence. I wasn't sure if I'd ever hear from her again. She didn't get to model my dress, because I hadn't gotten around to giving it to her until we were departing. She just kissed me without opening the box.

I hoped the dress would open the door to another occasion, or at the very least, make her reflect on our great time together in the dressing room.

I was curious how awkward the family holiday gathering would be for us, but it turned out none of the family wanted to get together this year. The year ended with no further communication from Elaine. I wondered had I not done something right to make her never call again. I replayed that day over and over in my mind. Maybe the dress upset her. I even backed away from just about all the other women.

Hopefully the New Year will bring good things.

PART TWO

Happy New Year?

16

Arnold

Sandy and I were having lunch at the little bistro we always meet at when she asked me, "Why did you call off the investigation so soon?"

"I don't have any more concerns with my wife. I let it go on for almost two months, and all she was doing was going to work, some lunch or business meetings, and home. Not only that, my wife gave me some loving for Christmas. Not just a little bit, but all of it. We've been doing great ever since then."

"I don't trust the bitch. I think you need to keep checking."

"Sandy, it's time to let it go. I'm happy. We're happy. I just need for you to be happy for us. Hell, maybe now's a good time for you to think about dating again. You've been divorced a year now. Let me hook you up with someone."

Sandy laughed. "I don't think so. I don't trust your judgment." She got serious and said, "I know you are happy now, but I just don't want to see you hurt."

"I'm not going to be hurt. We're talking about the A-Man. The A-Man can't be hurt."

Sandy laughed as she always does when I refer to myself as my superhero fantasy, The A-Man. "Okay, Mr. A-Man, but remember—you're not invincible."

"You always worry about me, but I'm more worried about you. I know you get lonely and long for a man's touch," I said, standing up and rubbing her shoulders. "Let me find someone for you, Sandy."

"Hell no! Like I said, you have piss-poor judgment when it comes to my sister, but I ain't gonna lie, that shoulder rub does feel good. Uhm!" she said, pretending to completely relax and soak up my shoulder rub. "Thanks, but no thanks. I'll stay on my own when it comes to finding my man."

I took my seat. "If you insist. I was just trying to hook a sister up."

She laughed and swatted me away. "Yeah, yeah, yeah. Now get away."

"So what's your New Year's resolution?"

Sandy pondered on the thought and gazed around the bistro.

Our nosey waiter was not servicing our table that day, but it didn't stop him from trying to get an earful. I'm sure he'd heard so much, he was probably going home and writing a book or a script about our lives.

"I am going to finish up with my degree. That's it. Oh, and I guess I can tell you first, I'm going to stop working for Charise," she said.

"Why? What happened? I thought you liked working on the magazine."

"I do, but I can't keep dealing with my little sister. She has some serious character flaws that I just can't seem to get past. I used to think that she changed—"

"Am I missing something? Is there something you're trying to tell me, Sandy?"

"No, Arnold. It's nothing I haven't said in the past. It's not that you're missing it. It's just that you refuse to see it."

"Sandy, I told you, me and my wife are doing well now. Yes, it's been rough before, but I'm getting some loving almost every day now."

"Do you know where she's at when she's not with you?"

"She's working. She runs a business. You know how demanding that is, right? And from what I understand, the magazine is doing very well. That's not an easy thing to pull off, and my baby is doing it."

"Yeah, she's working all right, but not on any business for that magazine. I run that damn magazine. I run that business because she's barely there. Every now and again, she'll show up in the office. I'm juggling my kids, my school work, and her business. I have been doing all that I can to keep the magazine from failing because it is a great concept with everyone's money in it except Charise's."

"So if she's not in the office, then she's more likely in business meetings. In order to run a successful magazine, she's going to have to spend a lot of time out of the office. If she knows you are there holding it down, then there's no need for her to be there all day," I said, defending my wife. "Besides, the investigator says she's at her office most of the time."

"I give up!" Sandy stood up from the table holding her hands up. "I give up, Arnold. You are impossible. I promised to be your friend, but I can't take any more of this. When you find that you need me, please call me. In the meantime, I can't just sit back and watch that girl destroy you. I have to go now, but call me when you open your eyes," she said with tears in her eyes before she dropped money on the table and left.

I sat there shocked by Sandy's behavior, as she walked away. *Where did all that come from? Maybe Sandy has grown romantic feelings for me and didn't want to hear about me and Charise being happy finally.*

The nosey waiter came by my table and said, "You better listen to her. That girl knows what she be talking about."

I was shocked by this no-boundary-having motherfucker. "You know what?" I said, standing up.

He took off out of my sight before I could get another word out. I added some money to Sandy's and left.

That night I arrived home to find Charise on a rampage. She had dumped all of my drawers out and pulled my clothes from the closet and thrown them all over the floor.

"What the hell is going on here, Charise?" I was already having a bad day, and I certainly didn't need to come home to this shit.

"So how long have you been fucking my sister, Arnold? What was this—her way of trying to get back at me for Lewis? Get your shit and get the fuck out!"

I was shocked for the second time in one day. Where was all of this coming from? Did Sandy lie and tell Charise we were having an affair to break us apart?

"Charise, what are you talking about? If you're talking about Sandy, I have never been with her romantically. Where would you get something like that from?"

"From my own fucking eyes, that's where. I saw you giving her a fucking massage at the bistro. I saw the two of you together, you bastard! Then I saw her get mad and take off crying."

I didn't know what to say. I laughed and Charise threw a book at my head.

"Oh, you think that shit is funny, motherfucker!" she yelled.

"Stop this now! It was not what you think. I had just asked her to let me set her up with a man because I figured she has to be lonely. Right at that moment you saw, I rubbed her shoulders and told her she could have her own man to rub her shoulders or whatever. I told her how happy you and I are, and I felt bad for her and just want her to be happy also."

"So why did she run off crying, and why have you been sneaking off to meet with my sister behind my back? How long have you been seeing the bitch?"

"Okay now with the unnecessary name calling. You make it sound so sinister, as though we've been having this crazy affair. If I run into her every now and again, I'll ask her if she wants to grab some coffee or something to eat and it has never gone beyond that," I lied. "She was upset about not being able to have what we have. That's all."

"Why wouldn't you tell me that you saw my sister someplace?" Charise asked, softening up just a bit.

"Because I wouldn't want there to be any trouble. I don't know what her work schedule is at your office, so I wouldn't want to cause any trouble if she wasn't in the office when she was supposed to be," I continued to lie.

"And you promise that's all there is to it, Arnold?" she asked, looking almost embarrassed. "'Cause I'll fire the bitch tomorrow, and she can go apply for welfare or something."

"Baby, that's not nice. You should know better than anyone that you are all that I want and need," I said, trying to reassure her as I took her into my arms.

"I know. It's just that I think Sandy still has it in for me sometimes. She says she's forgiven me, but then other times she acts as though she hates me. I see how she looks at me."

"There is nothing anyone could say or do to turn me away from my baby," I said, kissing her.

I wanted to make her pick up all of my stuff from the floor, but I wanted the cookie she was about to give me even more. She bent down and pulled my dick out and took it into her mouth. She wouldn't say, "I'm sorry," but I guessed a blow job would suffice.

I did want to go check on my son, but this was more pressing since I didn't hear him crying or anything.

17

Eric

I don't know, Sandy. I hate the idea of leaving the poor guy out there to suffer like that. Yes, we both know Arnold is living out there in La-La Land, believing Charise is faithful to him, but he needs us. He'll go insane when his world comes crashing in on him, and we know it will. It's just a matter of when," I said after swallowing a bite of my sandwich during our regularly scheduled lunch meetings.

She shook her head and dropped her fork onto her salad plate. "What I don't understand is, does he not pay attention to the details? I noticed many times Charise left the office with her hair one way and she'd return another way. I've noticed changes in her makeup, which would make me think she was somewhere sweating. At least four out of five days during the week, she comes in from somewhere smelling like she's been somewhere fucking. I just don't know how this bitch was able to give the private eye the slip. Arnold should have called Joey Greco from *Cheaters*. She wouldn't have given them the slip. They would be camped out at the front door, back door, the stairwells, and the elevators."

We laughed and then took a quick bite of our food.

"Well, if you said she'd leave with her hair one way and return with it another, shouldn't the P.I. have some pictures where Arnold should have noticed the changes?"

"Eric, I know he's our friend, but Arnold is a blind, foolish jackass. That's all there is to it. He doesn't want to see shit. We just have to sit back and wait for his world to crumble, and then we'll help him. We'll be there for him, but I can't be bothered with their shit anymore. Let Charise run her own damn company, and I'm going to focus on me, finishing school, and my children."

"I hear you. That's a solid plan. At least you got some experience running a company and working on a magazine. Perhaps when you're done with school, you can put together your own thing," I said. Then I laughed. "No, I'm still trippin' about Arnold trying to hook you up with somebody. That's funny."

Sandy gulped down the swig of water she just drank and laughed, looking as if she was trying not to choke. "Yeah, could you believe it? I thought so myself. But speaking of love lives, how is yours coming along? How is the Mandingo Jungle working out?" She laughed again. "How in the hell did you come up with that name for your little bachelor pad? That name automatically implies that there's some wild shit happening up in there."

"That would be putting it mildly. Everybody wants to check out the jungle. I hardly get enough rest anymore. When I want rest, I stay at Shawnee's guest house, since I know she ain't giving up any action."

"How is she dealing with that arrangement? I can't imagine my controlling sister being okay with your not being home every night."

"She won't say shit directly, but she'll say something like, 'your daughter sure missed her daddy last night.'"

Sandy and I both cracked up on that one.

"I can tell she wants me, but she won't just come out and say it. Your plan might actually work. You know, the one about not paying her any attention will make her want me?"

Sandy became semi-serious, but still had a forced smile. "I thought you might be enjoying your freedom and finally be ready to find someone that's going to treat you the way you deserve to be treated. Don't be like your nutty friend Arnold that doesn't know when it's a wrap and to just let go."

"Sandy, you just don't know how bad I want to settle down with one woman who is not just enamored by my physical. I want a woman I can have a friendship with, like you and I have now. I want a woman that's going to have my back through thick and thin. And more than anything, I want a woman who will respect me and love all of me, for me, unconditionally. The problem I have is, I wanted that woman to be my wife and mother of my children. Now Shawnee is the mother of my first child. I don't want my children living apart and not growing up to know one another as I did with my own siblings. Any new woman I marry and have children with will have to coexist with the likes of Shawnee, just so my kids can have a relationship with each other.

"You know Shawnee better than I do, but we both know Shawnee won't make our lives easy. I wanted her to be my wife, but I'll be damned if I'm going to be an Arnold. I'm not going to live like that in some fantasy world, married to some woman that don't love me, just for the sake of being a family," I explained. "Oh, I forgot, and she needs to be sexy as hell also. Whoever my wife may be, that is. Most importantly, she definitely has to be able to handle Big Willie." I laughed.

"Yeah, yeah, whatever!" Sandy laughed. "Damn, it suddenly got warm in here," she said, fanning herself. "Don't worry, Eric, your Cinderella is closer than you think. I know how you believe in all that fairy tale mess . . . Cinderella."

"Now you know damn well what I mean when I talk about Cinderella. We need to make sure it's a good fit. Big Willie doesn't like when he's left hanging because one of the stepsisters tried him on but couldn't fit him." I laughed again.

"All right now with the Big Willie talk. You got me sitting here sweating from flashbacks," she said before taking a long swallow of her water.

"Girl, you're just getting old. That's menopause."

Sometimes I try joking with Sandy because I can see this distant look in her eyes. It's almost as if her feelings might be hurt, but she acts like a trooper despite, which makes it difficult to get a good read on her true feelings.

"Fuck you, Eric!" She laughed. "I got your old. Menopause! Oh no you didn't go there. Your baby's momma is closer to menopause than I am. No, she's old!"

Sandy and I continued to crack on one another as we finished up our lunch. Afterward, I headed back over to my own restaurant to get some work done. Thankfully, I have a very competent staff that holds it down when I'm not there. My chefs are able to execute my dishes almost to perfection. Still, most of my patrons prefer when I prepare their meals. I did really good selecting each of my employees. I have yet to lose one. If for nothing more, I will always be eternally grateful to Shawnee for listening to my dreams and helping make them real. I guess that's another reason why I love her like I do.

Before I could step in the door my hostess Karen met me in the doorway to let me know I had a visitor. Karen's demeanor seemed a bit rattled, which let me know the visitor must have been attractive.

OH-NO! No, no, no, no! Why did this chick have to come to my restaurant of all places? Thank goodness Sandy didn't come here for lunch today instead of us meeting at the bistro.

If Shawnee found out, she'd have my balls for serving her a glass of water. But damn! That girl is fine as hell. I know she's being spiteful by coming here.

I walked to her table as if I was walking the plank to my death.

I flashed my professional smile. "My hostess told me you requested to see me. What can I do for you?" I said as though she was unfamiliar to me.

"I wanted to at least stop in to say hello since I was in town. It's not like we're total strangers."

I looked as if I was trying to place the face. "Yeah, you do look familiar. What was your name again? Forgive my memory. It's just that I meet so many people each day," I lied to throw her off.

Damn, she's fine! Down, Willie, down!

"Well, I guess a handsome man such as you would have plenty of women to take to lunch. You couldn't possibly remember us all."

She paused to take a sip of her water. "Tatiana. Tatiana Palmer," she answered with her sexy southern accent as she extended her hand for me to kiss.

It always amazed me how she had the accent, but her brother Todd didn't have it. Maybe she grew up watching and studying Scarlett O'Hara from *Gone with the Wind*, because that's exactly who she reminded me of—but super sexier.

"Oh my goodness! Tatiana, in the flesh! You're trouble," I half joked. "What brings trouble my way?"

"I don't have to be trouble. It's been a year since the man I loved passed away, and I think it's time for me to get out and live again. He'd want me to do what makes me happy. So are you doing what makes you happy, Eric?"

I had to take a seat at the table across from her. Somehow her statement made Willie want to show off. Perhaps it was the memories from the video tape of this woman in the raw.

"I'd like to think I'm happy, Miss Palmer. So, are you in town to visit your brother and mother?" I asked, captivated by her beauty. No wonder the old dude had a hard time choosing.

"No need for formalities; Tatiana will do. Actually, to answer your question, neither my brother nor mother are aware I'm in town. I came to see you."

"Me?" I asked, surprised by her answer. *Now I know this is trouble in the making.*

"Ever since that lunch we had a couple of years back, I have often wondered what you were all about. You were very charming, as well as handsome, and you don't seem like the kind of man who likes to play games or be played."

"But yet, you're here trying to incorporate me in some game of yours."

"Not at all. As far as I understand, you are no longer attached to the mother of your daughter, and I am done grieving over my loss. Yes, when I called you that first time, it was a game, but not anymore."

Damn Todd, with his big mouth!

Tatiana spoke so seductively. When she put her hand over mine, it shot sensations down to my groin. Even the way she sipped her water was turning me on.

Shawnee would die if she knew Tatiana, of all people, was back on the scene trying to claim me. I bet if I told Shawnee, she'd give me unlimited pussy as long as she thought Tatiana was sniffing around. She might even be willing to get married. But then again, Tatiana is hot as hell. I would love to make my own video with her like the one I watched of her and old dude.

"So you're not here trying to get back at Shawnee?" I asked suspiciously.

She laughed. "And how would I be getting back at Shawnee when she's basically discarded you like yesterday's news? I would have come sooner if that were the case. No, it's just that I saw something I liked, but the timing wasn't right. Now, I think the timing is right. Even my mother feels I should go after what I like. She's still a little pissy that I let Shawnee get Brad away from me. Well, Shawnee thinks she took him from me. What kind of marriage did she have while he was seeing me the entire time?" she asked, shrugging her shoulders.

"So you're not bitter that old dude left her all of his loot?" I asked out of curiosity.

"Not at all. Brad made sure I was well taken care of. He didn't want me to be burdened with having to run his entire company, so he left that to Shawnee. He specifically said he wanted me to be able to enjoy my life, while Shawnee was more fixated with climbing corporately. I don't detract anything from her. She's very good at what she does professionally, so I completely understood Brad's logic in leaving his company to her. Me personally, I would have sold it to the highest bidder and he knew that. I was satisfied with the funds he left me, along with the purchase of not one, but four Caribbean homes. Also, Brad told me of his illness before he shared it with Shawnee. He transferred a lot of things into my name prior to their marriage, including our home in Houston.

"I knew his marriage was more business than anything, but those looking from the outside would never understand that. I also know he left an inheritance for your daughter. At first I was annoyed by him leaving an inheritance for

Shawnee's bastard child, but then once I learned the child was yours, I was okay with it. I thought for sure the child belonged to Brad's driver."

"Brad's driver? Where the hell did that come from?"

Tatiana laughed. "Oh, I take it you didn't know about that little fling. Even Brad knew about that. His driver continually apologized about it to him, because he felt he betrayed Brad by sleeping with Shawnee on more than one occasion. He eventually apologized to me for putting me in a bad position with Shawnee, and had hoped I'd understand the pressures he was under. Yeah, your girl was out there. Probably still is."

I was fuming inside. *Ain't that about a bitch? Brad's driver?* She was certainly correct with the "she's still out there."

I couldn't think of anything else to say, but, "Wow!"

"So, to answer your original question, no, I am not bitter about Shawnee taking 'Brad's loot' from me. I would have preferred she got nothing, but I respected Brad's decisions. And I have no other agenda for being here today, other than trying to get to know you better—hopefully *better* in every sense of the word," she said, looking at me like a piece of chocolate during a woman's menstrual cycle.

Although my dick got hard again, I was feeling violated the way she was looking. I didn't know how, when, or where, but I wanted this woman. *Hell, at least she believes in being dedicated to her man.*

"Well, I kind of know you better than you think. I saw your video," I confessed. "I must admit, it was interesting to say the least."

She flashed a beautiful smile. "I can't believe Shawnee held onto that video. What part did you find most interesting?"

"It was all good. I see you have some skills," I flirted back as if I had a death wish.

"I mean, did you enjoy looking at my pussy?" she boldly asked, looking directly into my eyes with her hand back on top of mine.

She was making me nervous. I slid my hand from underneath hers. "Tatiana, like I said, it was all good."

"Ah, so you did recognize me today."

She chuckled and picked my hand up from the table and put one of my fingers in her mouth. For a hot minute, I forgot where I was at. The background noise faded away. I looked away from Tatiana's lips around my fingers when I felt Karen's eyes burning a hole in me. Karen looked as if she would jump on Tatiana any moment. I pulled my hand from Tatiana and excused myself.

I summoned Karen to follow me to my office.

"I know you are mad at me for staring at you like that, Eric, but I couldn't help it when I saw her sucking on your fingers like that," Karen pleaded before I could say a word. She was practically in tears.

"I'm not mad at you, Karen. I need you to save me from her. My ass was getting weak," I told her.

"Huh?" she asked, surprised. "What do you need me to do? You know I'll do anything for you."

I took Karen in my arms and kissed her deeply. I reached in my desk drawer for a condom, pulled up Karen's hostess mini skirt, laid her on my desk, moved her thong to the side, put my dick in her pussy, and stroked her until I was relieved. It didn't take long at all, but she was happy.

I left my office feeling back in control of myself. I was glad to see Tatiana was gone when I came back out. I was feeling kind of proud of myself for resisting her advances despite wanting to fuck her mercilessly. I just couldn't see letting myself get caught up in some crazy feud between her and Shawnee. Nah, I'm too smart for that silly shit.

"Hey Eric, this is for you," my waiter, Dale, said. He handed me an envelope.

Before I could open the envelope, I could smell Tatiana's scent on it. I opened the sealed envelope when Dale walked away to find a nude snapshot of Tatiana. It was a photo as I remembered her on the video. There was a note card telling me to meet her at the Beverly Wilshire, room 1401, along with an elevator access code. That messed me up all over again.

In about thirty-six minutes, I was knocking on the penthouse suite at the Beverly-Wilshire.

Tatiana opened the door. "Wow, you actually came. I didn't know if you'd come," she said, smiling ear to ear. She stepped back to allow me into the posh penthouse suite. "I didn't know if the photo would get you to come. I brought it just in case you weren't there when I came by."

Shit! I wouldn't mind living in this place. The suite had to be at least 5,000 square feet. It had marble mosaic flooring, crystal chandeliers, a double oven, stainless-steel kitchen with an island, and marble countertops. I would love to cook in that kitchen. There was also a media room with a built-in, white-lacquer entertainment unit holding a 55-inch flat-screen television. It was a sight to behold. Oh, that, along with Tatiana.

I couldn't believe I came. A part of me was screaming "run," but Big Willie was running this show, and he said we weren't going any-damn-where.

I saw she was wearing the hotel robe, so I asked, "It looks as though you were expecting someone, no?"

"I was about to run a bath. I wanted to relax my nerves. It was kind of unnerving being publicly shot down, but I figured I had it coming since you can't really be too sure of my motives, and I respect that. I figured a nice bubble bath with some strawberries and champagne might make me feel a little better. But now that you're here, well maybe . . . I don't know. Perhaps you'd join me," she stated, suddenly shy.

I walked over to the six-foot tall beauty, with natural hair flowing down her back, about two inches above her ass. She was more beautiful than I remembered from our lunch in New York. I pulled the tie that held her robe closed, hoping to see the lovely body I saw in the video, live.

The robe opened showing her body in the raw. I held the robe open as I just looked at her beautiful body. *Fuck Shawnee! Shawnee can't touch this.*

This girl didn't have a flab, stretch mark, fat, or any blemish that doesn't belong. Shawnee has a great body, but Tatiana's fit in a class all by itself.

Tatiana let the robe fall to the floor. My hands gently caressed her body, starting with her arms and shoulders and working down the front of her chest. Her nipples hardened from the anticipation of my touch. My fingers teased her nipples before they crept down her abdominal area.

She let out a moan. My hand hadn't made it to her pubic area. Instead, I walked behind her and admired her ass. I rubbed her back, getting close but not touching her ass. I stood close behind her, pulled her hair up, and let my breath hit the nape of her neck before my mouth covered her ear. My hands continued to tease her body, touching around her breasts and pubic area.

Tatiana pressed her backside up against my body when she couldn't stand the teasing any further. She took my hands and ran them over the front of her body. She worked to peel my clothes from my body. She gasped when she got her hand on Big Willie.

My hands continued to explore her body until I found her wetness. I bent down to get a sample taste of the wetness. I put one of her legs up over my shoulder to gain better access. She tried hard to maintain her balance as my tongue tickled her clit. She held onto my head for dear life, as my tongue went deeper within her.

Eventually I carried her to a king size bed in one of the large bedrooms, where she laid me on my back to give me a 69. While I was sucking that pussy, my fingers played with her clit. She was sucking my dick like it was hers, or wanted it to be hers for good. She stopped and turned her body around, bringing those beautiful breasts to my mouth. I sucked them as I had two fingers in her pussy and a finger from my other hand in her ass. She was going wild.

Then, without warning, she backed that pussy up onto my dick. When that hot, wet, tight pussy made contact with the head of my dick, I thought about my condoms in my pants pocket in the living room, but while I thought about it, my dick was being slowly immersed in that damn good quicksand. Her tongue was in my mouth, and she was in total control of every stroke. I was in love with this chick. She took my 14 inches in like a champ and handled it with ease despite the tightness of her pussy.

I think this was the first raw pussy I'd had in ages, and it was fabulous and worth the risks. When Tatiana finished showing me what she could do, I spent the next hour or so showing her what Mandingo could do. I didn't think she'd be able to handle it, but I was able to get the head of Willie in her asshole. It was enough to feel good to me, and make me cum in that ass. Shawnee had some serious competition here.

We shared that champagne bubble bath in the deep soaking tub like I didn't have any other care in the world. We made love again all over that designer bathroom.

Later, she whipped me up a nice meal to show off her cooking skills. I was impressed. We enjoyed great conversation. I learned Tatiana has a great sense of humor, which one would not expect by looking at her. And on top of everything else, she's very intelligent. Listening to Shawnee, I thought she was an airhead. Even better, she seemed genuinely interested in my life. After dinner we made love one more time for the road.

We spent about five hours together before I got a conscience and thought about my restaurant, home, or daughter. I hated to leave, but I had to get back to reality.

I definitely wanted to see this woman again, but I knew it would ruffle a lot of feathers. Todd would be pissed if he knew I fucked his sister—even more so, if he knew that was probably the best fuck of my life. Then again, had he not been running his big mouth to his family about me and Shawnee, his sister wouldn't have known I was currently available.

I used to think that was Shawnee was the best fuck, but not anymore. Tatiana hadn't been with any man since that old guy. I keep wondering how that old guy chose Shawnee to marry over Tatiana. If it weren't for my daughter, I'd flaunt Tatiana everywhere. And she's finer than fine too? Tatiana is more than just a fuck. I could really get into her if the situation wouldn't be so complicated.

"I'd like to see you again if that's possible. How long do you plan on being in town?" I asked.

"For you, as long as you want me to," she said, smiling. "You were better than I could have ever imagined and I totally enjoyed your company. I hate that you have to leave, but I understand you have your daughter to be concerned with."

"Damn, why couldn't I have met you first? Now I'm mad you sent me off with Shawnee when I met you back in New York."

She blushed. "Everything is perfect timing. Well, with the exception of your being biologically attached to that bitch."

I didn't know how to respond. As I kissed her before leaving, I almost got swept back in. I didn't want to leave.

I didn't want to live in Shawnee's guest house anymore just to see my daughter. I wished I could just go live in my own little crib I rented for my sexcapades, but I had to be at Shawnee's for my Shayla. I wished I could keep my daughter when I want and not have to go on Shawnee's property ever again. Yeah, she is a bitch.

Ironically, when I got home, who wants to give me some pussy? Shawnee. I told her no. I almost fucked her when she put those big nipples I love so much in my mouth. I sucked those titties and sent her to her own damn room all hot and bothered with an attitude. I went to the guest house and watched the video with Tatiana and enjoyed that instead. I would have preferred the old dude not be in there, but as long as she was in it and I could visually replace him with my own image, I was good.

18

Todd

Harmony decided she wants to lose weight now as her New Year's resolution. She even claims she's going back to work in March or April. She noticed I've been moping around lately, so she decided she wants to give me back the wife I married. Little does she know, the only thing she can give me back is her sister.

It's been over a month since I've heard from Elaine. I don't know what to think, but I know I want to feel her again. Damn, why won't she at least talk to me?

I pretty much cut off all of my extracurricular activities. Well, almost all. After Elaine, I really had no desire to be with any other, but in a weak moment, I had to call on ole reliable Cynnyyah to handle business. Not even Harmony. I've been to Houston two times since, and I only saw Roxana on that second trip to try and make myself get over Elaine.

I hate the thought of Elaine with Kevin, especially now that he told me about his and Charise's affair. Not once, but four times. He claims he ended it for good the last time. I could tell he was lying.

I had wondered if Elaine knew about it before and if that's why she fucked me. She did say she felt as though they were becoming distant before we slept together. Maybe her knowing is what pushed her to take it all the way. But then why won't she come see me again? Maybe she feels guilt because of Harmony.

I want so desperately to go to her shoe boutique to see her, but her watchdog brother and all of his gay friends would be in our business. I'm hoping she's not back prostituting. I would be more devastated than Kevin.

I really thought Kevin had some nerve getting all pissed about Charise screwing Kelly's husband, when he's screwing her himself. Kevin swore me to secrecy, and I had to honor that since I fucked up by telling him about Valerie and Cynnyyah. I didn't mention all the others.

Meanwhile, poor Arnold thinks he has the wife of the year now that the whore is giving him some pussy. His dumb ass got word from the private investigator that Charise was at Kevin's house.

Arnold chalked it up to business meetings because he'd never suspect Kevin, of all people, to be boning his wife. I even suggested he go over his own wife's financials and business affairs instead of Kevin. After all, he is just as business savvy as Kevin.

Arnold defended her needing Kevin to go over everything since he's the principal financer of her magazine. That's probably the bullshit line Charise fed him.

Now, I have owned my own practice for years. I may not be as business savvy as Kevin and Arnold, but I do have enough sense to know that "your bank" doesn't stay involved in your day-to-day operations when they loan you money. Hell, Elaine put up her money as well. Why isn't she involved in the day-to-day operations just the same? Because that's a bunch of bullshit!

Kevin doesn't need to be involved. He just wants an opportunity to fuck her. Probably always has, just like I was zoned in on Elaine from day one, but he is one sick puppy if that's where his lust began, because he first met Charise while she was in the hospital in a coma.

At least I'll get to see Elaine in Cancun when the four of us go for our anniversary celebration. I was laughing inside from Kevin's reaction when I suggested to him that we invite Arnold and Charise to Cancun with us since Arnold is happy with his wife once again.

Kevin practically spit fire through the phone. He made up every reason why they shouldn't come, to include Charise and Elaine might end up fighting. Elaine knows where to find Charise now if she wanted to fight. I just figured it would be comical watching Kevin squirm now that he fucked with a loose cannon like Charise. He now has to always worry about when that girl will start talking, and she doesn't give a shit about her husband. She has no problem treating him like shit every chance he allows her. Yeah, that would be some serious drama there.

Speaking of drama, now my crazy-ass sister has got me caught up in some more of her mess. She brought her silly self here from Houston to fuck with Shawnee's baby's daddy. Now that motherfucker's nose is all wide open for my sister.

He thought I was going to be mad when I found out. I wish it wasn't my sister, but I'm glad he finally got his nose out of Shawnee's ass. If it weren't for all the hell that Shawnee would cause, I wish Eric and Tatiana could have their relationship out in the open. Eric is good people and doesn't deserve what Shawnee does to him.

The way I know Tatiana, she's not going to be satisfied until she sticks it to Shawnee good, and if I can help her in any way, I most certainly will.

I don't know why Shawnee would sleep on my sister. Shawnee didn't even know that her so-called husband set my sister up for life. I'm just mad that Tatiana let that asshole put her second to Shawnee, when she was with him first, although I didn't know it back then. He didn't have to marry Shawnee to leave her to run his company. That dirty old bastard just wanted to have his cake and eat it too. The way I see it, Tatiana should have gotten everything and Shawnee shouldn't have gotten shit. Okay, so I don't like her. Never have, and never will. I wouldn't mind seeing her naked, but I wouldn't want to fuck her, though—well, maybe just once for the experience.

I would openly support Eric and Tatiana being together, but I know

I'd have hell to catch in my own house. Momma's happy about them being together as well. She likes Eric.

What she wasn't too happy with was when I told her about my encounter with Elaine. She said it was obvious to her that I was in love with Elaine and not Harmony, because I sunk into a funk after not hearing from Elaine. I told her I gave up just about all of the other women for Elaine, although Elaine didn't know anything about it. As sexy as Cynnyyah and Roxana are, they are no replacement for Elaine. Fucking them is like a Band-Aid on a gunshot wound. It's just not enough to fill the void.

The number of women patients has been increasing significantly. I don't know what type of word has been getting around, but I confused them all. Now I take one of the nurses in the room during the examination. My life is all business these days. I go home early once again, play with the kids, and then sulk. When I get horny enough, I go to Cynnyyah instead of Harmony, but other than that, I'm home being a family man.

"Dr. Palmer, there's a Mrs. Dobbs here wanting to know if you have a free moment to speak with her," the receptionist came and asked.

I lit up like a Christmas tree immediately. "Sure, send her in."

I tried to fix myself up before Elaine made it in my office. As quickly as she was in, I closed the door and gave her a big hug.

"Wow! What a greeting," she said, laughing.

"Elaine, Elaine, Elaine. You don't know what my life has been like since I last saw you. Where have you been?" I asked.

I sat on the edge of my desk because I didn't want to move too far away from her. She sat in a chair.

"How have you been, Todd?"

"Crazy! Everything's been crazy. I've been going crazy wondering what you may have been thinking about after our last time seeing one another. I haven't stopped thinking about you, dreaming about you, everything. Where have you been? Did I upset you?"

Now if the boys could see how I was acting, they'd strip me of my Playa card. However, right now, I don't care. I'll turn it in voluntarily.

"I've been spending time away at my other stores. I really needed to get away to process my thoughts of what I had done. I feel like I have wrecked my sister's life by sleeping with her husband. It's been a hard pill to swallow. The insane part is I loved hanging out with you before it went all the way. I started off trying to keep you occupied from cheating on my sister. Then I don't know what happened. I started wanting you to want me. I wanted you to find me desirable. As much as I thoroughly enjoyed being with you in every way, we know it's not right and we have to figure out how we are supposed to go forward as a family from here on out. We have this trip coming up to Cancun soon. Do you have any idea how awkward that will be? We have to clean up this mess."

I wasn't trying to hear that family shit. I wanted to hear about how we would hook up again. I wanted her to say we'd be able to sneak off together while in Cancun. I wanted so desperately to tell her that her husband is fucking her sister, so she shouldn't feel any guilt.

"Can we go have dinner and talk outside of this office?" I asked.

She hesitated. "Uh, well, I guess so. We've never had any problems with dinner."

I canceled the rest of my appointments. I was getting some today.

We went to the Bluewater Grill in Redondo Beach. It was pretty nice. We slowly but surely worked up to a comfortable conversation that included laughter.

After dinner, we took a walk on the beach, even though it was nippy outside. Somewhere along the way, our hands interlocked like two lovers. When we made a seat on the sand, she sat directly in front of me as I used my body to keep her arms and back warm. That closeness helped me to have access to Elaine's lips. She pulled away at first, but my lips weren't going to accept rejection, so I cornered her in my arms and took my mouth to hers until it had no place to run. Her kiss was hesitant, but she eventually reciprocated. My erection pressed in her back, letting her know I was hungry for her.

"Todd, we can't do this. It's not right," she said when breaking free from our kiss.

"Is your contracting vagina agreeing with your mouth? Are your hardened nipples agreeing with your decision?" I asked.

"I don't want to hurt anyone, Todd."

"I just want to make you feel good, Elaine," I said, taking hold of her mouth again. "You deserve to be happy, and I want to give you what you want. I want you. I desire you. I find you desirable."

She pulled away and stood up, holding her hand out for me to get up. "Come on, let's get going."

My heart sank. I didn't want our time to end. We walked in silence holding hands, but instead of walking to the car, she led me to a hotel a block away. I felt like doing cartwheels.

She's going to give me some! Yes! Yes! Yes!

When we got behind that door, I made love to Elaine as she would never forget. No I didn't fuck her. I made tender, passionate love to her. I even told her I loved her and have from the first day I saw her. She was okay with my revelation. She didn't have to say it, but I knew she was in love with me as well.

I knew I was going to have hell to pay when I got home, because it was after two o'clock in the morning when I left the hotel. I couldn't begin to think of a good lie to cover my excessively late-lateness.

When I got home, I decided to sleep downstairs on the sofa rather than to go and face Harmony, and probably fight all night. Surprisingly, I awoke to find a cover nicely placed on me to keep me warm. Even more surprising, my wife didn't ask a single question about the night before. I don't know whether to be afraid or not. This is not like the Harmony I know that's always reminding me about her crazy family in Detroit.

She had my breakfast ready and helped me get ready to go to work. I was scared to eat the food. Maybe Harmony is as crazy as the family she talks about. Damn, she was making me feel like shit, although I had no regrets about making love to Elaine.

19

Kevin

Kevin, I'm not going to be able to see you anymore."

"What?" I asked, shocked.

Charise just showed up in my office unannounced. I wondered where my secretary, Andrea, was at since she didn't mention Charise was present. I was having a rough day trying to make a deal go through, and I was hardly in the mood for any nonsense.

"What do you mean you can't see me anymore? Does this have anything to do with that Sean character?"

"Sean? No, I haven't been with Sean in a minute. I just realize that I actually love my husband. I want to work on my marriage. My husband loves me with every fiber of his being, and I want to at least try to reciprocate," she answered as though she may have actually been telling the truth. With Charise, that was a crock of bullshit.

"No! No, I will not just let you end things like that. I'm not going to just let you cut me off like I was some cheap thrill. Charise, I love you. I am not going to let you walk out of my life."

After looking at me as if I were stupid, she chuckled. "Kevin, you do know you are married to my sister, right? You are in no position to make demands. It's over. Get a grip!"

Charise was dismissing me as if I had no feelings. Why all this sudden bullshit to fix her marriage? She is not walking out of my life. That's all there is to it. Not now, not ever.

I don't know how or when my feelings have come to this, but I'm not going to let things end between us. We have been making love at least three times a week for the past month, and now she thinks she's just going to shut me down like I'm some toy? She better think again.

"Charise, I hear what you are saying, but you need to understand that what you and I have is not over. I don't want it to be over, and that's that. It's not over! You say you want to fix your marriage, but I don't think your marriage will work when Arnold finds out about you fucking Sean."

"What? Are you trying to blackmail me, Kevin? Not you of all people who was supposed to be in the church and super righteous?" She chuckled. "Furthermore, you can't prove I was ever with Sean. He'd certainly never admit it to you. How do I know? He told me you asked him that time I told you I was fucking him, but regardless of that, he and I are done just like you and I are now done. You have some nerve trying to blackmail me of all people, and don't forget—trying to wreck my marriage will only destroy yours and send your wife back to pulling tricks again. So, let's not go there, Kevin. See, I might have been willing to let you touch it one last time for the road, but for that blackmail shit, I don't play. Wrong bitch!"

I watched and let her say her piece. She was so full of herself.

"Oh, but you think it's okay for *you* to blackmail people and try to wreck other people's marriages, and think there's not supposed to be any consequence to it, Charise? Think again!" I said, equally as smug and sure of myself. "I don't need Sean's word that you were fucking him. A picture is worth more."

Charise looked as if she was thinking about what evidence I could have against her as she twirled a piece of her hanging hair and twisted one of her feet around in her five-inch heels. She didn't look so confident at that moment. She remained quiet.

I continued. "I guess you never knew Sean's one weakness, did you? Cash!

Cash money. For it, that prick would do anything—even tape himself fucking your naked ass. I myself was very disturbed watching the footage, but I knew it would come in handy one day. I also paid the snake to stay the fuck away from you."

Charise was clearly disturbed. Her mouth was opened, but words would not come out. I got up from behind my desk and walked behind Charise and rubbed her shoulders. She tried to pull away, but I wouldn't let her.

"You talk about my being all righteous, but you didn't give a damn that first day you came to my house trying to fuck me. You didn't give a damn about my wife—your sister—then. You also didn't give a damn when you attempted to blackmail me and was willing to wreck your family and marriage. Oh, and let's not forget how you blackmailed me regarding Lauren. Isn't that how you were finally able to get me?"

I let my hands fall to her breasts and cupped and fondled them through her blouse. I pressed my erection against her backside.

"So Charise, it's not over, because I didn't say it's over. And no, you weren't going to come into my office today, telling me you were going to just let me touch it one last time."

I reached my hand underneath her skirt and roughly groped in between her legs. "This pussy is mine, you got it? I don't want you fucking Arnold anymore either."

I pushed my fingers into her pussy with no resistance. My other hand made its way into her blouse to hold one of her tits in my hand. I pressed and rubbed my erection against her backside like an animal in heat. I have never fucked her in my office, but I wanted to right then. That's probably why she came to my office to break it off. She probably figured I would never risk having sex there, where all my employees are. She figured she could come, say her piece, and simply walk out.

My fingers were so far up inside of her, while she was pretending she was in control of the sensation. I had her blouse completely unbuttoned and both of her tits out over her bra cups. I made my way around her to suck them. I picked her up and laid her on my desk. I was both angry and horny, and I was going to fuck her good. I pulled my dick out and put it up in that wet pussy. It was feeling wonderful. She tried to lay there as if she wasn't turned on, but eventually Charise ended her resistance and began gyrating her pelvis with my strokes. She fondled her own breasts while I held her ass up from off the desk.

My secretary Andrea walked in my office holding a file. She stood frozen in shock as she watched my naked ass, with my pants wrapped around my ankles, banging my wife's sister on my desk.

Charise and I tried to quickly collect ourselves as Andrea ran out the door visibly upset by what she witnessed. Charise smirked and then left without a single word. I didn't know what to do or think at that point.

After getting myself cleaned up, I called Andrea into my office. She had been crying.

"Andrea, I am so sorry you had to see that. I can't even explain how it happened. I have never done anything like this before," I half lied. I just never did it in my office before.

"There is no need for you to apologize. This is your company and what you do in it, is your business. I should have knocked before barging in, but I didn't know anyone came into the office. I had just gone down the hall to check on that acquisition you asked me about. I was within view of my desk, but I didn't see anyone. I'm sorry." She cried harder.

I waited a couple of minutes for her to collect her emotions. "I guess there's no right time to stress this enough, but I do not expect to hear any more about this from anyone in the office. Have I made myself explicitly clear?" I said in an intimidating manner.

"Yes, Mr. Dobbs. I will not mention a thing." She looked afraid, and that's how I wanted her to be.

Two days later when Elaine left town again, I summoned Charise to my house to finish what I didn't get to finish the other day. She certainly wasn't her sassy self. She was more submissive, and I liked that. I had my way with her, and she did whatever I said to do.

Since Elaine had just flown out that morning, I was able to take my time with her sister. I was greedy. I kept her for 12 hours. I didn't let her go until 9pm that night. I would have never been so inconsiderate of her time or schedule when Elaine would be out of town before, but since she pulled that "It's over" stunt in my office, I had to teach her a lesson. I think the power trip was getting to me. I felt like the alpha male this time, and I was loving it. It made the sex feel better as well.

I wish I could tell Todd about it, but he just left to go to Houston to see his family. Well, maybe it's better I don't tell him I had to blackmail Charise in order to keep fucking her. I told him a while back I wasn't touching her anymore.

I don't know when the last time I have stepped foot in church was. Once my mind stepped out of my marriage, I tried to repent. I prayed and tried to fight the urges of revisiting a life I once knew, but ultimately I lost the battle. I figure I'm headed to hell anyhow; I may as well make it worth it. Now I have no problem doing what I need to have what I want. I even changed up how I do business.

When I returned to the office the following day, I had a notice that Andrea had resigned effective immediately. Thankfully she didn't provide a reason, but I already knew the reason. I'm not sure what I'm going to do now without her. Andrea had worked many years for me. Ironically, I got her into church. She's been grateful ever since. I also taught her to become a wealthy woman through investments. I could imagine how she must have felt by what she witnessed. I think she even idolized me, but what people fail to realize is that I am human and I get weak and make mistakes too. I didn't set out to get involved with Charise. She came to me and I got weak.

Elaine is not going to be happy when she finds out Andrea quit. She really liked Andrea. I just hope she doesn't push the issue to find out why. She's already trying to figure out why Lauren stopped coming around her. She thinks she must have offended Lauren in some manner with the whole makeover thing. I knew Elaine had to have been behind that makeover. Figures!! Nonetheless, I am glad our sex life has finally toned down. In addition to Charise, I was able to make it back to Lauren and finish what I never got to finish months prior. I thought after Charise, I wouldn't want to go to Lauren again, but it just seemed so unfinished and I don't like unfinished business. She is not someone to fuck after having been with both an Elaine and a Charise. I'm not sure why, but she could not make me cum to save her life. The whole time I was with her, I kept imagining her fat, nasty, greasy looking husband up in her. I ended up pushing her over to jerk myself off.

At times, I feel horrible about cheating on my wife because she trusts me implicitly. I hate lying to her. I hate that I have become so selfish, that I don't go with her to check on her New York and D.C. stores anymore. I used to go everywhere with Elaine and was always there for her. Now I practically push her out the door just to have the opportunity to be with her sister. I didn't even go with her to the airport this last trip.

Next week will be good for me and Elaine to reconnect. We're heading to Cancun with Todd and Harmony to celebrate our anniversaries. That should be interesting since I know Todd despises making love to his wife now. Maybe they'll get down there and fall in love all over again. Maybe I'll reconnect with Elaine enough to make me want to give up Charise. It would have really been awkward if Arnold and Charise were on this trip. I don't know if I could stand to watch Charise with him. I wanted to kick Todd's ass for suggesting it. I've been avoiding Arnold like the plague. Every time he asks about us getting together, I tell him I'm busy with something. I'm not trying to hear about all the "good loving" he's getting at home. I remember not so long ago, his "good loving" was coming outside of his home.

It's funny, last month when I had Sean make the video tape of him and Charise, I wasn't sure what I would do with it. I mainly wanted to figure out a way to get him out of Kelly's life. I knew that's what would make my wife happy. I may fuck around on my wife, but there's not much I wouldn't do for her. I know there isn't much she wouldn't do for me just the same. I figured I had to be careful of how I present the video without implicating myself. I don't know what I would have done if I didn't have it to hold onto Charise. Cutting Charise off is like cutting off oxygen. That just can't happen.

20

Sean

They should be back from Cancun by now. I want you to hit that joker up for some cash. I don't think he's in much of a position to bargain."

"Why would Kevin be fucking Charise when he has Elaine? I think you're wrong, Sean. I don't think Kevin would do anything like that."

I ran up on Kelly, ready to smack the shit out of her. I had to stop myself since she was standing in the kitchen washing the dishes and happened to have a knife in her hand at that moment. My gun was on the other side of the house.

"What the fuck did I tell you about trying to make that nigga out to be all high and mighty? I told you that I know he's fucking Charise. Why else would he be always asking me about her? You can just go straight at him like you know for sure that he's fucking both of your sisters, and tell him he needs to give you some loot to keep you hush-hush."

"And what's going to happen if he says no, and then tells my sisters?"

"Kelly, why are you acting all scared of the motherfucker? That sneaky nigga got all y'all fooled. You don't have to worry about him telling anybody."

I moved Kelly away from that sink and took her in my arms to sweeten her up. She's my soldier and I needed her to do what I say, but I can't have her all scary and shit.

"Baby, you have to do this for us. You want us to have nice things, and if we can hit his ass up, we'll be okay. Maybe we can take you to the doctor and find out why you can't get pregnant after we get this money," I said, rubbing her belly as if there was a baby in there already. I planted kisses on her neck to help her see things my way. "His ass is loaded. Hell, I wish I had some dirt on all of them niggas, 'cause I'd hit each one of them up."

"Sean, you don't know for certain about Kevin and Charise. I'd feel a lot more comfortable approaching Kevin if I knew he was really with Charise."

I want to strangle this bitch sometimes. I continued to give her a bunch of small kisses around her face and neck before I took her mouth. I went one step further and picked her up and carried her to the bedroom. I knew she'd feel more comfortable making love behind closed doors. That's when I can persuade Kelly to do anything. By the time I finished fucking her properly, she was asking me for the plan to extort cash from Kevin. My Girl!

A couple of months ago Kevin paid me 50 G's to fuck Charise on tape without her knowledge. That was the easiest paper I had ever made. I kind of figured there was something up with him and Charise, but I couldn't understand why he would want me to fuck her if he was fucking her. I thought maybe he was trying to take her company from her.

However, when I handed him the disk and he handed me another envelope with five thousand, saying that was for me to "Stay the hell away from Charise, and you better not ever lay a finger on her again," I knew he was doing her. Why else would he pay me to stay away from the ho?

Now I figure we can get all that we can from his ass. Surely he don't want his precious wife to find out. He was stupid to believe I wouldn't keep tearing that ass up every chance she gave me after he paid me. That girl likes getting her two dicks at once just like I enjoy my two bitches at one time, and she don't give a shit who the second dick is attached to. That was clear when she let me and my 430-pound sound engineer fuck her together. That didn't go too well, but she fucked him just the same.

I figure it's about time to hit his ass up for some more cash. We're going to hit him up bigger this time. If he wants to cut off my pussy supply with Charise, he's going to have to cough up more loot. My dick is about ready for some more of Charise's ass. She hasn't been coming through lately. Hell, all I'd have left is to watch that video of me fucking her if I can't get her. I need a new video. Shit! I could make a collection of them and sell those bitches for some real cheddar. I think I could get her dumb ass to go along with that plan. Damn, my dick is getting hard just from the thought.

It took six fucking hours for Kelly to return. She came home all distraught. I didn't know what to make of it.

"Well, what happened? Did you get the loot?"

She cried harder. She shook her head, no.

"What the fuck happened? Did you follow the plan?"

"Yes. I did what you told me, and said everything you asked me to say," Kelly responded.

"I know you fucked something up. You're stupid like that. For all I know, he was probably trying to fuck you too. What did he say? I just want to strangle you for being so stupid sometimes."

Kelly dug in her pocketbook. "He told me to give you this," she said, handing me a DVD.

"What the fuck is that? What am I supposed to do with a DVD? Does it have some type of info to get me my loot? I can't spend that shit."

Then it hit me: *Could that be the video of me fucking Charise, and he gave it to Kelly to give to me as payback for coming at him like I did for more dough?*

He must think I'm stupid to play that thing in front of Kelly. I took the DVD from her and tried to play it off as if I didn't care about what was on it. I placed it on the kitchen counter.

"You're not going to look at it?" Kelly asked suspiciously.

"I don't give a fuck about some dumb DVD. That ain't paying any bills."

"Sean, I really am sorry. I tried with everything in me, but it just didn't work. I don't want you to hate me, but I'll understand if you will," she said, attempting to hug me.

I pushed her away. I didn't want to hear that shit. That last line sounded out of place. I wasn't sure what to make of it. When I saw that pathetic look on her face, I hesitantly hugged her back. I'm not all-monster, even though I really wanted to smack the shit out of her for not coming back with some cash. She might be stupid as I don't know what, but despite it, I do love her and could never see letting her go.

She went in the bedroom and laid down with all of her clothes on, still crying. Since the bitch didn't seem like she was about to cook our dinner anytime soon, I decided to head on down to the studio, but first had to make my pit stop at Roscoe's. I was certain to take the DVD with me. I wasn't going to leave it for Kelly to see it. She obviously didn't see any video of me and Charise together, otherwise, she wouldn't have been upset about letting me down.

But why was she so messed up? Why did it take so long for her to get back? Was she really that messed up about not getting the money, or is she afraid he's going to tell her dumb ass sisters? Why would she apologize to me if she saw me fucking her sister?

Hell, maybe it would be good if Kelly knew so I could suggest that threesome with the two of them. After all, she doesn't want me hating her and all, so she'd be willing to do just about anything right now. There's no telling how she would have come at me if she knew I fucked Charise, but then again, my bitch already knows better than to come at me stupid. So what I fucked her sister? She'll get over it. It ain't like she's going anywhere. That bitch would never have the heart to leave me.

I left Roscoe's with my food in tow and headed to the studio, where I was able to check out the DVD. Sure as shit, it was me and Charise. That nigga thinks he's slick sending Kelly to deliver that DVD. Too bad for him, I got my bitch trained. Ha-Ha! That shit blew up in his face. She wouldn't watch it without turning it over to me first.

I did a little work after watching the video and then found one of the groupie bitches in there to come give me head. I needed something to take away the aggravation from my day.

That held me over for a few hours more of work, but then I wanted some pussy, so I found yet another bitch in the studio. That video had me horny. As I was fucking the second groupie in her ass, I had a thought. What if Kelly fucked Kevin to get back at me? Could that be the reason she was worried about me hating her?

My thoughts became so intense that I didn't realize how bad I was hurting the groupie. She was bleeding out of her ass and crying. She wasn't going to complain for fear of her not being able to do any possible upcoming videos. I pulled out of her ass as soon as I noticed the blood on my dick. I wouldn't apologize. I just dismissed her.

How can I find out if Kelly fucked that nigga? Maybe that's why she went and laid down, 'cause she was all exhausted from fucking. That's why she took so fucking long to come back. I thought they were at the bank getting my money all that damn time. I'm going to kick that bitch's ass.

I went in the bathroom to clean the groupie's shit off my dick, so I could head home to fuck Kelly up. This bitch thinks she's slick. I know she fucked him. It all makes sense now. Why would that bitch try to play me like that? Don't she know I'm too fucking smart for her dumb shit? She couldn't begin to think of any shit to get back at me. Fucking some other nigga is the oldest game, and she just played her fucking self.

That Kevin motherfucker will pay as well. As soon as I finish with Kelly, I'm going to round up my boys and fuck his ass up as well. He fucked with the wrong wife.

I got to the garage to pick up my car and it was gone. I stood there wondering, *Who steals a car from the garage?* I stood as though my car would somehow reappear. I tried to use my cell phone but couldn't get any signal. I know whoever got my car had to have a gate card to get out. I went to the attendant to inquire about my car's whereabouts.

"Yo! Where's my fucking whip at?" I yelled, scaring his scary ass.

"Uh . . . uh . . . I-I wasn't on duty at the time, but I was told a tow truck carried it out. He said they had a repossession order."

"What the fuck you talking about? My shit is all paid for. That wasn't a fucking repo."

The scary looking guy shrugged his shoulders, flinching. "I-I don't know. I just know what the other guy told me before he left.

"Ain't this a bitch! Somebody stole my shit."

I called Kelly to come pick me up. She said "Okay" without asking why. That was strange to me as well, but right now I am fuming because I need to know what's up with my ride. Why would someone be claiming to repo *my* shit? I don't owe anyone for my ride. Taxes? Nah. The feds? I don't know why they would be fucking with me.

Two hours went by and Kelly still hadn't arrived at my office. It doesn't take that damn long to get here. We live in Santa Monica, and my office is on Avenue of the Stars. That's 15 minutes, tops. Well 30 minutes, tops, with any traffic and lights. *I'm going to hurt that bitch. She knows how I feel about waiting.*

I called her again. "Kelly, where the fuck are you? It's been two fucking hours. Don't make me come punch you in your fucking throat."

"Oh, I thought you were going to call me when you wanted me to pick you up. I figured you were waiting for the police to get there to make a report," she responded.

"Ain't nobody tell you to think or figure shit. I told you to come and get me two fucking hours ago. You know damn well I ain't calling any fucking police. I'll handle this shit myself. Somebody fucked with the wrong car. That's all there is to it. Now get your ass down here and pick me up!"

Then it dawned on me: *I never told her about my car missing.* "Hold up! How the fuck—"

There was a dead silence.

"Hello? Hello? Kelly? Kelly!" I yelled.

I know this bitch didn't hang up on me.

I tried calling her back, and the call went straight to voicemail. I figured she must have been trying to call me back. I waited a few minutes and still no call back. I called her again and got her voicemail still. I waited another 30 minutes before I had one of my boys from the studio drive me home.

That's one thing I never allowed: I never let any of my boys know where I lived with Kelly. I didn't want any of them dropping by when they know I wasn't home and end up trying to get with my wife. When I first met Kelly, I was staying in a phat-ass crib not too far from where we are now. Niggas would drop by all the time unannounced. Kelly thought it was my house when we met. You can find a lot of nice house-sitting gigs in L.A. That's how I got that house.

When we pulled up to the crib, I was all set to beat Kelly's ass but saw Kelly's car was gone. She must have gone to get me after all. I tried calling her phone again and still got her voicemail. Maybe her battery was dead on her phone.

"You need me to go in with you?" he asked.

I chuckled. "Nah, man. We good. I'm gonna roll up in here and handle business, but I'm gonna get with y'all later about some other shit that needs handling."

"Cool. Just let me know."

My boy dropped me off outside and left. I could see the light on in the window when I got out of the car, but when I opened the door, I noticed it was dark. I was about to reach for my Glock but realized I didn't have it on me. It was in my car along with my briefcase and my .38. Then I figured it was my sons, and Kelly must have left them alone to come and get me. *Grounds for another ass beating when I catch up with her.*

When I came to, I was tied to one of our dining room chairs. It was hard for me to focus my eyes. There was a bright light shining in my eyes. I had a bad pain in the back of my head. My hearing started to readjust. I heard someone say, "Oh, the little bitch is finally coming to."

Eventually I realized there were three big niggas and one thick chick in my home. I didn't see Kelly or my sons.

"Where are my boys? Where the fuck are my sons?" I demanded to know as I struggled to free myself from the chair.

The quad all laughed. The woman walked up to me and punched me in the eye, and one of the guys kept my chair from falling over. I could feel instant swelling. She said, "I don't think you're in a position to be trying to jump all bad, bitch. Funny, I didn't hear you ask for your wife."

This chick must be the brains behind this operation, but who is she? She doesn't look familiar. This bitch must be at least six feet tall and around 250 solid pounds. Her back-up looks like they eat nuts and bolts for breakfast and human people for lunch and dinner. They have to be a minimum of 300 pounds each. The rope tied around me was tight enough to make it hard to breathe. The ones around my hands were so tight, they were cutting in my skin. I could barely feel my hands.

Where is Kelly? Her car was gone. I don't hear my sons anywhere. I tried to wiggle, but it was pointless. The ropes were firm.

"What is this all about? I don't know you," I said.

"You're right, you don't know me, but I understand you have some bad habits that need straightening out. Do you know Charise Wiggins?" she asked.

When I didn't answer, she punched me in my jaw. This big bitch had a powerful punch. I could feel my teeth loosen. *What the hell does Charise have to do with this? What kind of mess is she into? Does she owe these people money?*

"I asked you a fucking question, you little bitch. Don't get all brand new now, motherfucker," she said to me. Then she said to one of her goons, "Tiny, untie this bitch. I want to kick his ass fairly."

Is she kidding? There wouldn't be anything fair about a fight with her. If I try to hit her back, those goons would all take turns on me.

Of course "Tiny" had to be the biggest of the three, so I tried to quickly answer her before Tiny could untie me. "Yes. Yes, I know Charise. She's my wife's sister."

"Your wife's sister, huh? Well your wife's sister just so happens to be my first cousin." She paused and looked up in thought. "Uhps! Well I think that makes your wife my first cousin as well. Their first cousins also," she said, pointing to the three big men. "I understand you like to beat on women, fuck women and their sisters, take all of their money, fuck women in front of innocent children, and fuck over people in general." She made a sour look on her face. "Which is too bad for you, because we don't like bitches like you. Especially when they fuck with our family. That's the ultimate no-no.

"So, let me tell you what's about to happen. You are going to go get all of the money that you have ever taken from my cousin over the past year or so, and get it back to her within the next twenty-four hours. How you get it is not my problem. It's yours. Next, you will sign the divorce papers giving her everything, and you'll stay the fuck away from my cousin—your wife. You will keep your sorry ass out of those kids' lives as well. I don't give a damn if they are your sons. Not anymore! You will leave Charise and the rest of my family alone one way or another.

"Today, you're just going to get a small sample of a Detroit-style ass-whupping. You don't do as I say, those samples will get larger, until you exist no more, and no one has to be concerned with you being a menace to society. Oh, and if you're wondering where your car is, we have it in safe keeping. We left you the other car to go get that paper you need to get within twenty-four hours. Now the way I figure, you owe my cousin Kelly, uhm, let's just say about a million. You owe Charise at least, uh, a hundred gees for her pussy. And then there is our fee for having to intervene. I'll just make that only a hundred gees, since this is our family rate. Oh, and I'm sure I don't have to mention what will happen if you get police or anybody else involved. As far as your boy Deondre, his body won't surface unless you fuck up with the plan. Your thirty-eight that killed his ass won't surface either."

I couldn't believe what I was hearing. *They killed Deondre? What did he ever do to anybody?* Tears filled my eyes, but I couldn't let them fall. *They killed my boy and plan on framing me for his murder? What did they do with my sons? Where the fuck am I supposed to get that kind of loot within twenty-four hours? A million for Kelly? Man, please! And Charise is a ho. Her pussy's hardly worth a dollar let alone $100,000. Yeah, right! These motherfuckers came in from Detroit? Detroit just don't know. They fucked with the wrong nigga.*

"Get his ass untied, 'cause he has work to do. He'll probably lose an hour trying to get around with broken ribs."

Huh? I didn't understand what she meant about broken ribs, but I found out real quick when her big ass foot crashed into my side. The chair fell over and then she kicked me in the jaw. That time I did feel teeth come out.

"Now untie him," she said, wiping her shoe off as if I contaminated it. "Keep in mind, your every step will be watched, so don't even think about doing anything stupid. I don't like using kids as leverage, but that'll be up to you. The money better be here in twenty-four hours, not a minute later, and your bitch ass better not think about trying to run to save yourself. Trust me when I say you can't run, nor can you hide. No one has ever succeeded."

One of the guys pulled out a switchblade and put the blade to my throat while he wore a wicked smile. He poked enough to draw blood, but not to do any real damage. Then he cut the rope in one slit.

My mind raced as to how I was going to handle the dilemma on my plate. My ribs were killing me. I felt short of breath. I felt like I was going to pass out. I must have, because I opened my eyes and no one was there. But for the pain, I would have thought it was all a dream.

Her family is straight gangsters!

I couldn't believe Kelly was behind this shit. I have been nothing but good to her ass. So what I fucked her sister? She acts like that was the end of the fucking world. Everybody fucked her sister. Why would she involve my sons in her mess? They have the nerve to hold *my* kids hostage. Kelly will pay dearly for this shit. I'll get her the money, but she won't be spending a dime of it. I have to find my kids. Thankfully that bitch never got pregnant. She probably did that shit on purpose somehow. I know that bitch is probably hiding out at one of her sister's houses. All of them will be dead after I get my sons back.

Man, I can't believe they killed Dre. Why did they have to do that shit? This was between me and Kelly. He didn't have anything to do with this. Damn!

Dre had some cash stashed in his safe. He didn't believe in banks. *I can go get that cash and get my kids. I'm sure he wouldn't mind under the circumstances. I think I have about 250 gees in my safe at the office. Where am I getting 1.2 mil?*

I tried to clean myself up some so I could make some moves. I tried to find as much jewelry I had that I could pawn. I also thought about all the people I could get some cash from. Thankfully I had put some money in the bank when I was trying to get custody of my boys. *I forgot all about that. I sure need it now.*

I arrived back at the crib, and the big bitch was waiting there. This time she had three other big bitches with her. I didn't see the guys. I didn't know if that was a good thing or not. I was able to scrape up 1.1 million. I was still a little short.

"You're still a little short, aren't you? I think you forgot about our intervention fee," she said, as if reading my mind.

How the fuck did she know I was short 100 gees? She didn't even count it. "I still have two more hours. I'm working on it."

"Uhm, well see now, our fee has increased since my girls said they want a piece. I figure for all the women you've fucked over in your life, you owe at least, let's say two-fifty. Yeah, make that two hundred and fifty gees, and you got three hours to make it happen. Don't come up short again, 'cause hopefully now you are convinced that your every step is being monitored. Drop that bag and get a move on it," she ordered.

I was exhausted and in pain. I hadn't eaten since my meal from Roscoe's. My mind couldn't think about how to come up with another 250 G's. If they didn't have my sons, I wouldn't bother. I can't imagine them letting me walk away alive. They already killed Dre, and he didn't have anything to do with this shit. Why would they spare my life? *Who the fuck did I marry? Maybe I should have checked her ass out before I married her.* She better hope they kill me because she will die when I get hold of her ass.

I wish I knew how many of them were with the big bitch. Then I could round up my niggas to handle their asses. They think Detroit can roll their asses up in here and just declare a fucking war? I don't give a fuck about them being from some damn Detroit.

I made it to the crib with eight minutes to spare. Kelly was there this time, along with one of the big dudes and the other four big bitches.

"Kelly, why are you doing this to us? Yes, I fucked up messing with your sister, but all of this isn't necessary. Where are my sons? Kelly, we love each other," I said, trying to appeal to Kelly's soft side.

One of the big women karate kicked me in my side, causing me to hit the ground. It was the same side I was kicked in the first time. Then she put a hand up in the air, shaking her head and said, "I'm sorry. I just can't stand a lying motherfucker with all that love shit, while he's poking your sister." She spat on my head while I was on the floor.

Kelly's eyes were filled with tears. One of the other women kicked me in my face. "See? This nigga done made my cousin cry. I don't like that shit." Then she kicked me repeatedly in the groin.

I didn't have a chance with these rough bitches and their black Timberlands. Thankfully they weren't steel-toed shoes. I could see the big guy's shoes are steel-toed. His kick would have probably finished my ass off.

"I . . . I . . . uh . . . I got all the dough. Let me have my boys and I'll leave," I spoke through intense pain, still curled up on the floor.

The original big bitch said, "I told you yesterday that you wouldn't see them again. Now you will sign these divorce papers and be on your merry little way?"

"I'll sign the papers, but give me my kids. Please."

Everyone but Kelly erupted into laughter. I could tell that she didn't appreciate what was happening. I was hoping Kelly would get a backbone and stop her crazy-ass family from interfering in our lives.

One of the girls helped me sit up so I could sign the papers. After I signed them, Kelly walked closer sniffling as tears poured from her eyes and said, "Sean, you won't be getting the kids back. You have traumatized both the boys and me for the last time. You have raped me repeatedly, in front of them no less, as they helplessly watched and would always beg me to leave your ass. Well guess what? It was them that decided they don't want to see your ass again. They don't want to go back to that trick mother of theirs either. They asked me to have you put in jail for the rest of your life so you can't hurt anyone anymore.

"They told me how you showed them the video of you fucking my sister and got paid to do so long before you sent me to Kevin's. They told me how you drugged me to get me in bed that first time. They told me how you said you had to find a 'ho with some money' so 'she' could watch out for them. They told me how you brag about all of your hoes and bitches you fuck or get head from in the studio every day. They told me how you said all women are stupid with the exception of your whore-ass mother, who so-called taught you how to be a man.

"I also haven't forgotten about when you ripped my shirt off of me when we were in your studio, because you said I was trying to show off in front of your boys, but then had them all looking at my breasts like I was an animal in the zoo. Speaking of zoos, I will NEVER forget when you stripped me naked, tied me up, and had Dre's nasty-ass pit bull to hump on me and lick me between my legs, and then snapped pictures to keep me hostage. I should have killed your ass that day. At least you had sense enough to never go to sleep around me. And don't think I have forgotten the countless times you have put your hands on me or had me sucking on your fucking gun of all things. Even worse, you putting that damn gun in my pussy, and then got mad because it wasn't making me feel good. Or how about that time you again humored yourself by pretending to pull the trigger, thinking the gun was empty? That shit had a fucking bullet in there, Sean! That was God saving me, not you. And you better pray He saves your tired ass. No, I haven't forgotten shit, Sean, and the only reason your life will be spared is because I want you to remember just the same. I want you to remember why you'll never be able to look at your kids again. I want you to remember the reason you'll never see another sunrise or sunset. I want you to remember why you lost everything. And like I said to you the other day, hopefully you won't hate me when you understand why things had to be the way they had to be. Your ass think you got so much game that you played your damn self. I knew your predictable ass would never call the police when I had your car removed from the garage. You think you're such tough shit, but you look like a little bitch right now." And then she too spat in my face. "And while those rats are crawling up your ass, let's see how much you get a kick out of bestiality then, which is the only other reason I don't want you dead—YET."

Damn! She played me like that over some stupid shit? She knows damn well we were just playing with the dog thing. She's being ridiculous. What couple doesn't have their problems or try to have fun? We even laughed about the dumb dog since that time.

Her people were looking at both of us like they were hearing this stuff for the first time. I guess she never did tell anyone. I couldn't understand what she was talking about: *not seeing a sunset?* If I'm not dead, how does she expect me to not ever see one again? I wonder if this is what she meant about not wanting me to hate her. The bitch!

"You can have him now. I'm done with him," Kelly said with no emotion to no one in particular. She flipped her hand and walked out of the house accompanied by the big guy. The guy took the bag of money I brought the first time.

"Get the lye so we can burn his fucking eyes out. I should just snatch those bitches out of their sockets," I heard the original girl say. "I can't believe that shit I just heard my little cousin has been through. I know she wants him alive, but this pig certainly deserves to die."

"I agree, he does need to die," another girl said. "I'll take care of these hands, so at least he'll never touch another soul again."

What the fuck?!! Burn out my eyes? My hands? What kind of shit are they on?

One of the girls asked, "I thought we were going to drop him down in the homeless district first?"

Homeless district? I guess the bitches aren't too smart after all. Someone will recognize me and get me help. I can tell anyone to get their asses.

"We'll get him there soon enough," the original big bitch said. "Man! I should just kill his ass. Kelly won't know."

"Yeah, I know, but we promised we'd let him live."

"That was before I heard about all this other shit," the original chick said as she was pacing the floor. "Okay, we'll just make sure those rats will find his asshole tasty."

What the fuck is that supposed to mean?

"I think we need to remove that tongue as well. We'd hate for his rat-ass to snitch. He likes to talk shit with that mouth," another said.

"Just snip his tongue up in a few places and underneath the tongue. The rats will have a feast on the rest of it. You don't always have to take the whole tongue out," the original told her, laughing.

Damn! These bitches are crazy for sure.

"Put the skag in him to keep him subdued while we do what we gotta do. I should give that motherfucker a roofie since that's what he likes to give other people. And make sure you put his fresh print on that thirty-eight. At least when the police find it, the prints will match up with this loser," she instructed the others.

They are really out to destroy me. I didn't know what the hell "skag" was until I saw them cooking up heroin. *Fuck it! They're going to have to kill me.* I yelled out, hoping maybe a neighbor would hear me.

One of the girls kicked me in the mouth, while another yelled out, "Yes, baby. Fuck me! Tear this pussy up, big daddy. Fuck me, baby!" all while tying the tourniquet on my arm.

The women laughed, a needle was inserted into my arm, and I don't remember anything after that.

When I came to, I couldn't see. My eyes were burning and my head hurt big time. My thumb and forefingers were snapped from the joints but still attached. My wrists were broken. My tongue was swollen in my mouth. It was hard to breathe. The rats crawling on my legs let me know I didn't have any clothes on. I felt this super throbbing pain in my genital area. I reached down in a slow motion to try and grab hold of my Johnson. It was super swollen beyond any erection I had ever had. I only had boxers on, and my dick was sticking out of the opening. The back was also ripped open. I felt something in my ass. It turned out to be a large black dildo. I could also feel rats crawling around near my ass. I was laid on my side. I felt newspaper covering my upper body and some on my legs. I couldn't move to get up. I tried to yell out for help, but no words came from my mouth.

I heard a woman speaking over me. "Looks like you messed over the wrong people, but I see that dick of yours is still looking for some action. You give me five dollars, I'll suck it dry. Oh, I guess you like it up the ass, I see. I'll do that for you too."

I grunted and groaned. I needed this stupid crack-head bitch to get me some help and get this shit out of my ass, but all she could think about was making a dollar to get her next hit. I was hoping someone down there in the District would recognize me. Most people know I'm the man in L.A. and Oakland.

"Well you don't have to get funky with me. You probably ain't got shit anyway," was the last thing she said to me. "That motherfucker over there thinks he's too good to let me suck his dick. That's why somebody beat his ass up already and left a fat stick up in his ass," I heard her tell someone at a distance.

Moments later, I felt someone standing over me. When I grunted, I was kicked in the groin right before the foot stepped on my still overly erect dick. I tried to holler, but my swollen tongue was cutting off my air supply when I did. Then the dildo was pushed deeper inside, causing me to shit on myself.

"Eww, you na'ty mot'afucka! We don' like s'itty mot'afuckas comin' out here try'na show off. You 'eed to put tha' s'it back in ya drawls fo' you lose it," a man said, sounding as if he may have been missing many teeth. I could hear many others nearby, laughing. "You 'on't come ta Vegas try'na to sho' off. Take yo' ass where you come from." *VEGAS??? Vegas? What the fuck?!*

Why didn't Kelly just kill me? I hope she's happy now. No one will ever recognize me here. I think that was her plan. I can't believe that bitch pulled this shit off on me. That's why I said before: a bitch immune to getting her ass kicked can be a problem.

21

Eric

Tatiana and I have been going strong for the past three months now. Thanks to her, I was able to pay Shawnee off for my restaurant. Shawnee was pissed, but what could she do? Not a damn thing. She knows I am seeing someone, but she has yet to find out it's Tatiana. She figures I found "some wealthy white woman to buy a black man." I let her think what she wants.

Every now and again, Shawnee tries to give me some, but now that I have Tatiana, I don't want Shawnee anymore. Well, I did get weak one time for those nipples on Shawnee. Shawnee just knew she was getting Big Willie up in her. Wrong! I sucked those titties and went home and fucked my woman. Tatiana.

Tatiana and I aren't really living together, but I'm there just about every night. And I enjoy waking up with her in my arms, unlike I had with Shawnee.

Tatiana told me she'd understand if I slipped up and slept with Shawnee, since I was in love with her for years, but she doesn't want me to. I assured her I have no desire to sleep with Shawnee.

I really feel like Tatiana could be my Cinderella. She has no silly inhibitions or hang-ups, and she does everything to stroke my ego and make me feel like a man. Shawnee would do everything to strip my manhood.

Shawnee's going to hit the roof when she receives those court papers for joint custody of my daughter. Tatiana helped pay for that as well since she knew that was the one hold Shawnee has on me.

I took Tatiana with me to D.C. to meet the family. They all loved her. I went to Houston to meet her family as well. She said she had never taken men home to meet her family. We even received Todd's blessing, although his wife is still unaware. He understands why I want to keep things quiet for a while. However, I am letting Arnold meet her today when we get together for lunch at my restaurant. I couldn't let Sandy meet Tatiana just yet. From what I understand, there's some bad blood between Tatiana and Sandy stemming back from the old guy's funeral last year.

"Wow! You are more gorgeous than my man Eric described," Arnold said, kissing the back of Tatiana's extended hand. "No wonder you have all the women hatin' on you. You fine as hell!" he said before we all laughed.

"Glad you could make it for lunch," I told him. "I figured it's about time you met my lady, the infamous Tatiana."

"I think I had just missed you in Cancun that time at your brother's wedding. I met your other family and they didn't look anything like you," Arnold said to a blushing Tatiana.

Tatiana showed her wonderful smile, "Oh yes. I heard about that. You had just left when I arrived. Trust me, you didn't miss much."

"So how has your reception been since you've been in L.A.? I know things are not too good with you and your brother's new family. My in-laws."

"Well, no one really knows I live here now. I only stayed because of Eric. My mother is happy that I'm here. I've also been able to see my brother's children. They are so adorable. I just wish I didn't have to sneak to see them. Hopefully soon all that will change. I hear you have a beautiful little three-year-old. You have pictures?"

Arnold proudly whipped out his phone and showed Tatiana his many photos of his son, plus the photos in his wallet. "Yeah, this is my little man."

"Oh, Arnold! He is absolutely precious. You are so lucky to have him."

"Yeah, I think so," Arnold answered, grinning ear to ear. "Have you two ordered already?"

"No, we were waiting on you," I told him.

"I better hurry then, 'cause I have a meeting shortly," he said.

We summoned the server and ordered our food. As we ate, talked, and laughed, I was beaming with the pride of having Tatiana. Not only could I tell Arnold was smitten by her, but everyone else walking by would stare at her.

The staff members I had fucked before Tatiana came along weren't too thrilled with her presence, but there was nothing they could say or do about it. I took a chance having lunch at my own restaurant this time. Although I was hoping not to encounter any of the Wiggins women, I felt it was time I allowed Tatiana to openly be a part of my world. Hell, she paid for it.

Sex with Tatiana goes beyond any man's fantasy. I never get tired of being with just her. It hasn't been but three months, but she goes out of her way to make sure I am satisfied, which isn't easy. Because she puts forth so much effort to keep me satisfied, it makes me want to go the extra mile in making her happy in any way I can. Her being financially loaded is an added bonus. I don't have to take a back seat to her job, since she doesn't work anymore, and although she doesn't work, she doesn't try to smother me.

I was hoping Tatiana didn't slip up and tell Arnold that I brought Shayla around her a few times when Shawnee went out of the country. Tatiana would make an excellent mother someday. I'd be wishing Shayla belonged to Tatiana instead of Shawnee. Shawnee is a good mother, but I don't think motherhood is her priority. Shawnee has more than enough money to not have to work or run that old man's company. Yet, Shawnee is so hell bent on staying away from the illusion of a family with me, she leaves town every chance she gets, leaving her own daughter.

A lot has been going on, but everyone's trying to be tight-lipped. However, Todd tells his mother everything and his mother tells Tatiana. I was sick when I learned Kevin has been having an affair with Charise on the regular.

I told Arnold long ago to lose that ho.

What's worse is, Todd's having an affair with Elaine. They had the nerve to go to Cancun together to celebrate their anniversaries back in February, and try to play like all was great.

Somehow Kelly went to work for Kevin as his secretary until he can find a replacement. Not sure about that whole story or how that came about, but supposedly Kelly's presence is making it difficult for him to hook up with Charise on a regular, and it's pissing him off. I'm just wondering where Sean's grimy ass is at. He wasn't letting Kelly out of his sight, and now she's working for Kevin? Interesting.

One thing I don't like about Tatiana's mom, although I'm grateful she encouraged Tatiana to pursue me, is she encourages Todd to be with Elaine since that makes him happy. She claims Todd and Elaine are in love with each other and should be together although others will be hurt by it. So, I'm thinking, if I married her daughter, and her daughter wanted to hook up with Arnold or Kevin, she'd think that shit was all right?

Damn, at least when I stepped away from Shawnee, I didn't get involved with her sisters. Yes, it's the one person she hates more than anyone, but it certainly wasn't intentional on my part. And yes, I was previously with both Elaine and Sandy, but I didn't know at the time they were sisters.

I don't want to see Shawnee tonight as she provides me all the rules for keeping my daughter while she goes to New York for two days. The girl is a year old already. What does she have to orient me on? I think orientation is just her cheap attempt to seduce me. Now that I haven't been touching her or showing any interest, she suddenly wants me. Typical woman.

"Hey, where's Shay-Shay?" I asked when I entered the house to see Shawnee wearing an outfit that made it clear she wanted some of Big Willie.

The short white tee-shirt she had on covered less than a bra would, but she was not wearing a bra. Her breast peeped from the bottom of the shirt, but her nipples were visible through the fabric. She showed off her tight abs she's been working on, and she had on some gray shorts that were fitting like a thong. I ain't gonna lie; the sight was a turn-on.

"Oh, I didn't know you were going to be here so early. Shayla is napping and I was trying to get my workout in."

She may have been telling the truth about the workout because I could see the sweat on her body and face, as well as the wetness on her outfit. I was just wondering why she wouldn't have on a bra while working out. I also didn't understand why she would be working out in the den rather than her gym downstairs. However, that bullshit about my being early—I was there at the exact time I told her I would be.

"You can go wake her up if you want. She's been asleep for twenty minutes already," Shawnee added, trying to make me aware of the amount of time potentially available to fuck her.

"Well, I really hate to wake her, when she hasn't been sleeping too long. That girl gets funky when you mess with her nap." I chuckled.

"Suit yourself." She tried to play nonchalant, because she knows I don't like disturbing my daughter's naps. I wondered why she was napping so late. I don't dare ask, though, because Shawnee would think I was challenging her parental abilities. She does it whenever I ask the slightest question, which she won't ever answer or "justify" as she puts it.

Shawnee laid on her floor mat to do sit-ups or crunches. It just so happened that I had a clear view between her legs. The shorts covered nothing. Then, as I expected, her boobs came from under the shirt when she raised her arms to put her hands behind her neck. When she raised her upper body, she wouldn't look at me, but both of her tits and her twat were looking me dead in my face. My dick was getting hard. She knew what she was doing. I couldn't even get up to move from the view, so I played like I was really reading the magazine I was holding. I tried thinking about Tatiana to keep me faithful. Instead, thoughts of Tatiana made my dick harder. I thought about how that old guy must have felt having both pussies to fuck at will.

While my mind was racing on how to get my erection down, Shawnee got up from the floor, walked to the large sofa I was sitting back on, took my magazine away, straddled me on the sofa, and put one of those scrumptious tits in my mouth. While I was sucking, she guided my fingers inside her pussy. I finger fucked her and sucked those nipples like a man just released from doing a twenty-five-year bid. I was so into it and it felt good when Shawnee freed Big Willie from my pants. She was grinding on Willie while my fingers were still inside of her, but then my phone rang. I was ignoring it, but then there was a second call.

I was hoping it wasn't Tatiana calling because she knew I was going to be at Shawnee's house. Nonetheless, my erection went away and Shawnee started bitching.

"Why didn't you answer your phone? You need to let your insecure bitch know that she doesn't need to be calling you while you're spending time with your daughter. I'm not going to tolerate your bitches calling you every five minutes when you're with your daughter because they're all insecure and shit."

I looked at her in disbelief. Technically, I wasn't spending time with my daughter; I was about to fuck her mother, I wanted to say. I can't wait for the delivery of those court papers. Shawnee walked off upstairs still loudly bitching about something or another.

I quickly peeped at my phone to see who called. It was Michelle. I wanted to call her back because I figured it had something to do with the restaurant. Michelle never calls me otherwise. I was scared for Michelle to hear Shawnee bitching in my background and get word back to Tatiana.

I wanted to just tell Shawnee that the call came from Michelle at my restaurant, but Shawnee might think it is okay to finish what we started. Also, I didn't really have any way of knowing if Michelle's conversation was going to be strictly business.

I decided to wait until after I spent time with my daughter to call Michelle back. Good thing!

"Eric, this is getting very difficult for me. How do you expect me to just forget about how good you made me feel? I can't get what you have from another man. I need you, Eric. Please, I promise I won't interfere with your relationship. I just need you. I won't get greedy. I'll take whatever you're willing to give me."

I was shocked by her desperation. "Michelle, I really can't do that. I'm sorry, but that part of us is done. It's been months. I don't want to hurt you, but I am really serious about this lady in my life."

"But I promise I won't cause any problems. I have never said anything to Karen or Ariana—because everyone knows you fucked them. Eric, please," she pled, sounding as though she was crying.

"Michelle, I have to go now. I'll see you tomorrow," I said, pulling up in front of Tatiana's new house, and my second home.

"Will you at least think about it?" she asked, still pleading. "Gotta go now." I ended the call.

I felt like I was coming home from war. I had to fight off Shawnee and Michelle. I almost lost the first battle.

When I got inside, my woman was looking fine as ever with dinner, a candlelit bath, hot oil massage, and it was all topped off with some good, good loving.

22

Arnold

Charise has been so moody since Kelly came back on the scene. I don't know what it is that drove a wedge between the two of them. I thought Kelly was the main one she was always the closest to of all of her sisters. I also don't understand why she would have a problem with Kelly filling in for Kevin until he gets a new secretary.

Personally, I'm glad Kelly finally got away from that crazy dude. I'm surprised he just up and left his sons and company. I heard they tracked his car to Las Vegas but don't know where he is. They think it may have something to do with his friend's murder. The news said the friend's house was ransacked and Sean's prints were on the safe as well as other ransacked areas. They found the guy's blood and a bullet in the guy's house, but then found the gun and the guy's blood in Sean's truck. No body was found. No one knows if Sean is dead or alive, but they suspect Sean dumped the body in the desert somewhere, and is lying low somewhere in the state of Nevada.

I would think Charise would be a bit more supportive of everything Kelly is dealing with. She's planning on moving back to D.C. and taking her instant children with her as soon as she gets a clearance from the courts. Charise said the sooner she goes, the better for us all.

Whatever it is bothering my wife, I wish would go away because it's interfering with our sex life. She's hardly in the mood anymore. I tried meeting Kelly for lunch one day to see what all I could learn from her. She was still very emotional and tight-lipped. That was a waste of time.

Charise couldn't have picked a worse time to start cutting back on the cookies. Samantha called to let me know she went on and took the position with the law firm in L.A. She said that she'll be patiently waiting when I'm ready. I did go by her new office just to check it out, and there were plenty of brothers in there. It looked like it would be a woman's paradise in there. As I sized them up, I felt jealous at the thought of one of them with my Sam, but I can't keep leading her on. I have a wife, and I have to let Sam live her life.

Sandy and I barely speak now since things have been going well in my marriage. I miss our friendship. I really wanted to be able to talk with her about Sam's return, but I already know where Sandy stands on the subject. Now that my marriage is experiencing some turbulence, I don't want to turn to Sandy. I also don't want Sandy asking me about Eric and his new girlfriend.

I can't understand why Eric would hook up with the woman, knowing the character she's shown when she and Shawnee were involved with the same man. Not only that, he knows how Shawnee detests the woman, along with her sisters. On the other hand, she is fine as all outdoors. Everybody in the restaurant was checking her out. A lot of times you see fine women, but they are either lacking boobs or ass or something might be wrong with their body. There was nothing wrong or lacking with Tatiana. I know Eric's big self is tearing that ass up all day, every day. I would be too. I guess I can't knock him really. He's doing what any man would do if given the opportunity.

"Thanks for meeting me, Arnold," Kelly said when I rode out to her crib in Santa Monica. She looked stressed and held her temples as if she had a headache.

Her place was really nice. I don't know why I expected her to be living slum-like. I was the first to see her place since she got it. Sean wasn't having anyone in his home—not even family. I was surprised to get her invitation, particularly after such a difficult lunch last month. Maybe she just needed some time before she was able to talk about her ordeal. Maybe she got some new news about her husband or the courts about the children. Maybe she just wanted to use me to contact Sam to get information to help her legally, I speculated.

"No problem. I was surprised to get a call from you," I replied. "So how have you been holding up with everything? You get any new info on Sean?"

"No, and I'm not looking for any," she answered bitterly. "That's part of the reason I had you come here. There's something you need to see. Someone sent me this and it involves you just as it involves me."

Now I'm sitting here wondering what the hell Kelly and I would have in common.

"Has Charise seen it?"

"Actually, she has. She didn't think much of it. She really doesn't have much regard for anything."

"She hasn't mentioned anything to me." I was both curious and annoyed that Charise knew of something that affected me, but never mentioned it.

"I have sat on this for some time, debating whether or not I wanted to say anything to you. But then thought about how I felt about being kept in the dark and whether or not I would want to know the truth," she said.

I could feel my air supply cutting off. *Please don't let her be talking about my wife with her husband.* What else could Kelly and I have in common, that Charise wouldn't mention to me?

"Kelly, I'm not sure I want to see this." I started bailing out.

Kelly grabbed my arm to keep me from leaving. "I didn't want to either. Not sure who said it, but the truth shall set you free," Kelly answered stoically.

She hit the play button on her DVD player. There was my butt naked wife on Kelly's seventy-inch screen television, fucking Sean. I didn't want to watch this. I was about to get up and leave, but Kelly stopped me again.

"You need to come to grips about who you are involved with: Your wife, my sister, with my husband. Stop running from the truth, Arnold. Sandy told me she tried to tell you in the past that Charise has been cheating on you, but you didn't want to hear or accept it. Now you can see it with your own eyes. That's my husband's office there," she said, pointing to the television. "That's my husband, Arnold, with your so-called wife, and apparently, she's been fucking Sean's friend and business partner as well. If you keep listening, you can hear her say, 'I like having both of your dicks inside of me at the same time,' but he declined. Now if that isn't one stank ho, then I don't know what is. Do you see the date on the video, Arnold?"

Kelly stood up to point at the date and time stamp on the bottom of the screen. It was a time while we were clearly married, and a time I wasn't even getting any.

Kelly continued to torture me. "Sandy said she tried to warn you long before you were even having sex with the nasty tramp. I know she can't stand me working for Kevin now, because I know she has designs on his ass also. I tried to warn him to stay away from the tramp before she wrecks his marriage. I don't understand why she has to call Kevin every day about her magazine or visit him. He has plenty of businesses that he's involved with, but they don't call him every day.

"When I questioned her, her smug ass told me not to be mad at her because I didn't know how to take care of my man. Every time she goes to see Kevin, she always wants the door closed, and then wants to come out trying to pretend she just finished fucking him. He'll tell her to stop behaving that way with me, and she'll just laugh. I have asked him why he indulges her visits, and he says it's because she doesn't have any real friends. Every day that she comes to his office, she tells him that he needs to fire me. He acts like he's scared to say anything that will hurt her feelings, which makes me wonder if she has something on him."

Kelly sighed and resumed holding her head.

"I think the girl has some mental defect that causes her to go after all of her sister's men or whatever is forbidden. I'm sure there are others that she is fucking, because Charise is not capable of being with only one man at a time. I know you want to preserve your family, Arnold, but the truth is, you're living a lie, just like I was. My husband was fucking everything under the sun and would tell me it was because I did something wrong. But I'm done living lies, and you need to be done also. I want you to just take your son and boot that bitch to the curb once and for all. She's evil. Pure evil. And just to give you an idea of how evil, she named your son after one of her ex- boyfriends. It was the only decent relationship she had ever had in her life, but, as always, she cheated on him also. Three times."

Kelly was practically yelling at me as I slipped deeper and deeper into a catatonic state. I felt my whole world coming apart, and she wasn't pulling back any punches. It was like she was mad at me. I couldn't breathe anymore. I could hear Kelly calling my name, but my mouth wasn't responding. When I came to, the paramedics were there working on me, trying to bring me back to my ugly reality. I was disheartened with Kelly when I saw she didn't have the decency to turn the television off. The paramedic extras were standing around totally engrossed in my wife's amateur porno flick.

My head was pounding and I still couldn't bring myself to speak, so the decision was made for me that I was going to the hospital. Kelly was crying as if I were her husband. Maybe she was feeling guilt for having brought this condition about, by exposing my wife in the manner as she did.

I was in the hospital for four days. During that time, Shawnee, Elaine, Sandy, Harmony, Kelly, Eric, and Todd, along with my own family, came to visit me. Even Tatiana snuck up for a visit when the others were not around.

Now, of course, by this time I was wondering where my wife was at. Eventually I began wondering why Kevin also never came. I thought we were supposed to be cool. I kept Kelly's words in the back of my mind about

Charise's designs on Kevin. Perhaps Charise viewed Kelly as some sort of intrusion between her and Kevin. Could they be involved? Would he, of all people do that to me? I dismissed that thought. He's probably just busy with work as Elaine stated.

It did my heart good when Samantha came to see me. Even her mother flew in to see me (well partially because it was Mother's Day weekend). I felt bad about how I treated Sam and felt I didn't deserve her love. She cried as if I were given a death sentence when she came to the hospital.

The bottom line on my diagnosis was shock. I went into shock. I never knew that was a real condition that could happen to people, most of all myself. I don't know why anything Charise does would shock me.

They had me evaluated by a psychiatrist in the hospital and got me on some antidepressants. I guess they're worried about me killing Charise. The bitch wouldn't even let Sandy bring my son to see me in the hospital. When Charise was hospitalized for her rape, I wasn't with her anymore. On top of that, she lost her parental rights to our son, and I still brought him to see her because I thought it would help with her healing process. I feel like one of the slaves who was freed from Egypt, and then begged to go back into their life of bondage. I was free and clear of Charise. I had a good life and a good woman by my side. I was there for my son, but I traded it all in to go back into a life of hell for me and my shorty.

Right now, all I can think about is getting my son away from her ass. I thought about taking him and leaving, but that bitch is the one who's getting out. I even thought about killing her. The psychiatry people at the hospital keep asking me if I am having thoughts of hurting myself or anyone. I'm sure they mean Charise.

If I knew for sure Kevin was boning my wife, he might be second. Sean would be at the top of my list if I knew where his ass was. Nah, I think Kevin would have to be at the top because that motherfucker is the one who's been cheesing and grinning, acting like we were family. I foolishly answered "yes" the first time the doctor asked me. I ran off at the mouth about how I was going to kill that slutty bitch and anyone else who I find out is fucking her. They immediately started me on some new medication when I said that.

The medication hasn't taken away my thoughts, but I don't feel like I could do anything if I wanted to. Now I just feel like a killer trapped in a paraplegic body. They weren't going to let me out of the hospital until they were convinced no one was in any danger of me retaliating.

My mother wasn't helping matters because she kept saying to me in front of the staff, "You better beat that bitch's ass when you get out of here."

I think her talking shit made them increase my medication dosage.

Eric and Sandy took me to my house. They didn't want me to get there and kill Charise. When we pulled up, Charise's car was there. I was hoping she would have had sense enough to be gone from my house. My mother had already picked the baby up before I got there because she didn't know what was going to happen once I made it home. Charise tried to give her a hard way to go when picking him up. My moms don't be playing. She doesn't like Charise. Charise handed my son over.

These antidepressants ain't no joke. I feel so subdued. I feel like a bunch of people are physically holding me back, but my mind is trying to push forth and kick her ass. I don't think I could knock her ass out if I wanted to. She could probably knock me out right now.

"Why are they here?" she had the nerve to ask when we entered the house. "You and I need to talk. We don't need a bunch of visitors."

"Girl, you have bumped your head," Sandy told her. "You are the visitor, and we only came to safely remove your ass out of the house. Hell, they're worried about Arnold killing your ass, but don't think my memory is so short that I don't remember you fucking with my husband also. We figured you'd have sense enough to be gone. Didn't they serve you with a stay away order or something? Why are you here?"

"Fuck you, Sandy. It ain't my fault you didn't know how to satisfy your man, and he had to come looking for someone who could."

Sandy almost leaped across the sofa at Charise, but Eric was able to grab hold of her.

"Let me go, Eric," she yelled.

"Nah. Sandy. That ho ain't even worth it," Eric said, struggling to hold her.

Charise stood with her arms folded, smug as hell. Little did she know she also had to worry about me leaping at her ass. Well my mind wanted to, but my body wouldn't cooperate. All I could do was sit on the sofa.

I took out my cell phone and called the police. I wanted to do damage control before Sandy ended up in jail. I would kind of love to see Sandy beat Charise down for once and for all, if not for herself, but for me, since I can't do it myself right now.

"And Eric, Mandingo, or whatever your name is," she said, targeting Eric for no reason, "Was that Tatiana you've been flaunting all over town? The same Tatiana who tried to take my sister's husband away? You know my sister—your baby's momma?"

Sandy stopped struggling to get free from Eric's hold. The shocked look on her face made it clear that the news didn't sit well with her. Charise smirked. The change of Eric's dark chocolate skin tone made it impossible for him to lie or deny. Charise is evil. How could I have not known that before?

"Eric, tell me this bitch is lying," Sandy said, showing a mixture of emotions.

Eric just stuttered, "What . . . I . . . Why . . . Sandy…"

"Oh no, Eric. You didn't go there! Why? You know that girl is bad news."

"Look, I just came here to keep my boy from killing this bitch," Eric finally spoke up. "I didn't come for any stupid shit, but yeah, I am with Tatiana. The same Tatiana. There, now it's out in the open. If Shawnee wanted to be with me like I wanted to be with her, there wouldn't be any Tatiana." He zoned in on Charise. "Now how does who I am with have anything to do with you fucking three of your sisters' husbands? You trick bitch!" he spat.

Three? Where did he get three from? Maybe he meant to say two but said three by mistake in his anger.

"And all three of them couldn't get enough of this pussy," she said, pointing to her genitals. "Maybe if you knew how to fuck my sister right, she would have wanted your ass."

She also said three. Who is the third? It could only be Todd or Kevin. Kevin. It's gotta be Kevin.

"So how long have you been fucking Kevin, Charise?" I asked, slurring as I spoke.

"You sound like a fucking retard. You need to save your breath. What's it to you anyway? If you knew how to handle this," again pointing to her genitals, "I wouldn't have to fuck anyone else. Hell, the only reason you got some pussy was because I had to fuck you and pretend you were one of the others when I couldn't be with them."

My body was jumping up to attack this woman—in my mind.

Sandy took a seat next to me on the sofa. She was overwhelmed with emotions. She took my hands into hers. She was shaking her head as if that would make the words go away. It also occurred to me that Eric had to have knowledge of Charise and Kevin's involvement.

"Eric, how long did you know about this?" I asked. "I just found out not too long ago," he confessed.

"I am so sorry, Arnold," Sandy said with a slow stream of tears falling. "I don't know why my sister has to do this." Then she turned her attention to Charise. "Charise, why did you have to do that to Elaine? She did everything to help you get your life together. She even paid to have your messed-up face repaired after it was all fucked up. Why did you have to sleep with her husband? Forget about my husband and Sean. They were both dogs and assholes, but Kevin?"

"Because he wanted this pussy and I wanted him to have it!" she said as ugly as she could. "Elaine's a prostitute anyway. What's it to her? Her marriage was doomed from the start. No need for Kevin to have to suffer."

Damn this medication!

I felt my body trying to jump up from the sofa still. And still I was unable to. I don't know what kind of drugs they gave me, but they were surely saving Charise's life right now. I don't think Eric would have stopped me from killing her at this point. Neither would Sandy.

Charise continued bragging. "But you know what I really wish I could have? I want Lewis for breakfast, Sean for lunch, and Kevin for dinner, or all three at once. I could have one dick in the mouth, one in my pussy and one in my ass. I would have Eric for dessert, but obviously he ain't man enough for either you or Shawnee. I don't have a hole available for him anyhow."

"You nasty bitch!" Eric said in response, laughing in disgust.

"Don't get mad. Maybe I could let you suck on these double-D's. Or maybe you could be good for something," she said, fondling her breasts while laughing and making facial expressions as if she were having an orgasm. "I know you be thinking about how this pussy would feel on your dick just like all the rest of them." Charise pulled up her tee-shirt and slid her bra down. "Look at these beauties, Eric. Tell me you won't be fantasizing about them tonight while you are fucking your bitch." She pulled her shirt back down and kept laughing.

Eric just shook his head.

This woman is a true nut. What the hell did I marry? I was wondering what happened to those police I called. I didn't know how much more shit Charise was going to talk before someone jumped on her.

Just as I thought it, they knocked at the door. They told me without a restraining order or Charise actually doing something, they couldn't make her leave the home, but they advised Charise to leave after we explained the situation and the words she had shared just moments prior to their arrival. They knew all three of us were ready to hurt her.

"I think I'll go check into a hotel tonight and call my man to come join me. We've been enjoying our time together while you were in the hospital these past few days," Charise said in response to the police's request of her to voluntarily leave the home. "I wouldn't get any good dick staying here tonight anyhow."

I couldn't help but wonder what she did with my son while she was taking up with Kevin, since she didn't let Sandy take him. Knowing her nasty ass, she probably was screwing right in front of him, just like she did a couple of years back when we were in Houston.

There weren't any words between Sandy, Eric, and me at first. I didn't know how to deal with Eric's knowledge of Charise and Kevin, while Sandy was having a hard time dealing with the Tatiana and Eric situation. I'm sure Eric was thinking I told Charise about Tatiana, but I really wouldn't do something like that.

I did ask after Charise left with the police, "Is Elaine aware of Kevin and Charise?"

Sandy answered, "Apparently not. What I never told you that day last fall when we had lunch was, Charise tried to seduce Kevin after the Fourth of July cookout, but Kevin told Elaine. I'm just shocked to learn that things went further than that. I wish you would have left her long ago. Now they have you all drugged up behind her mess. I have to tell Elaine about Kevin. I liked his ass. I can't believe he went there."

"So you could have saved me a whole lot of grief a long time ago, and Kevin—fucking Kevin—was my boy and didn't say shit to me about my wife coming on to his ass?"

Sandy sat silently as she shook her head and covered her mouth.

Eric spoke next. "Sandy, I know you're upset about the whole idea of my being with Tatiana. I had every intention on telling you first. I just wanted to deal with the joint custody issue first because I didn't want my relationship to play any part in the proceedings."

"But why, Eric? I know Shawnee acts like a damn fool, and you had every right to be with someone, but Tatiana? I just don't get that. Was that a way to get back at my sister? This will crush her. You do know that, right? Hell, I'm crushed by the news. What's worse is Charise is armed with the info. How her little ass gets her information is beyond me. You're gonna have to come clean before Charise gets word to Shawnee somehow. Thankfully you weren't fucking Charise too. I guess you and Todd are the only other decent ones besides Arnold."

Eric's eyes looked away with guilt.

"Eric, you've been fucking my wife also? I thought it was just the three?" I asked.

Eric looked ultimately offended. "Oh, hell no! I wish I would touch that walking disease."

"Todd?" Sandy asked just as concerned as I.

"Please don't make me do this. It's not what you think," Eric said, half defeated.

"Come with it now!" Sandy demanded.

Eric sat down then put his face in his hands. Then he took deep breaths before covering his face again. "Don't do this. Todd is not messing with Charise." His words were muffled and barely audible.

"Then who?" Sandy asked. "Who is Todd—" she stopped mid-sentence as though she figured out her own answer. "But how? Why? Why would Elaine do something like that? I can't believe her ass. She fucked you knowing you used to be my boyfriend. What the fuck is wrong with my nutty fucking family? Why must everybody be fucking everybody else's man?" Sandy said, getting louder by the minute and again becoming emotional. "You know what? The more I think about it, I hope you're happy with Tatiana, 'cause Shawnee's ass don't deserve you anyway. That bitch had no problem fucking you and kept fucking you when she knew I had a problem with it and Harmony told her to stop it," Sandy said to Eric. "Shawnee deserves this good kick in the ass. I take it, it was Tatiana that helped you buy your restaurant from Shawnee?" She laughed. "That shit pissed her off. Serves her right. She's been wanting to know how you got from under her control. And then she was glad she had Shayla to control you with. Don't worry about any backlash from Shawnee concerning Tatiana and getting joint custody. I'll do whatever I can to help you, because I am about sick of all these nasty bitches. And tell Tatiana I apologize for my role in attacking her last year at the funeral. She probably did have genuine feelings for that man, unlike my sister who was out making a baby with you and fucking God knows who else. Better yet, I hope you get full custody, just so you don't have to deal with any of Shawnee's shit, ever."

Sandy was on a roll. She was no longer teary-eyed, but full of rage. She was scaring me.

"And I guess Charise must have known something when she said Elaine was back prostituting. First, she was prostituting with Shawnee's first husband, and now Harmony's husband. Now I guess it's my job to tell Harmony. The bastards! Didn't they all go away together to Cancun a few months back? I wonder who was fucking who. Elaine was probably there fucking both Kevin and Todd, while poor, unsuspecting Harmony was somewhere clueless. Now that I really think about it, Elaine's always been out of town the same times when Todd is gone to Houston. No wonder Kevin was able to fuck Charise."

Sandy was pacing back and forth. Me and Eric couldn't get a word in whatsoever. "Arnold, are you going to be all right? I have to get home to my own kids. Hell, I need to pack my family up and head back to Maryland away from these bitches. Here I thought it was going to be nice having my family all together again. Wasn't I a damn fool? And so was Harmony. She brought her husband into this shit."

Sandy sat down as a thought came upon her. "Oh my God! Those poor precious babies. What's this going to do to those kids?"

"I guess you should be asking that for all of our kids, including your own," I finally was able to interject.

"Wow! You are so right," she said, and Eric nodded in agreement.

After Sandy and Eric left, I thought about calling Samantha over, but then I decided I just wanted to be alone. I slept that medication off, and the next day I was up, out, and able to get a restraining order against Charise, since I was hospitalized as a result of her actions. I also got to retain custody of my son, who carries another man's name. I went and filed for an immediate divorce. Actually, I filed for an annulment.

I decided to stay away from Kevin, since I figured he was about to get his soon enough. I also decided I would not get back with Samantha, because that's obviously not where my heart is at. Hopefully when she gets over the fact that we're not going to be together anymore, we can have a good friendship like Eric has with Sandy.

For now, I am just going to focus on my career and my little man. Thanks to Charise, I learned how to be abstinent. I still can't believe that bitch had me celibate for a whole damn year, while she was out fucking everyone else. Well, she didn't know about that time with Samantha, but nonetheless, she had me sexless. Let her be some other nigga's problem. She won't be mines anymore.

23

Todd

I don't know what the hell I am going to do. It was like some conspiracy with both Cynnyyah and Roxana deciding to wait until they were five and six months pregnant to tell me. Roxana said she was planning on telling me when I came to town, but I had been so busy avoiding her since I had been seeing Elaine on a regular. I don't know how I didn't pick up on Cynnyyah being pregnant. She's been carrying small and neat. Now Cynnyyah, I did sneak and fuck twice while I've been seeing Elaine. I just couldn't help myself. Her booty was getting bigger along with her tits. Perhaps that should have been my clue.

I don't know who I'm more worried about finding out: Harmony or Elaine. I can tell Harmony knows I'm having an affair, but she just doesn't know the "who." It's almost as if she doesn't care what I do or when I'm gone away anymore. I took her and my mom out for Mother's Day and that was the extent of that. No loving or anything else. Why would I?

Elaine and I have become more of a couple than either one of us are with our spouses. The Cancun trip was difficult because I didn't like seeing her with Kevin. We didn't get a free moment to steal away. I watched his hands as they were all over her body. Needless to say, I was miserable as hell.

Elaine is ready to leave Kevin to be with me only, but she doesn't want to hurt Harmony or the kids. She told me she loves me. Lord knows I probably love her more than I do my own wife. She said she doesn't love Kevin. She thought she did by his attentiveness when they first met, but then him making them hold out for sex made her more pressed to get married, although she didn't realize it back then.

Elaine also told me she suspects something going on between Kevin and Charise, because they have far too much unnecessary communication despite Charise making a pass at him a while back. Elaine didn't appreciate having to cover Kevin's absence when he didn't go see Arnold in the hospital—while Charise was also missing. She understood Charise not going to the hospital, but why not Kevin since we were all friends. You don't know how bad I just wanted to confirm her instincts.

Every chance I get, I sneak away with Elaine somewhere. Each time I've recently gone to Houston, she went with me. She'd stay at the hotel spa while I would visit my sons. She hangs out with me openly when I'm with my brothers (without their wives, of course). I feel like the luckiest guy in the world when she's with me. Even my brothers wish they had her.

Her love making skills are so great. I want to brag to anyone willing to listen. As I expected, we are totally compatible sexually. She has a high sex drive that goes perfectly with mine. Sometimes I think if I just leave Harmony to be with Elaine, Harmony would have no choice but to accept it. I mean, after all, Elaine is who I love, am in love with, and always have loved from day one. She's not just a piece of ass like Charise.

Charise is just a piece of ass to all the men she's with. Kevin couldn't possibly love Charise. He just loves the forbidden thrill of it all.

I wanted to fire Valerie the day she let me know she caught on to me and Elaine. That silly broad had the nerve to blackmail me to "tighten her up." I really didn't want to fuck her, but felt I had no choice. I ended up confessing it to Elaine. Thankfully she understood my predicament. She decided not to visit my office during Valerie's hours anymore, hoping that would make Valerie less aware.

I just want to come clean with Harmony and stop playing this charade and sneaking to be with Elaine. Instead, now I have to worry about losing Elaine because of Cynnyyah and Roxana. I don't think the news of the babies will sit well with her.

"Dr. Palmer, there's a Miss Wiggins here to see you. Clearly related to your wife," one of the secretaries called to me.

Who would that be? Elaine? Maybe she's going back to her maiden name. No, they've seen her many times. Could it be Shawnee? But why?

"Send her in," I tell her.

In walked an angry looking Sandy. She didn't look pleasant at all. I attempted to greet her with a hug, but she dismissed me as she closed my office door and took a seat without an invitation. Then she gestured for me to take my seat.

"Todd, I am going to just cut to the chase. Why the fuck are you sleeping with Elaine? Cheating on Harmony is one thing, but with Elaine? You couldn't find another bitch to put your pecker in?"

I was shocked. *How did she find out? Who told her?* I didn't know how to answer her.

"I sat on this for a few days as I decided the best road to take with this. I don't want Harmony to find out, so I'm simply going to suggest you work on your marriage and stay the hell away from Elaine. Now I could have told Kevin that you are fucking Elaine, just as I could have told Elaine that Charise is fucking Kevin, but Harmony would be the only one really hurt, and the only one who doesn't deserve to be hurt. The rest of you nasty asses deserve everything you got coming to your selfish asses."

"Sandy, I love Elaine. Always have from the first day I met her. I am ready to walk away from my marriage to be with her, and I hope she'll walk away from hers as well. We love each other and we belong together. While that's not what you want to hear, it's the truth."

Sandy was obviously taken aback by my unexpected admission. Hell, I couldn't believe I just said it. The truth was out. I was only one hurdle away from having the woman that I love. Well, the new babies make two hurdles.

"I can't believe you, you selfish motherfucker. If you loved her from day one, how'd you marry Harmony?" she said, sounding like a scene from the Exorcist. I'm bigger than her, but that shit was scaring my cornered ass.

"I-I-I know how this may seem to you," I stuttered, "but I didn't really know how I felt until Elaine came to Cancun for the wedding. I actually felt my heart doing flip-flops when I was around her. I could smell her scent long after she'd be gone from a room. I know you'll never accept it or understand it, but we are in love. As for Kevin, he's free to have Charise to his heart's desire. I care for Harmony, and hate that I'm hurting her, but I'd be hurting her more by staying and not loving her than if I were to leave."

"But you were happy being with Harmony the whole time you were in Houston. As soon as you have access to Elaine, you can't keep your dick in your pants? How long, exactly, has this affair been going on between the two of you? Did you move here to L.A. to be with Harmony and your children or for Elaine? Why did Elaine marry another man if she was so in love with you?" Sandy asked.

"She married another man because she felt she couldn't pursue her feelings for me due to my marriage. We're tired of being bound to ungratifying marriages. Long story short, I am not staying with Harmony, and if you feel the need to be the one to tell her, then you'd be making my life that much easier."

Sandy stood up and looked at me like she was about to kick my ass. "Oh, so you think I'm supposed to do you a fucking favor now? Oh no, bitch! You got the wrong one now!" she shouted. She opened the door and then yelled, "You nasty, sister-fucking ho!" and left my office.

I will say I was a bit embarrassed, but at least I was a hair closer to being with my Elaine forever.

I thought for certain Sandy would have made it to Harmony before I arrived home. There was no apparent change in behavior. I didn't know whether to get comfortable in my home or if should I start packing to leave. As always, when I don't know what to do, I go ask Momma.

"What am I supposed to do? I don't want to wait for Harmony to find out and probably try to kill me, but I don't want to just walk out on my children."

"Toddy, you knew this day would come sooner or later. I know you love that girl, but is she worth losing your kids again? You missed out on a lot of your first two kids' lives because your first wife couldn't get over your infidelity. I think you need to walk away from both of these women if you know your marriage is over. You can't go on like this, and those children are going to be the ones to suffer. Your wife is not going to accept you leaving her for her sister. I wouldn't let my children anywhere near either of you if I were Harmony."

"But Momma, Elaine is going to leave her husband so we can be together. She told me today that she's leaving him," I pleaded for my mother's validation to my infidelity.

"I understand what you are saying. You both are in love, but what's going to happen to your children, Toddy? They're not even two years old. What if your wife has a mental breakdown when she finds out you've been with her sister? Do you think she'll be able to handle raising your children in that state? Do you think your wife's sister wants the responsibility of raising your three babies? These are her nieces and nephew. I doubt it. I want you to be happy, but right now, I have to speak up for these babies. What's going to happen to your kids once I go back home to Houston? I can't stay here forever, and I certainly couldn't see myself moving in with you and that other girl. You wanted your wife to hurry back to work, so now she's back. I think you should just ask Harmony to forgive you and stay together for those children."

"Momma, are you kidding? Stay with my wife? I thought you said I should be with Elaine because she makes me happy? My wife doesn't make me happy and I'm sure she's not too happy to be with me right now. I'm sure the only reason she hasn't left yet is because of the kids."

"That's my point exactly. She's putting her children before herself. She should have left your butt long ago, but she stayed for her children. On top of that, she's still a good wife to you. She still makes sure your needs are taken care of when you get home, no matter what the hour. And not one time does she have you coming home to a contentious household. Don't think she's not aware of you cheating on her. She just doesn't know who. Still, she puts it aside for her children's sake like I had to do for my children.'"

"For your children? What is that supposed to mean?" I asked, annoyed.

"Oh Todd, don't act like you don't know your father was the biggest whore in all of Texas. I figure that's where you get it from. Despite it, all these years later, we are still married. Even now, don't think I don't know his old ass has a bunch of young hussies—younger than Tatiana—but he's still my husband until the day I die.

"Because we stayed together, we have a very tight-knit family, and all of our children are successful and have successful spouses. Look at your son sitting in jail for the rest of his life. Do you think his life could have been different had you stayed in your first marriage? I don't want to encourage you or tell you to leave your wife, but I will say this—if you leave her, you don't need to take up with the sister as her replacement. That will mess the babies up. Then you'll probably have more kids and won't be a father to any of them. Thankfully, none of your siblings have children beyond their one spouse. Not only are you on your second marriage with now five kids, but you're about to throw that away for a temporary floozy who has no class or decency about her. Otherwise, she wouldn't steal her own sister's husband from his children. When I said I wanted you to be happy, I figured you just needed to satisfy your loins like your daddy did when he slept with your aunt, my sister Flo, forty-eight years ago, but I figured you would get it out of your system real fast like he did."

I was shocked by her callous words.

Not my daddy and Aunt Flo. Aunt Flo was my favorite aunt. Oh, hell no! Aunt Flo's not a skank, is she?

She continued. "This fling has been going too long, and you're throwing everything away for that temporary gratification. It's not right, Toddy. Your wife has been busting her behind to be a good wife for you. She may not have lost all the weight, but she's lost a good chunk of it to try to be more appealing to her husband. The ball is now in your court. You have to make some concessions for the sake of your family. This is your life, and I have a feeling you are going to do what you want despite what I say, so I'm just going to stop wasting my breath and go to bed now so you can make your own decisions. I'll still be your mother no matter what you decide." And she was off to her room, leaving me at the kitchen counter more confused and pissed off to figure out my life alone.

I wish I would have just come out and told her about Cynnyyah and Roxana's babies. I think she'd understand why staying is not an option. She'd smack me a couple of times, but she'd understand.

24

Kevin

What do you plan on doing about your affair with Charise?" Sandy asked, storming into my office and catching me off guard.

"Sandy? What? What are you talking about?" I asked.

"Don't play dumb with me. You're fucking Charise, while Todd is fucking your wife."

What the fuck?! Todd is fucking my wife? Is she kidding?

"What did you just say?"

"Which part do you need me to repeat—the part about you fucking Arnold's wife, or Todd fucking your wife? Kelly told me how you provided the video of Charise and Sean. Were you jealous and wanted Sean gone so you could have her all to yourself? Are you the reason Sean is missing? You had something to do with it, didn't you? Were you going to make Arnold disappear as well just to have Charise all to yourself? Or were you trying to fuck Kelly also? You do know Elaine plans on dumping you and Todd plans on dumping Harmony so they could be together. They're supposed to be so in love. Elaine confirmed it. I guess I'm doing her a favor by telling you for her, but I just want you to know that each of you deserves what you get. You nasty asses!" And then she was out the door as quick as she came.

Todd and Elaine? If his wife wasn't so big, I'd fuck her for the hell of it. That low-down motherfucker had all those other bitches. How did he end up fucking with my wife? I ought to go give him a piece of my mind.

I tried to call Elaine on her cell, but she didn't answer. *She's probably somewhere fucking Todd right now. The whore!*

I didn't know who the new guy Charise had been fucking lately was, but she'd been trying hard to avoid me. I needed to find her now, 'cause fucking her was about the only thing that'd make me feel better.

I wonder does Arnold know about Charise and me. Why hadn't he said anything if he knew? *No, I need to go kick Todd's ass. Wait a minute! Was she fucking him while we were in Cancun? Oh, no! I need some answers. No, I need some pussy.*

Pussy had been making me think better lately. Celibacy makes for poor judgment, like getting married to a hooker.

"Charise, where are you? I need to see you," I demanded when she finally answered her phone.

"Kevin, have you not heard? Everything is out. Everyone knows about us, including Arnold. I will not be seeing you anymore."

"Fuck that! I need some, and I need it now. Where are you? I'll come to you."

"I guess you didn't hear me the first time. My marriage is over. You can't threaten me anymore Kevin."

"Well I guess your business is over as well. I wonder who can I sell the business to?"

"You wouldn't."

"I'll say it again—I want some ass, and I want it now. Where are you?" There was a long silence. "Charise? Don't fuck with me! I am not in any mood right now."

"Kevin, why are you doing this to me? I don't want to be with you anymore. Be with your own wife."

"Oh, don't get all righteous on me now. You didn't give a damn about my wife that first time you came throwing your pussy in my direction," I yelled, not even paying attention to the fact that I was still in my office within earshot of my employees.

After another long pause, she said "I found a little place to stay off of Wilshire. You could meet me there in about forty-five minutes."

And forty-six minutes later, I was deep into her pussy. I was pounding her as hard as I could. I sucked and nibbled on her nipples so they'd be sore. At times, I'd choke her, and watching her struggle made my dick harder. I was angry, and Charise let me take my frustrations out on her body. She was obviously depressed and, for the moment, I didn't give a damn. She brought this on herself.

When I'm done here, I'll be bouncing Elaine's ass out of my house. I guess you really can't make a housewife out of a tramp.

"I'll call you when I'm ready to see you again. Don't make me wait so long again. Right now I have to go deal with that bitch sister of yours," I told Charise as I was getting dressed.

"I told you she was still hooking. I knew it," she answered with excitement. Charise was coming to life. It was like my words against her sister spoke life into her.

"Whatever!" I responded, not at all amused. "She's getting the fuck out of my house today. I don't know what made me think she could be trusted."

"Don't feel so bad. At least you've been getting you some good pussy the whole time," she said, now completely happy with the revelation. "Aren't you glad you didn't pass up on this?" She was caressing her own body. "Well, now you know where to find me."

I chuckled and shook my head. Charise is something. Little did she know, I didn't want her for anything but sex. She certainly would never be my woman, let alone wife. She's a bigger tramp than Elaine. At least Elaine had the good sense enough to get paid for being a whore.

I arrived home to find Elaine moving out.

What the fuck?! Oh no! She thinks she's going to just move out. No, I'm putting her ass out.

"What the fuck are you doing?" I asked her.

"Leaving. What does it look like?" she replied nonchalantly.

"How the fuck are you just going to move out and we haven't talked or anything?" I asked, getting more upset by the minute.

I didn't like the idea of her leaving me.

"There's really nothing to talk about, Kevin. The divorce papers are on the kitchen counter. I don't want shit from you but my freedom. No need for a discussion, fight, or argument."

"Oh no! No! Absolutely not! You owe me some sort of explanation. You can't just leave me without any discussion. We haven't tried to work out anything. How can you just leave without trying to fix the problems? We need to talk about this, Elaine. I am not going to let you go. We are married. You don't just give up like that."

I couldn't believe the words coming from my own mouth. I was begging Elaine to work things out. I couldn't stop myself. "Please, Elaine, don't do this. We both fucked up and made mistakes. We can work through this. Please just stop and talk to me," I said, following Elaine back and forth as she loaded her truck with her belongings.

She paused just long enough to look at me as if I were stupid then continued as she was.

"Elaine! Elaine! Please! Tell me what I have to do. Please don't leave. Yes, I fucked up. We both fucked up, but we can get past that."

"No, we can't!" she finally stopped and snapped. "Everything about you is a fucking lie. Everything about us is a lie. Here I am fucking my sister's husband because I'm supposed to be getting back at your trifling ass for not only fucking my sister, but lying to me about Yolanda."

I fell in a seat. *How did she know about Yolanda?*

"Yeah, motherfucker, have a seat, because I know all about you fucking Yolanda and her sister, causing both deaths. I should have dropped your ass to the curb the minute Mary Banks, Yolanda's sister, came to see me in my boutique months ago. And then what do you do? Fuck my sister. I should have fucked your brother instead of my sister's husband. Where was the justice in that? Better yet, I should have bounced your ass the minute you stuck your fingers in Charise's pussy last fucking July, only a month after our big wedding. And yeah, I knew about that too. Did you think that big mouth bitch was going to keep that to herself? I left the door open intentionally to see what the fuck you would do. I guess your dumb ass forgets that Charise confides everything in my brother Angelo. I also know you had the nerve to be pissed off about Charise fucking Sean. You were so busy focusing on Charise, you didn't even give a shit about me slipping away more and more. I was hoping to be gone while you were at Charise's, fucking her today. I guess you were only able to manage a quickie, huh? Yeah, I know. Charise told Angelo you were on your way and that you threatened her business. The only thing I will agree with you on is selling her business so I can get my money out.

"See, Kevin, I left you enough rope to hang your damn self. You have dug your own grave, now lie in it. Our whole marriage was a sham. I loved and respected you for your commitment to God and the church and your ability to stay celibate. Guilt? I think so, being that was right on the heels of Yolanda's death. Funny after we married, your commitment to the church seemed to diminish. You've become so ugly; you don't even bless your food before eating anymore. You've just turned into the trifling man you said you once were and now you cuss more than a damn sailor. Contrary to popular belief, I have not reverted to prostitution, and I wanted to believe you would somehow get back on track. I know how men think. I know sometimes they just need to get shit out of their systems in order to fix shit in their households. I wanted to believe that about you.

"You know, I may have been able to forgive you for sleeping with my sister, Kevin, but I can't with all of the other shit, like lying about your past, lying about your religion, your blackmailing and jealousy of my sister. Then I learned yesterday that you fucked my sister in my bed. Not one of the many other beds, but *my* bed, every chance you could get. No! Enough is enough. I have allowed myself to get caught up in your stupid shit and then take up with my only decent sister's husband, of all people. You and I are so done, Kevin. I ought to take your ass for half of everything you own, including this house since we didn't have any prenuptial agreements, but in the end, I wasn't any better than you. So for that reason alone, I'll walk away with nothing extra, and hopefully I will become a better woman as a result. You? You'll have to deal with yourself."

I stood up from the chair Elaine had me cornered in as she spoke with her hands in her back pocket. I put my arms around her waist. "Elaine, we can work through this. I want to be a better man. I don't know how I fell so far from grace. I promise I'll do whatever I need to do to fix all the damage I have caused. I understand that you need to step away from this marriage, but please don't end it. Give me the opportunity to make up and prove myself to you. As a matter of fact, you stay in the house and I'll stay elsewhere or wherever you say. I'll even buy you a new house if you want one. I'll get back into church. I'll do whatever to keep you, Elaine. I'll go to counseling. We can go together."

Elaine sat down and cried. She sobbed uncontrollably. She hit me a few times, but I grabbed hold of my wife and held her. I cried with her. Suddenly I felt so filthy-dirty. I didn't have the decency to wash Charise off of my dick, but now I'm pleading with my wife to give me another chance. I could tell Elaine was confused. I know she didn't want to go.

"Why couldn't you just tell me the truth about Yolanda? Why did you have to lie about your last relationship?" she asked. "I opened up to you about everything."

I took her asking questions as a good sign that we were going to work things out. "Elaine, I didn't lie about my last relationship. I just never mentioned Yolanda. The woman who came after Yolanda really did leave because she couldn't deal with my celibacy. Probably I was an asshole then too. She was the first person I tried to date after Yolanda's death. I caused both Yolanda and her sister's death. I did the same selfish bullshit, and Yolanda died in a car accident after she walked in on me and her sister. Her sister committed suicide as a result of her guilt. After everything I learned about Charise, I felt it was best to hold back that bit of info. I never in my life thought I would have crossed the line with Charise. I couldn't understand how Sandy's husband did, but after the day she targeted me, I got so weak and would find myself lusting all the time. That lust was the driving force to make me cross the line. After that, it was her always telling me you reverted to prostitution that kept me coming back. I will admit that my feelings got caught up in there somehow. I just became totally screwed up in the head."

Elaine wiped the remnants of her tears and asked, "Why would I believe that you can stop fucking her all of a sudden? You have resorted to blackmailing her because she no longer wants to fuck you. That's crazy. Absolutely no one on the planet has to blackmail Charise for sex," she said. "And what's worse is you're up in my face right now smelling like her pussy. Did you just finish eating her pussy or something? Tell the nasty bitch to get a douche."

I put my face down in my hands. I was disgusted with myself. What could I say? The truth was, I didn't know if I could just stop fucking Charise. I wanted to. She's like a drug.

Elaine sat looking at me as I remained silent. "You can't say, can you, Kevin? That's why we can't work this out. I can't live with always wondering if my husband wants me or my sister. I was a prostitute. I know how men pretend one woman they are fucking is another woman they want to fuck." She stood up and was back in control of herself. "I refuse to be the wife, while my husband is pretending I am the other woman—my sister. I'm going back to New York. That way I can at least leave my sister's marriage intact. I don't think our marriage is repairable. There's too much damage and too many lies, Kevin. Your life and your roots are here in California. You need to stay here. My roots are on the east coast. Angelo will run my boutique here, and I can head back to my roots. If you want Charise, you can have her to your heart's content."

I wasn't sure what else I could say. She was right and her mind seemed made up. She could have made my life so much uglier, but she chose to be the bigger person and walk away empty handed.

"Elaine, at least let me help you. You are still technically my wife. That should count for something. I don't want you to go back to New York and struggle. At least let me help you financially. I owe you at least that."

"You don't owe me anything, Kevin. It was an experience. Some good, some bad, but nothing I'll ever regret." Elaine was so stoic and I was feeling smaller and smaller. I knew she'd be too proud to take anything from me.

"Fine, I'll just put something in your account. If you need it, it'll be there for you. If not, then it'll just sit there and collect interest until you do need it."

"Is this the way to relieve your guilty conscience?" she asked.

"Maybe," I admitted. "Maybe not, but I do know I will hold on to the hope of being rejoined with my wife one day soon. I'd just hate the thought of you struggling in the meantime. I also want to know that you are doing well."

Elaine slightly smiled. "I guess I can live with that. I'll hold off on filing the divorce papers, but you're going to have to sign them now."

"You're killing me. Could I hold off on signing them?" I asked.

"I'd prefer you didn't, but, I will hold onto them. I'll see how things are going in a few months, and then I'll know for sure what to do."

I didn't want to hear that, but I accepted it. Then she was gone. My wife left me. I didn't give her the boot or anything like it, but she left me.

The next day I put three million in Elaine's bank account and signed over some shares of my stocks to her. I thought that would help alleviate some of my guilt. Unfortunately, I only made it two days before I was back between Charise's legs. I was hooked, but still I held onto the hopes of being reunited with my wife.

PART THREE

It's a Wrap

25

Eric

I can't believe all the mess that Charise causes. She breaks up all kinds of families. I have to shamefully admit, that night I left Arnold's house, I went home and fucked my woman thinking about those big juicy-ass tits Charise flashed my way. Truth be known, as pissed off as she made me that night, my dick got hard at the sight. I wanted my face smothered in her tits. I wanted to see them again. I wanted to touch them. Suck them. I even imagined her in a porno flick, fucking three different men at one time. That's one bad bitch if she can do that. After seeing her exposed tits, I understood how Kevin got sucked in when she stripped naked for him that first time. I guess it was good she didn't catch me alone when she pulled that stunt. I would have probably been up in her just the same, merely for the experience.

After that night, I have wondered why all men seem to go crazy or want her so badly. Hell, even Todd once confessed he found her body attractive and fuckable but said he couldn't or wouldn't ever touch her. I've seen plenty of big tits and nice asses plenty of times, but I don't know what it is about that girl, and now she moved Elaine out of the picture and completely has Kevin to herself. Like I said, she's bad. You have to admit; she sets her mind to shit and gets what she wants.

I often wonder how she knew about Tatiana. I figured Arnold's pussy-whipped ass had to have told her and probably told her not to tell anyone. That's the only way she would have known it was a secret. I kind of lost respect for him behind that one, but I'll check in on him every now and again.

As soon as I got my joint custody, I didn't care who knew about Tatiana. I did feel bad because Sandy and Shawnee fell out over Sandy helping me at my custody hearing. Sandy told me not to feel bad because she was pretty much done with Shawnee anyhow for many other reasons.

Shawnee went on an absolute warpath when she found out I was with Tatiana. I hate to say it, but she beat Tatiana's ass. Now Shawnee has pending legal charges. I think the whole thing was stupid, because she might lose her freedom and I'll still be with Tatiana. Tatiana wouldn't even fight back. Not that I was there at the time of the fight.

I left Tatiana at the restaurant one afternoon while I went right up the street to drop some food off to one of my favorite customers. Ironically, Shawnee picked that very moment to show up and saw Tatiana. Karen said Shawnee rolled up on Tatiana as if she knew she was there without me. She was even wearing tennis shoes instead of heels. Tatiana, on the other hand, was looking like a million dollars in a dark pink tank dress that fit her curves like a glove and matching stilettos.

Shawnee basically snuck Tatiana, I guess some shit she got from growing up in D.C. She pulled a D.C. move on my unsuspecting girl. My girl didn't stand a chance. It took four policemen to get Shawnee off of Tatiana. Karen called my phone, but I couldn't make it back fast enough. Everybody watching acted like they were afraid to help get Shawnee off of Tatiana. Shawnee practically ripped the entire dress off of Tatiana, exposing her nudity to anyone watching. Supposedly, she seemed more focused on ripping the dress off of Tatiana than anything else. She dragged Tatiana all over the ground by her hair, kicked and stomped her, cracking a rib. She also broke Tatiana's nose. Tatiana was taken to the hospital, while Shawnee was taken to jail. When I saw what Shawnee did to not only Tatiana, but my restaurant, I wanted to beat her ass myself. Instead, we decided to handle things legally to keep me from going to jail.

On a positive side, I was able to go back to family court and take my daughter from the stupid ass. Tatiana was ready to leave me because of the beating, but I had to convince her I wanted her to stay, with an engagement ring. Now we are officially and blissfully living together. I finally relinquished the Mandingo Jungle.

Sandy came and made peace with Tatiana upon my request. I was glad about that because I wanted to be able to keep my friendship with Sandy. Thankfully, Tatiana is okay with my friendship. Actually, the two of them talk like they are cool with one another. Sandy said she doesn't want her and I to have to sneak to be friends, and feel it is only respectful if she were okay with my fiancée as well.

Michelle quit working for me because she couldn't deal with my relationship and my not being with her anymore. The others don't have a problem with it. They like Tatiana and are glad that I am happy, although they can't experience the Big Willie again.

Just as I expected, Tatiana has been a wonderful mother figure to Shayla. Shayla gets happy whenever she sees Tatiana. I was glad Harmony accepted my being with Tatiana, because now Tatiana takes Shayla on play dates with Harmony and the kids.

While she is out on bail, Shawnee isn't allowed visitation until she completes anger management and parenting class. That is just for the family courts. She tried to run that crap about her being the mother, and her daughter needs her. The judge told her she didn't seem to give a damn about being a mother or about her daughter's needs when she placed herself in a situation that would give her jail time. That judge said she wished she could sentence Shawnee for her criminal case, because she would give her the maximum for being so childish and stupid at her age, over a man she can't have, who obviously doesn't want her.

Shawnee still has to deal with the criminal courts. Tatiana has no intentions of backing down from making sure Shawnee gets prosecuted. She also filed a $250,000,000 civil action against Shawnee. She went for $250,000,000 because the fight was posted on YouTube by an onlooker, showing all of Tatiana's goodies. She wasn't wearing panties either. Shawnee refuses to settle, like she thinks she's not going to have to cough up some dough. Her own attorneys are trying to get her to settle and take a plea deal on the criminal, but she seems to know more than her four attorneys.

I was able to get my restaurant damages paid immediately for her to avoid prosecution for that as well. We have all kinds of restraining orders on her. She can't come near my restaurant, our home, our church, or Tatiana's yoga class. She's not allowed to go near Shayla or the daycare center. She had to surrender her passport and can't even leave for business. They consider her a flight risk.

Tatiana and I are planning on a June wedding. She wants a big wedding. I personally don't need a big wedding with all that fluff. Just so long as I have Tatiana as my Cinderella, I'm good. It's crazy—never did I think there was a woman capable of taking my heart away from Shawnee, but here she is in Tatiana.

26

Kevin

The need to blackmail Charise is gone. She was glad to be with me, believing I kicked Elaine out to be with her. I was having nonstop sex with Charise. I was sucking on those big tits any time I wanted to. I didn't have to sneak or hide her any longer. We'd go sex toy shopping all the time to find things to keep us both excited with one another. We have sex anytime, and anyplace, and I love it.

She was all too happy to take Elaine's place in my bed on a permanent basis. I moved her into my home the same week Elaine left, so I could have my dose of pussy whenever the urge hit.

I would find all kinds of ways to keep our life together hot and spicy. I took her to my condo on Catalina Island on my yacht. I took her on a cruise to Hawaii. I'd take her shopping to buy sexy outfits for her to wear for me. I also love how all the men lust for her when she is with me, because I know I would be the only one fucking her. For whatever reason, I didn't mind Charise wearing provocative clothing, but I don't think I could have tolerated it had Elaine dressed in the same manner. I took her to a topless resort in Mexico, just because I wanted to see everyone going crazy when Charise pulled those melons out for all to see. Charise got turned on by the attention as well, because that was probably some of the best sex we had. Even the women were staring at Charise. I could just squeeze and suck her titties right out there while everyone was looking. Her thong bikini bottom left little to the imagination. All of that big booty was visible for anyone wanting to see it. It didn't take anything to move that bikini over and get my dick up inside of her on the beach. I loved eating out her pussy on our quick flights just for dinner and a show in Las Vegas on my private jet. I can always count on my dick getting sucked any time we're in my limo. I love burying my tongue in her delicious ass when we're in the shower together. Whew! I get excited just telling you about her.

Yep, life with Charise is fabulous. The thought of trading Charise in to fix my marriage became a distant thought, very quickly. It didn't take long for me to stop thinking about Elaine altogether.

For once, Charise seems genuinely happy. I love being able to do things to make her happy and keep her happy. I am glad to finally be that one capable of making this woman happy. It's like some challenge or something that I conquered. All she needed was someone who's able to give her unlimited dick and have enough money to not have to worry about going to work and depriving her of the dick that she needs.

Charise likes to be pampered, wined and dined, and I like giving her all of that, for her to give me what I need: Her body. She doesn't make any demands on me. She just allows me to be the alpha male. I call all the shots, say how things will be, where we'll go, what we'll eat, how and where we will fuck, and she is completely submissive. I love it!

Sandy was right when she said I would get what I deserved, because every man deserves to have a Charise in their bed every night or anywhere else. They just can't have my Charise. I guess if Sean is still alive, he's somewhere wishing he never put his grimy paws on Charise. I paid a half of a million dollars to make his ass disappear. The crazy thing was, I had to talk Kelly into it. She wasn't going to leave the hood-rat. Even after I paid him to stay away from Charise, my private investigator told me he was still fucking her. Then he tries to get Kelly to extort me for more money. He should have known deep pockets could make anyone do anything.

That day Kelly came to supposedly get money from me, she asked to see the video tape that her stepsons told her about. She only watched two minutes of it and didn't want to see any more. She started to unbutton her blouse in front of me, but I stopped her. She wanted to get back at Sean. She ended up having a meltdown and told me all the horrible things Sean had done to her from the very beginning. She thought about leaving him but was afraid he'd find her. She also didn't want to leave the kids with him because they hated him and their own mother. Kelly thought if she slept with me, that would somehow even the score.

First of all, I had no sexual interest in Kelly, and by this time, I was sleeping with both Elaine and Charise. I didn't need Kelly as well. Second, her sleeping with me hardly evened the playing field for all that he had done and would continue to do to her. Third and finally, he was fucking with my pussy, even though I paid him to stay away, and fucking with my money is the ultimate no-no. No, at that point, he just needed to go. He needed to disappear along with that troll-looking friend of his that wanted to keep messing with my pussy.

I remembered a conversation some time ago where Harmony threatened to call her crazy family in Detroit. I asked Kelly about it, got them on the phone, and had 12 of them on the next flight. Then I had four of my guys trailing Sean's every move along with Kelly's family. I thought about just killing him, but I figured the police would pursue Kelly, so I had to dig back into my past and how I did things back in the day (before I got saved). Not only did I have to make him disappear, but I had to make it so he couldn't tell anyone. I had to make it whereas if someone were to ever find him, he'd get locked up for his friend's murder. So I made the decision to drop his ass in Vegas where no one would recognize him anytime soon. I made sure Kelly got paid well from the arrangement to ensure her silence. She wouldn't dare tell anyone what I did without implicating herself.

So now with Sean out of the picture, I have Charise all to myself. I also had to talk Kelly into telling Arnold about Charise and Sean to get him out of the picture. It was rough having Kelly working for me during that short period of time, because it was hard for me to fuck Charise in my office with Kelly in the midst, suspicious as hell, but I needed Kelly near to make sure she wasn't unraveling with the police, and I needed her around to convince her to tell Arnold about Sean and Charise. I let her know to keep my identity out of it. It did piss me off that she told Sandy about the video tape I gave her. I didn't want to be connected to anything.

Charise doesn't know I know, but right before Arnold found out about Sean, she hooked up with some other married joker. I guess she must have liked him because she thought she was going to just blow me off for him. When she started avoiding me, that guy found himself in a nasty car accident. He survived, somehow, but he had no more, good use for Charise's talents.

Once Elaine was out of the picture, I was able to devote the time and attention to keep Charise happy. Now I have her all to myself and I don't have to worry about sharing her with any other. So therefore, I am happy—for now. Hopefully I don't have to have any others removed.

27

Todd

My wife and I are now separated. I didn't tell her about my two new additions. I took the coward route and left before they were born. Cynnyyah had a boy, and Roxana had a girl. The paternity tests confirmed them both my children. My mother is livid and won't have anything to do with the babies. She smacked me up as I anticipated she would once I told her. She's still living in the house with Harmony when she's not in Houston.

Harmony lost about 85 of those extra pounds, but I still just wasn't feeling her. Her self-esteem seemed to have gone to the dumps. She was no longer the person I used to know. Or maybe it was just because she was not Elaine and never will be. She would never do for me sexually, half of the things that Elaine did for me. Whew! There was no end to her creativity. I wondered if she used to do all those things on her customers when she was prostituting. It would be no wonder that she became a wealthy woman from her skills.

I couldn't believe Elaine left me right along with Kevin. She said she didn't want Harmony to know about our involvement. I still didn't want to stay with Harmony though. I've been enjoying my freedom.

I go by to see my kids a few times a week, but that's about the extent of things. Roxana wants to move to L.A. so she can be nearer to me, but I advised her against that. I still see Cynnyyah every now and again. Of course she uses our son as the reason to hook up for sex. I get with Valerie every now and again also. Like I said, I'm just enjoying my freedom right now. Eventually I'll decide what's going to happen with my marriage. Thankfully, Harmony's cool with Tatiana now. I still want to kick Shawnee's ass for what she did to my sister, but she'll get hers soon enough. That's why she's going to have to cough up some of those dollars that should have been my sister's in the first place.

I heard Kevin is out in the open with Charise now—so open that Elaine got word and filed her divorce papers. I remember he once said he wouldn't trade his wife for all the money in the world. Instead, he traded her for a trashy tramp like Charise. I did fly to New York to see Elaine one weekend. Although we made love, she let me know that it would never happen again. Now I just sleep with as many women as I can to fill the void. The void still is not filled.

Speaking of Kevin, he came to my office one day to confront me about sleeping with his wife. He caused a big scene, but when I reminded him he was with his wife's sister currently, he backed off.

Then like a preteen, he wanted to share how great the sex is with her and how they have sex anyplace and multiple times a day. He bragged how he and Charise have more sex than he and Elaine ever had, and he was sure to say, loud enough for everyone in the office to hear, about how "super succulent" Charise's tits are, which were way better than Elaine's. He talked about how "super juicy" her ass is, and that's why he's in it every day.

He asked me, "Who do you have?"

I wanted to belt him just because I knew I didn't have Elaine any longer. I started to tell him that I could fuck Charise if I wanted to, but I just didn't want to. I thought I'd probably sound as ridiculous as he did, but at least he didn't have to work here. I just decided to let him say his piece without giving him any rebuttals. That way he'd look like the jackass. And he did.

Arnold is just doing his thing. I think he's been seeing some new girl now. He doesn't talk to me anymore. I only heard from Eric that he's doing okay.

As for Sean, he just disappeared. No one found his ass. His family got on television and accused Kelly of his disappearance, but they shut up quick when they were told that Sean was wanted for the first-degree murder and robbery of his friend Deondre. Then the family was on television saying they hoped he stayed where he was at, because Sean committed a capital crime. His family is as nutty as he is.

Kelly took Sean's boys to Maryland and no one has heard from her since. Not even Harmony or Sandy. They did check to make sure she's okay through mutual friends. I also heard Kelly sold Sean's company for a nice piece of change. I guess her $50,000 investment paid off after all.

If anyone were to ask my advice about getting caught up with one of these Wiggins sisters, I'd say run for the hills as quick as you can. The sex is great, but the consequences are greater. Don't get involved unless you are willing to pay the price. Now I have all these extra babies to take care of because the one sister I had was making me crazy. Then the other sister broke my heart. Like I said—RUN!

The End

28

Sean

But HOLD UP! This can't end just yet. Oh fuck no! I ain't getting written out of this motherfucker.

Okay, so the bitches left me down in the dumps somewhere out in North Las Vegas. I've been getting around and hearing things, blending in with the rest of the homeless people out here. I heard that the police are looking for me 'cause they think I killed my boy. I'm just staying low until I can get well enough to make my move. Thankfully, those motherfuckers messed me up pretty bad, and I am not easily recognizable. I've heard the police walk right up to me to see if I was the guy they were looking for, but then I'd hear them say, "Nah, that's not him." Now, I do have a problem with the fact that they should be able to clearly see that someone messed me up, but they're not interested in trying to help me. I guess they figured I must have gotten beat down in the District.

Those bitches tried to burn my eyes, but somehow, I'm starting to get some shadows back. I think the previous swelling from them hitting me may have helped. I still don't have any real use of my eyes, though. Someone gave me a makeshift splint for my broken hands and fingers. It's been helping the healing, although it's hard to manage with them on. I also was able to get my ribs wrapped tightly to help them heal as well. Homeless people can be very helpful as well as resourceful. One guy helping me said he used to be a doctor but got hooked on his own prescriptions. I still wish I knew who the motherfucker that stepped on my dick when it was swollen was, 'cause I'ma get his ass the first chance I get.

I have been getting a little help from some volunteer chick I met at one of the shelters. She was probably the only one smart enough to recognize that someone messed me up intentionally to keep me from being able to communicate. Not even the police were able to pick up on that.

She eventually recognized me as the WANTED: Sean Greene. She has been trying to help me learn how to speak again with my tongue being messed up, and she also has been trying to help me get use of my hands to the point where I could use them myself and start writing again. Her gracious ass took me to her place to get me cleaned up, and she bathed me. I guess she liked what she saw, 'cause she ended up giving me some pussy once I was all cleaned up. She tried putting her titties in my mouth, although I wasn't able to suck them yet. She said there's nothing wrong with getting practice for when my tongue is all better. I like her logic.

I've been staying with her ever since she brought me in. She keeps me tucked away because she doesn't want the police to find me before I am able to get better and help defend myself. I think she's keeping me tucked away because she's enjoying this dick more than anything. I love when she presses her thick lips up against mine. She makes me feel like I still got it, and soon will be back on top again. I just keep hoping this bitch ain't dog ugly and nobody wants her. She's bigger than I'd prefer, but I won't complain.

I feel myself getting stronger every day. Something about getting pussy that makes you stronger. Hopefully I'll get my sight back again. I know when I do get better, I won't be going to jail until Kelly is a dead woman. They will be looking for her body in all different places. She should have just killed me when she had the chance. And then she got my sons somewhere. As soon as I am able, I'm going to have this new girl track down Kelly and my sons, and Kelly will die. At least my sons will know I came back to save them. Oh, this story won't end until Kelly Wiggins-Greene is dead. So we'll just say . . . **to be continued** . . .

Keep Reading for an Excerpt from Book 4:

THE EVOLUTION BETWEEN SISTERS

Synopsis

The men had their say in book three, and the Wiggins' Sisters are not taking it lightly.

Kelly's on the run with Sean's sons, but running with them is worse than being with Sean. When pushed over the edge, she makes an attempt to unload them on an unlikely bunch.

Lessons are never learned for Charise, and she's always a glutton for punishment. However, as she continues on a path of destruction, the layers of her life begin to peel back. Finally, Charise's truths are revealed.

Elaine falls on the wrong side of the law and has her sister's antics to thank for it. Through her own treachery, she finds the doors of yesterday opening up and she soon learns it's never wise to bite the psychological hand that feeds her.

Harmony comes undone after having a "loving" husband expanding his family outside of the marriage. She is on a warpath with anything in her way, including family.

WAR is the only thing on Shawnee's mind after an unwanted visit from Tatiana. The competition heats up, and there will only be one winner as far as Shawnee is concerned. However, Tatiana is not her only opponent.

Sandy finally finds romance in her attempts to get over Lewis, but she's part of the Wiggins family, which means there's not much chance of it lasting.

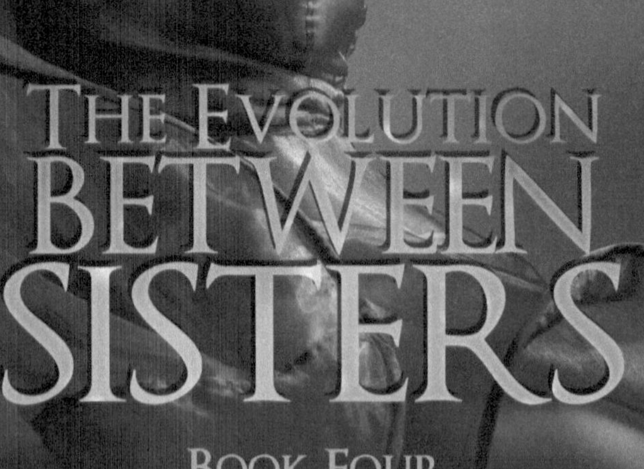
The Queen
PRESENTS

A WIGGINS
FAMILY SAGA

THE EVOLUTION
BETWEEN
SISTERS

BOOK FOUR

PROLOGUE

1

"Angelo! You won't believe what I just found in a box in the attic," Charise said to her younger brother.

"It must have something to do with a dick, because that's about the only thing that gets you this excited. Kevin's got a box of dildos hidden up in his attic? Let me find out Kevin's fine ass is getting down like that." Angelo laughed.

"Eww! That's just nasty! Can you not refer to my man in that manner? I hate to burst your bubble, but my man is all about the pussy," Charise shot back.

"But you're the one always talking about your anal sex life," Angelo reminded his over-sexed sister.

"Kevin loves this ass, all day and all night, anytime and anywhere, and from *any* opening. He is not interested in sticking his thing in a man. Not while I have anything to say about it. Anyhow, let me tell you why I called you. You got me all sidetracked with some box of dildos and what not."

"What! What's so important then? You know I have to run this boutique. All of us can't just sit home on our asses having sex all day, and we definitely don't have any rich men taking care of us."

"See, that's what you know. Hater! We haven't had sex in the past six hours." Charise laughed.

Angelo screeched loudly. "Oh my Lord! Somebody call 9-1-1. The girl is going to die soon. She's suffered six long hours without any dick. Help her before she withers away."

"Whatever, Angelo! For your information, I've made it twelve whole hours once before." Charise laughed again.

"Oh Lord! The girl has suffered twelve excruciating hours without any. Why hath you forsaken the fool? Help her, O' Lord. Help her!"

"You're the fool." Charise was cracking up at Angelo's theatrics. "As I was saying, I was trying to hurry up and get the Christmas decorations out before he gets home, 'cause you know what time it is when my man walks through that door."

"Trust me, I know. You remind me every chance you get, girl. Anyway, hurry up and tell me what you found so I can get back to work. Elaine is supposed to fly in this week, and I don't want to hear her mouth."

"Well after I tell you what I found, she won't have shit to say to you."

"Hmm. Go on, I'm listening," Angelo said, sounding skeptical.

"I found her client book hidden up in the attic," Charise answered in an excited whisper, as if someone was suddenly within earshot.

"Her client book? What the hell is that? From the boutiques?"

Charise devilishly laughed. "Her book with all of her johns and tricks."

Angelo screeched again. "Shut up! You're lying!"

"I have it in my hand. I'll bring it the next time I come to the spa."

"Stop it! You know you need to stop!" Angelo was unsure whether to laugh or cry. He didn't want to accept his older sister being a former prostitute, but the thought of her having a client book was amusing.

"Boy, stop acting like you don't know your sister is a ho."

"Which sister are you talking about? 'Cause you have them all beat in the ho department, hands down. Charise knows she's the biggest skank on this side of glory." Angelo laughed.

Charise chuckled. "I'm not a ho. I have a man. One man and a damn good one at that, thank you."

"Hell, he was your sister's man first. He was her husband at that before he became your man. Your skank ass took both Sandy's and Elaine's husbands."

"Well, that just goes to tell you that all pussy is not the same. I can't help it if their men always prefer my stuff over theirs," Charise defended with pride.

"Uhm-uhm-uhm! Girl, let me get off this phone with you. You're a certified nut for sure. You need to tell Kevin that you need to go back to work on your magazine. You have way too much time on your hands," Angelo said with a disgusted laugh. "I would suggest therapy, but we all know that was a massive fail. Talk about a waste of time and dollars. You should ask for a refund."

"Shut up, stupid! Besides, my man said he doesn't want his woman to have to work. He wants his pussy available at will," Charise shared with pride in her voice.

"Oh Lord! Yeah, whatever! I gotta go, ho!" Angelo laughed before hanging up on his nutty sister.

PROLOGUE

2

Harmony? What are you doing in New York?" Elaine opened her door for her elder sister. "I was just leaving to go find some dinner. You want to join me, or have you already eaten?"

Harmony barged her way past Elaine into her elaborately decorated hi-rise condominium.

Elaine was shocked by Harmony's behavior. "Okay, perhaps you don't want to eat," Elaine said, closing the door. "Well, have a seat."

Harmony stood directly in Elaine's space. "You know, while the bunch of you were running around doing all that man-sharing shit, I warned you all about ever crossing the line with me and fucking with my husband, but of course your nasty ass had to go and fuck my husband. Being a hooker and having your own husband wasn't enough dicks for you?"

Before Elaine could say a word, Harmony punched Elaine on the side of her head. Elaine tried to restrain Harmony to no avail.

Harmony grabbed Elaine in a head lock and flipped her over as she screamed every profanity that she could think of.

"You slutty fucking bitch! I'll teach your ass to fuck with what's mine. I told you not to sleep on my ass, you bitch!" she yelled as she straddled over Elaine on the floor, still beating on her.

Elaine tried to protect her face from her sister's continual blows. Harmony continued until she exhausted herself. Since she realized Elaine wasn't fighting back, she rolled over onto the floor, crying, lying side-by-side with Elaine.

"Why'd you have to do that shit to me, Elaine? What have I ever done to you?" Harmony yelled through her sobbing.

Elaine cried from her guilt more so than her whipping. "I'm sorry, Harmony. I swear I'm sorry. I didn't ever mean to hurt you."

"You had to know sleeping with my husband would hurt me. He's the father of my children for crying out loud. That was so unfair."

Elaine tried to reach over to hug her sister. "Please forgive me, Harmony. I could hardly live with myself. Please, Harmony, forgive me."

Harmony pushed Elaine away from her then made her way up from the floor. "I can't forgive you, Elaine. I won't ever forgive you for this. You took my husband and broke up my family." Harmony shook her head. "No! Absolutely not. I can't overlook this one. Charise takes your husband from you so you get back at him by taking my husband? I don't think so."

Elaine quickly got off of the floor before her sister could attack her again. She tried to put a safe distance between them.

Harmony continued. "Did you think you could just up and move back to New York, and that would make everything all right, Elaine?"

"I just felt like I didn't want to cause any more damage. I didn't want to break up your family. I was just plain selfish, and I understand that. I am trying to change. I'm trying to grow up, but I messed up. I don't know why I keep messing up. I just wish that one day you would find it in your heart to forgive me," Elaine pled.

"Elaine, my husband left me because he was in love with my sister. I can't forgive you for that."

"I know I messed up big time, but Todd didn't leave you for me. He left you because of his own selfishness."

"What in the hell are you talking about? Fucking you was his selfishness. And yours too!" Harmony yelled, foaming at the mouth. She was about to chase Elaine, but Elaine kept her distance.

Before Harmony could make her way around the furniture, Elaine blurted, "Todd has two new babies only a month apart in age. That's why he left you. He didn't want you to find out about them. Hell, he didn't want me to find out about them either."

Harmony shook her head repeatedly. "Uh-uh! NO! That's bullshit! Don't you dare lie on my husband like that! Don't you do that!"

"Ask Angelo. He found out from Charise and told me. He has a daughter in Houston with one of his former patients and a son in L.A. with another of his patients. And I know for a fact that he was sleeping with his nurse at his office. He told me that himself."

Harmony took a seat. She was filled with grief. "Where would Charise get that bullshit from?"

"Harmony, you know Charise always seems to get her info on everything and everybody from only God knows where. However, Angelo confronted Todd about it and he asked that no one tell you about it."

Harmony jumped back up. "Don't tell me? How would he expect my own family to keep something like that from me? Why would you not tell me right away? Why wouldn't Angelo tell me?"

"I didn't want you to find out about my involvement. I told Angelo he needed to tell you, but obviously he didn't. Todd left you after I left because he found out he had two babies on the way and didn't know how to deal with the situation."

Harmony collapsed on the sofa and cried again. "That bastard will pay if it's with my last breath I breathe. That dirty dog. So all of those times he was claiming to go to Houston to see his sons, he was making a daughter with one of his patients? Wait! His patient in Los Angeles as well?"

All Elaine could muster was a nod.

After Harmony cried some more, she asked, "Well when did he have time to fuck you? How many women was he fucking—obviously with no protection?" She cried some more. "I tried to be a damn good wife to his ass even when I figured he was cheating on me. I should have never taken his ass back. I should have left him in Houston. That dirty scum of the earth! Am I the only one who didn't know about those babies? What about Sandy and Shawnee? Why didn't they say something to me?"

"I don't know, Harmony. I really don't know. I haven't spoken to anyone other than Angelo since I returned to New York. I was surprised when you called me. I thought when you asked for my address, it was to send a Christmas card, but here you are," Elaine answered.

"You had to have known I'd hunt your ass down when I found out about you with my husband."

Elaine plopped down in a chair across from Harmony, still keeping her distance. She sighed deeply before saying, "Actually, I was hoping you'd never find out. Although I was, I didn't want to be a home wrecker."

"What I want to know is, how did the two of you begin sleeping with one another? How did something like that happen?" Harmony asked.

Elaine sat reflecting on the origins of her fiasco. "Stupidity! Pure and simple stupidity. I called myself getting to the bottom of why he was alienating you and your marriage. It started off with me trying to do you a favor. I hung around more to keep my eye on him. Eventually, I turned out to be the one to keep an eye on."

"Did he initiate things or did you?" Harmony persisted.

Elaine pondered on a truth that she could tell Harmony without causing her to attack again. Elaine remembered vividly the day in the dressing room where she asked Todd to touch her breasts. She also clearly remembered pressing her naked body that she invited Todd to see, up against his erection.

Elaine decided to lie. "I really can't remember."

"Yeah, I bet you can't." Harmony paused for a moment. "Why wouldn't you fight me back? What happened to all of your kickboxing? I wanted you to fight back so I could really beat your ass."

"I didn't fight back because I already felt as though I've hurt you enough. You didn't deserve what I did to you or what Todd did. I deserve any beating you want to give me. I was way-wrong. There is no excuse for what I did."

"I really wanted to do you like Shawnee did Tatiana, but Shawnee was just sentenced to a hundred and twenty days in jail, three years of probation, and she has to cough up a hundred million to Tatiana. It might be more than that. I really didn't feel like going to jail also. That was your only saving grace."

"Are you serious? Shawnee was actually given jail time for a bullshit fight? Hell, most of D.C. would be locked up right now for that, if they implemented L.A. laws. Who has Shayla?"

"Ironically, Tatiana and Eric. Eric got custody because of the fight, and Tatiana is the main one raising her now. She brings Shayla over to play with my kids at least once a week, more than Shawnee would ever do."

"Wow! No wonder you didn't come over here and kill my ass. People could actually lose custody of their children for one stupid fight?" Elaine asked. "Isn't that a bit extreme?"

"That wasn't one stupid fight. Shawnee hurt that girl bad and then someone posted the fight on YouTube. Shawnee pretty much was beating on a helpless, naked woman after she ripped that dress off of Tatiana. I saw the video myself."

"That is crazy. That's how we used to fight when we were kids. Remember? We'd always rip the shirt off whoever we were fighting? They wouldn't know what to do after that. It was either cover yourself up and get a beat down or fight back knowing your boobies were flopping around for everyone to see."

"You all like to hang onto all of that street-hood mess. Just because that's where we came from doesn't mean we have to behave that way," Harmony responded.

Elaine gasped before laughing. "Harmony, did you not just come up in here with that 'street-hood mess' and whip up on me?"

Harmony raised her eyebrow at Elaine. "That's because you know you deserved a beat down. I'm not Sandy. You ain't gonna fuck my husband and think, at the very least, I won't knock the shit out of you. Hell, maybe if Sandy would have beaten Charise's ass way-back-when, she would have had second thoughts about going after your husband.

"Charise, Charise, Charise. Now that's somebody I really want to beat up just once. That girl is out of control. I can't even talk to her anymore. She has totally taken over your husband and household. He takes her everywhere, which made me wonder, how come he never had time to take you anywhere?"

"As far as I'm concerned, they deserve each other. Angelo told me Charise caught him screwing another woman while I was still with him, so he screws Charise to keep her from telling me. Now how retarded is that? What pissed me off was, Lauren was like a friend, the only one besides Renee. I was the one that gave her a makeover. I gave her discounts at the boutique. Yeah, Charise deserves him," Elaine said, getting angry.

"Well, speaking of makeovers, I think it's about time I go for mine. Now that I finally got rid of all of the baby fat, my husband has his other two families to tend to. Now it's time for me to do my thing. I'm tired of playing the victim. I'm a damn psychologist. I would bitch-slap one of my patients for trying to tolerate the shit I have tolerated from Todd. He'll always be the father of my kids, but it's time for Harmony to do Harmony. I'll be forty soon. I'm too old to be so stupid, and I am too cute to be acting so old."

"I wanted to tell you that you look great when you walked in my door, but you didn't give me much of a chance."

"Yeah, yeah, yeah!" Harmony laughed. "Okay, I'm ready to go get that dinner now. I'll even let you treat since you owe me—for life."

"Life huh?" Elaine chuckled. "How about we find some nice jazz and dinner? I miss doing that."

Harmony broke out into a roaring laughter, while Elaine looked confused.

"Do you remember the Megaplex?" Harmony continued laughing. "That place was like the beginning of hell for all of us. We actually were like sisters back then. Somebody had to insist on going to see some strippers at the Megaplex.

We were fine with our weekly dinner and some jazz. Wasn't that Kelly? Kelly was the one who suggested Megaplex and you were dead-set against it. Since then, you dropped Russell to sleep with Mandingo, knowing that was Sandy's ex-boyfriend. Shawnee started with Mandingo just the same. Charise found Arnold, started taking up with Lewis, and all of your nonsense sent me packing to Houston to get away from you all. And the saga continues because Shawnee has a baby with Sandy's ex, and the baby is being raised by Shawnee's former husband's mistress.

"I ought to write this stuff up for a soap opera and get paid. I'd change the names to protect your identities. I'd call the show, "Between Sisters," because you all think EVERYTHING is supposed to be shared between your damn sisters and would step on your own sisters just to have what you want. I'd make a fortune. Society seems to like that kind of smut, just like all of you seem to get some kind of thrill out of living this crazy lifestyle." Harmony paused. "And speaking of crazy and Kelly, have you heard from her? No one has heard from her."

To continue reading, be sure to get your copy of
The Evolution Between Sisters: Book Four

Note from the Author

Thank you for reading *Between Sisters, Between More Sisters, and now Caught Up Between Sisters.*

If you enjoyed these three novels, be sure to look out for the continuation of the Wiggins Family Saga:

Book 4: *The Evolution Between Sisters*
Book 5: *Revenge Between Sisters*
Book 6: *Sister's Daughter*
Book 7: *Never Again Between Sisters*

To find out what other books Queendom Dreams will be releasing and other authors with Queendom Dreams Publishing, please visit us online at www.queendomdreamspublishing.com.

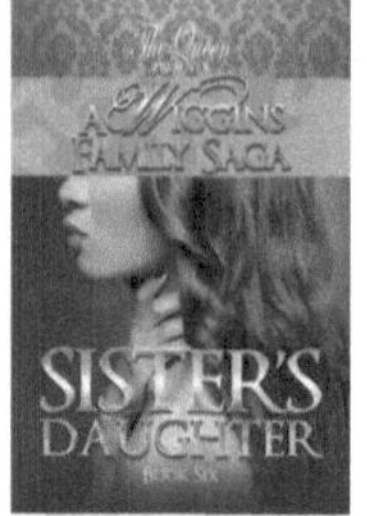

Queendom Dreams

About The Queen

The Queen has been writing for many years, ranging in short stories, poetry, plays, professional and other writings. She is a native of (Queensbridge) Long Island City, New York. Her debut novel was *Between Sisters* (of the Between Sisters series). Her education includes Business and International Business Administration, as well as Travel & Tourism. When she's not writing, she loves to travel to sunny climates with clear and turquoise waters or near mountains for inspiration.